Talking Equity in Polarized Times

How can teachers help students navigate tough topics in an increasingly politicized world? Featuring perspectives from teachers and students across the country, this unique book provides hope, applicable knowledge, and practical skills for teachers to address a range of current issues – including race, LGBTQIA+ advocacy, diversity and equity, civic engagement, ability and disability, school safety, social-emotional learning, immigration, and environmental justice.

Each chapter addresses one of those controversial issues and examines how teachers are grappling with it in their own classrooms. Each chapter is also informed by youths' insights, drawn from the authors' work with the Youth Research Council and the Through Students' Eyes project. Features include suggested resources, reflection questions, and talking points to support teachers in framing discussions of the topic positively and accurately.

With the voices and skills in this book, you'll be able to work with these issues no matter your own teaching contexts.

Meagan Call-Cummings, PhD, is an Associate Professor at the Johns Hopkins University School of Education. As a research methodologist, she emphasizes the meaningful inclusion of those who are often excluded from the knowledge creation (research) process – including teachers, young people, and communities of Color.

Kristien Zenkov, PhD, is Professor of Education at George Mason University. He is a long-time co-teacher with high school and middle school teachers and a dedicated boundary-spanning teacher educator. He's most proud of his teaching, research, and advocacy work that recognizes youths and teachers as key informants for what teaching and school, at their best, might look like.

Jeff Keller is a high school history teacher and a doctoral candidate at George Mason University where his work focuses on how students and teachers experience teaching and learning about controversial issues in today's political climate. He has taught for more than fifteen years, earning multiple honors at the school, local, and state level.

Also Available from Routledge Eye on Education
(www.routledge.com/k-12)

Identity Affirming Classrooms: Spaces that Center Humanity
Erica Buchanan-Rivera

Identity-Conscious Practice in Action: Shaping Equitable Schools and Classrooms
Liza Talusan

Gender and Sexuality in the Classroom: An Educator's Guide
Marni Brown, Baker A. Rogers, Martha Caldwell

Tangible Equity: A Guide for Leveraging Student Identity, Culture, and Power to Unlock Excellence In and Beyond the Classroom
Colin Seale

Creating Citizens: Teaching Civics and Current Events in the History Classroom, Grades 6–9
Sarah Cooper

"The insights in this important book come directly from the connections with students and their teachers. As discord spreads in their communities, youth often depend on how their teachers see, hear, and work with them – and that can bring thoughtful discourse across differences. As we hear these diverse voices speak their truths and grapple with their needs, we can envision a future where schools take the lead in shaping a better future."

Kathleen Cushman, Fires in Our Lives, Fires in the Bathroom, *and* Fires in the Middle School Bathroom

"Call-Cummings, Zenkov, and Keller have written a book that serves as an amazing guide for pre-service, in-service, and school administrators to support not only their thinking but also their practice when working with diverse students and learners. The book has voices from the field that everyone 'in the trenches' of schools can connect to as it is the lived experience of so many educators. Further, this book is an excellent jumping off point for professional learning with a staff. As a current Superintendent of Schools, I would love to use the vignettes and chapters as conversation points with our leadership to identify how we, as an organization, create a set of conditions for all to succeed. The chapters scaffold that opportunity with excellent questions and reflections for the reader. This is a book every school person should have on their shelf!"

Peter J. Noonan Ed.D., *Superintendent of Schools, City of Falls Church (VA) Schools*

"It is essential as educators that we become comfortable with being uncomfortable. By modeling vulnerability and growth mindset, we can create a learning environment that embraces every learner. Call-Cummings, Zenkov, and Keller have written a volume that will assist in building collaborative relationships with students, parents, colleagues, and experts is critical in developing learning experiences that allow students to construct their own understandings of the world based on facts rather than opinions. We must strive to teach in a way that ensures all learners feel seen, heard, and represented, and this book can be a powerful tool in accomplishing that goal."

Sheila Peterson, *2024 North Dakota Teacher of the Year*

"This book examines and reveals the insights of classroom practitioners and students as they navigate the overt and sometimes covert systemic inequities plaguing many of our schools. Through introspection and action, one can create a more inclusive environment for our most marginalized population. I highly recommend this book!"
Michael Houston, *2024 Minnesota Teacher of the Year*

"This book is an essential addition to any educator's library. The firsthand accounts amplify teacher voices, creating the feel of a conversation among colleagues and professionals. It equips educators with practical strategies to foster environments where teachers can uplift and empower their students. Guided by principles of hope and forgiveness, this book reminds us that educators are the key to overcoming divisiveness and promoting an inclusive future for all students."
Eric Jenkins, *Indiana Teacher of the Year 2024*

"*Talking Equity in Polarized Times* is a vital resource for educators navigating today's contentious climate. This book delivers a powerful toolkit for teachers to bridge divides in today's classrooms, and is an indispensable resource and must-read for creating a positive impact in education."
Kurt Russell, *2022 National Teacher of the Year*

"Meagan, Kristien, and Jeff have compiled a thoughtful guide to tackling the hot topics of public education. By tapping into their own experiences and the varied experiences of other front line educators and students, they provide a wholistic narrative of how the issues affect the American public education classroom. They also provide possible solutions and practices to combat the struggles that hinder student learning. This book is a great read for anyone who wishes to stretch their views on American schools and increase their capacity to lead systemic change for our community youth."
Louise Smith, *2024 Mississippi Teacher of the Year, 2024 NEA Foundation Horace Mann Award Recipient*

Talking Equity in Polarized Times

Stories and Strategies from Teachers and Students

Meagan Call-Cummings, Kristien Zenkov, and Jeff Keller

NEW YORK AND LONDON

Designed cover image: filo / Getty Images

First published 2025
by Routledge
605 Third Avenue, New York, NY 10158

and by Routledge
4 Park Square, Milton Park, Abingdon, Oxon, OX14 4RN

Routledge is an imprint of the Taylor & Francis Group, an informa business

© 2025 Meagan Call-Cummings, Kristien Zenkov, and Jeff Keller

The right of Meagan Call-Cummings, Kristien Zenkov, and Jeff Keller to be identified as authors of this work has been asserted in accordance with sections 77 and 78 of the Copyright, Designs and Patents Act 1988.

All rights reserved. No part of this book may be reprinted or reproduced or utilised in any form or by any electronic, mechanical, or other means, now known or hereafter invented, including photocopying and recording, or in any information storage or retrieval system, without permission in writing from the publishers.

Trademark notice: Product or corporate names may be trademarks or registered trademarks, and are used only for identification and explanation without intent to infringe.

Library of Congress Cataloging-in-Publication Data
Names: Call-Cummings, Meagan, author. | Zenkov, Kristien, author. | Keller, Jeff (Jeffrey W.), author.
Title: Talking equity in polarized times : stories and strategies from teachers and students / Meagan Call-Cummings, Kristien Zenkov, and Jeff Keller.
Description: New York, NY : Routledge, 2025. | Series: Routledge eye on education | Includes bibliographical references.
Identifiers: LCCN 2024032212 (print) | LCCN 2024032213 (ebook) | ISBN 9781032732923 (paperback) | ISBN 9781003468769 (ebook)
Subjects: LCSH: Educational sociology--United States. | School environment--Social aspects--United States. | Students--United States--Social conditions. | Educational equalization--United States. | Teacher-student relationships--United States.
Classification: LCC LC191.4 .C35 2025 (print) | LCC LC191.4 (ebook) | DDC 306.430973--dc23/eng/20240829
LC record available at https://lccn.loc.gov/2024032212
LC ebook record available at https://lccn.loc.gov/2024032213

ISBN: 978-1-032-73292-3 (pbk)
ISBN: 978-1-003-46876-9 (ebk)

DOI: 10.4324/9781003468769

Typeset in Palatino
by SPi Technologies India Pvt Ltd (Straive)

Access the Support Material: www.routledge.com/9781032732923

Dedication

This book is dedicated to teachers, who simultaneously care for our kids every day, do their best to engage children and young people with ideas and actions that help them to be healthy and successful, and collectively nurture our most unifying institution – school.

Contents

Support Material	xiii
Acknowledgements	xiv
About the Authors	xv

Introduction 1
  Context of the Book 1
  The Ground Rules 3
  Why This Book 6
  What Are the Issues? And What's The *Issue*? 6
    Race and Racism 8
    Immigrants and Immigration 8
    Civic and Political Engagement 8
    LGBTQIA+ Advocacy 8
    Ability and Disability 9
    Diversity and Equity 9
    Social-Emotional Learning 9
    School Safety 9
    Environment and Climate Justice 10
  Why Us as Authors, and Teachers and Young People as Experts? 10
  How Might I Use This Book? 12
  Teacher and Youth Introductions 12
  References 16

1 Race and Racism 17
  Critical Concepts 19
    Racial Consciousness 19
    Structural Racism 20
  Teacher Stories 22
  Teacher Strategies 26
  Youth Stories 30
  Taking Action 31
  Resources 33
  References 34

2	**Immigrants and Immigration**	**36**
	Critical Concepts	38
	Ethnocentrism	38
	Collectivism and Individualism Spectrum	39
	Teacher Stories	41
	Teacher Strategies	45
	Youth Stories	52
	Taking Action	53
	Resources	54
	References	55
3	**Civic and Political Engagement**	**56**
	Critical Concepts	58
	Civic Action Deficits	58
	Teacher Stories	60
	Teacher Strategies	66
	Youth Stories	74
	Taking Action	75
	Resources	77
	References	77
4	**LGBTQIA+ Advocacy**	**79**
	Critical Concepts	80
	Heteronormativity	80
	Teacher Stories	82
	Teacher Strategies	92
	Youth Stories	99
	Taking Action	100
	Resources	101
	References	102
5	**Ability and Disability**	**103**
	Critical Concepts	104
	Ableism	104
	Teacher Stories	107
	Teacher Strategies	114
	Youth Stories	117
	Taking Action	118
	Resources	119
	References	120

6	**Diversity and Equity**	**121**
	Critical Concepts	122
	Intersectionality	123
	Teacher Stories	125
	Teacher Strategies	128
	Youth Stories	135
	Taking Action	136
	Resources	137
	References	138
7	**Social-Emotional Learning**	**139**
	Critical Concepts	140
	Trauma Informed Practices	140
	Relationality and Holding Space	141
	Teacher Stories	142
	Teacher Strategies	149
	Youth Stories	154
	Taking Action	155
	Resources	156
	References	156
8	**School Safety**	**158**
	Critical Concepts	159
	Implicit Bias	159
	Teacher Stories	161
	Teacher Strategies	167
	Youth Stories	172
	Taking Action	172
	Resources	174
	References	174
9	**Environmental Justice and Climate Change**	**176**
	Critical Concepts	177
	Courageous Conversations	177
	Teacher Stories	180
	Teacher Strategies	184
	Youth Stories	191
	Taking Action	193
	Resources	195
	References	196

10 Caring for Kids	**198**
Closing: How and Why Teachers Care for Kids	198
Youth Stories	205
Taking Action: Ten Ways to Start Now	207
Appendix A: Self-Reflection Worksheet	**209**

Support Material

There are additional resources online to supplement the book. To access the materials, go to the book product page at www.routledge.com/9781032732923 and click on the link that says Support Material.

Acknowledgements

We are endlessly grateful to so many colleagues, mentors, friends, family members, students, co-conspirators, and educators that we could never offer a complete list of those who have given us the encouragement, space, and inspiration to complete this project. We would like to acknowledge our editorial assistant, Hannah Sroka, as well as the team at Routledge for making this book possible at a time when listening to teachers is so crucial. And we owe a professional debt of gratitude to Kathleen Cushman for modeling how to listen to young people and teachers and why we should trust their expertise.

Meagan would like to highlight her partnership with Courtney Bell, Amy L. Best, Khaseem Davis, Giovanni P. Dazzo, Jeff Keller, Bethany Monea, Katharine Rupp, and Emma Vetter on the Youth Research Council (YRC), along with over 100 YRC Fellows, who have inspired so much of this book.

Kristien would like to acknowledge the young people who have participated in some form of the Through Students' Eyes project over the past twenty years – at last count over 1500 youth from across the United States and five other countries. This work started with Jim Harmon and Piet van Lier in Cleveland, where we recognized that every teacher and every student need and deserve to be listened to. We will keep listening.

Jeff would like to echo Meagan's comments: Our YRC partners and youth Fellows are amazing and provide endless inspiration. He is also thankful for his students and public school colleagues who bravely tackle so many of the issues described in the book: this is for you!

About the Authors

Meagan Call-Cummings (PhD, Indiana University, Bloomington) is an Associate Professor at the Johns Hopkins University School of Education. As a research methodologist, she emphasizes the meaningful inclusion of those who are often excluded from the knowledge creation (research) process – including teachers, young people, and communities of Color. Her work most often takes participatory forms and is always action-oriented. She is particularly proud of the *Youth Research Council* and *Summer Institute in Anti-Racist and Decolonizing Research Methods*, which she co-founded with her co-conspirators and friends, Amy L. Best and Khaseem Davis.

Kristien Zenkov, PhD, is Professor of Education at George Mason University. He is a long-time co-teacher with high school and middle school teachers and a dedicated boundary-spanning teacher educator. He's most proud of his teaching, research, and advocacy work that recognizes youths and teachers as key informants for what teaching and school, at their best, might look like. This work most often finds form in the Through Students' Eyes project but increasingly through critical, project-based clinical experiences with future teachers.

Jeff Keller is a high school history teacher and a doctoral candidate at George Mason University where his work focuses on how students and teachers experience teaching and learning about controversial issues in today's political climate. He has taught for more than fifteen years, earning multiple honors for his teaching at the school, local, and state level, including being named the 2024 Virginia Teacher of the Year.

This book would not have been possible without the constant, hilarious, and patient assistance of Lin Rudder, our key contributor and colleague.

Introduction

Context of the Book

Schools and schooling are institutions and phenomena with which virtually all of us have considerable experience: schools and the practices of formal education may be the singular most unifying organizations and procedures we have as citizens and residents of the United States. Oddly, almost nonsensically, even if we attended night and day institutions – one of us a massive, urban, inner-city high school in Chicago, another of us a tiny, rural secondary school in Idaho – we would count these experiences as shared. We might have attended vastly different forms of this most common of institutions, but by the time we had earned a high school diploma, we have come to conflate them: We all went to *school*. We all "did" school.

The results of this false fusion of educational experiences are numerous, but a few outcomes are most important – and troubling – to us in this book. First, it seems reasonable that we are all experts in what school *is* and what school *should be*. Second, we all feel informed enough about the professional practices of teachers that we believe we are entitled – maybe even obligated – to express opinions about educators' pedagogies, training, and, increasingly, even their political perspectives.

As Bobbi shared, today's teachers are aware of this erroneous and deflating idea that *everyone* knows as much about their profession as they do:

> It's hard for me to explain to people who aren't teachers how skilled I am at this, how much training I've had, and how I take this so seriously. They seem to think that because they went to high school, they know what's going on, and they can weigh in and question me again, not only for *their* child, but for *all* children. There is not that respect toward people in education. Ninety-nine percent of parents are wonderful, but that 1% is certainly the loudest; we hear from them a lot. It's tricky to navigate these things, because I think that the students don't agree with their parents. I think students want to read books that are mirrors and windows. They want to read perspectives that are different from their own. But their parents don't want them to learn those things, or perhaps they don't want to learn those things in schools. And so, I'm constantly fighting to stay focused on what's best for kids.

It might be the case that the general public's assumptions about our shared expertise in all things school and teaching are the natural result of these institutions' focus on the young, arguably the most vulnerable in our society, and certainly the most malleable and impressionable. How accurate is any of our childhood recollections, even those formed over 12 years of experience? Not enough to make us experts on the institution where we encountered those experiences, particularly not when we often frame these experiences as something we all *endured* rather than as phenomena to be *honored*. Most of us attend some form of schooling almost from birth until adolescence, when we are suddenly and absolutely deemed ready to make that transition to adulthood. But it defies reason that we would unconditionally trust each other's, and our own, impressions and memories of what occurred during those years – certainly not so absolutely that we would base political decisions on these recollections. But we do.

Given our complicated relationships and experiences with school, it's entirely reasonable that at some point in our nation's history we would encounter a perfect storm of societal and political forces that would call into question the very existence of this, our most common institution. In 2024, these forces are leading us to question whether this institution – school – might, in fact, be our most shared and insidious *enemy*. Combine the complex factors above with political actors who see opportunity and ultimately significant financial gain in calling into question our institutions, creating chaos, and sowing doubt amongst schools' constituents – which, by the way, is *all* of us, though not everyone values schools similarly or equally – and you'll find yourself in today's America.

But because schools are institutions that are filled with and focused on the young, they are just as vulnerable and subject to society's whims as the demographic of our society that they serve. In short, they are easy targets, and they cannot defend themselves. They count on us – those who care about them and want the best for them, for the children and youth they care for, and for the adults (teachers, administrators, paraprofessionals, counselors, etc.) dedicated to serving their students and schools themselves – to do so. It is with all of these ideas and realities in mind that we have crafted this volume. While external forces may call into question schools' existence and teachers' pedagogies, we believe it may only be through the internal expertise and the voices and insights of the teachers and young people in these institutions that we might do more than *defend* schools: we might move them *forward*.

The Ground Rules

We have composed this volume with several guiding principles – ground rules, really. These are rooted in our own personal, professional, and pedagogical commitments, and they are drawn from the teachers and young people whose voices we will foreground throughout this book.

First, while all of our school experiences were *not* the same, our consideration of what is working and what might work better in schools is something in which we should engage as a community. Alfonso spoke to this ethic:

> My biggest obstacle was when a parent yelled at me during a parent-teacher conference. Fortunately, there was a follow-up email by the parent apologizing, but also asking what my qualifications were to be teaching. But I've always been good with parents – where they're coming from, their hesitation, their concerns, and their worries for their students. So, rather than saying that what that parent did was okay, and rather than saying that parent was the worst possible person ever, I saw it as "That's the way that they chose to release that concern and that worry." I keep that in the back of my head at all times, and from the very beginning I communicate with them in both English and Spanish, letting them know that "Hey – we're in this together."
>
> We are on the same team for your child. There are going to be times when you get an email that maybe you don't like. But I just want you to know that it's with their best interests in mind. Because in this classroom we have control over what happens, but later on,

in college or at the workplace, they're not going to get those training wheels. And they're not going to have that safety net. So, let's work on these things now.

Alfonso's approach with his students' families will be our orientation with this volume, and one we will ask readers to adopt as they dig into chapters, as they listen to the teachers and young people whose voices and ideas we are highlighting, and as they consider how to engage with educators and neighbors and policymakers. Division and critique are easy and lazy; the first steps toward finding and implementing the solutions our schools need in this time may be assuming the best of each other, actively appreciating that we all want the best for our kids and communities and that we can agree on what this looks like.

Amy shared an insight that illustrates our second ground rule:

> I think it's important for people who are interested in going into the teaching profession to know that you aren't just a teacher. There are so many different hats you have to wear. You're a bit of a counselor. You're a little bit of a surrogate parent. You're sometimes like an older peer or mentor. A lot of what you do is not necessarily your content area. In a given day I do English instruction, but a lot of my day is filled with all sorts of things that are not that. So, if you go into teaching, you go into it with a passion, knowing that it is challenging. It's very worthwhile. Every day I feel like what I am doing is making a difference to at least one kid that day. I don't want to be just booping buttons on a computer. I want to be doing something meaningful for society.

While Amy's comment is explicitly a heads-up to prospective teachers, it's also a window into the rich realities of teachers' roles which must be acknowledged. Teachers are experts in their content, yes; more importantly, they are experts in caring for our kids. Ultimately, why should we listen to them about how our schools might serve young people best? While we're generally pretty reluctant to use military analogies to communicate a point, this is an instance where such a comparison is nearly impossible to avoid: teachers are the primary adults in our society who *choose*, over and over and over again, to work on the front lines of serving youth. This is not meant to overlook the nature of parents' and families' commitments or contributions to our kids' well-being, nor to diminish the work or roles of counselors or caregivers or coaches, but just to appreciate the teaching profession and individual teachers' pledges and persistence.

But teachers showing up every day isn't equivalent to their just clocking in for a shift; it's a conscious decision that represents their faith in young people, in the good in youth, and the good they (teachers) might engender in adolescents.

Amy also spoke to the third ideal that guided our construction of this book:

> You know, teaching can be a very overwhelming profession. Being an educator can be really hard. But I think, whatever you can do to help yourself keep perspective, and remember why you became an educator in the first place is really important. Find your trusted people within the school. It can be hard to know who you can trust, who you can say certain things to. But find the people you can let off steam with. It's that shared experience of venting frustration that allows you to stay. We really do love the kids – so deeply. And it's a privilege to teach. A piece of advice I got from my mentor when I was student teaching, she said, "Every parent just wants you to *see* their child, and if you can do that, if you can let them know that, then you're doing exactly what you need to do."

Max echoed that idea:

> I still believe that the best learning is done with people and groups grappling with big ideas. And I still think about why did I become an educator? There's something still so very mundane but also magical about this idea that you have 25 to 30 totally different people made to be in this space together and we can consider "What are the possibilities that otherwise would not happen?"

One of the principles that orients our work as teacher educators and teachers is forgiveness. With the populations of children, young people, and future and current classroom teachers with whom we work, we make intentional decisions to forgive. To forgive lessons not yet learned, forgive disengagement, forgive grammar mistakes, forgive forgotten homework, forgive every act of a student – be they in elementary school, high school, or graduate school – that does not *yet* represent their best selves and their best efforts. Growth is almost entirely about one's openness to it, to new people, ideas, texts, and experiences. And openness is also about efficacy, about one's sense of their abilities to learn something new. Our (almost) unfailing expressions of forgiveness give our elementary, middle, and high school students the seeds of hope they need to try again in our classes – and sometimes just to come back to our classes again tomorrow – and perhaps discover the knowledge that will make their relationships to our content and school more positive and their own. Teachers need not be blindly optimistic, but they must live hope and forgiveness and model these qualities for future teachers.

Why This Book?

As the everyday experts on what serves young people best, teachers might not just inform administrators, policymakers, and caregivers about how to depoliticize the act of caring for the kids in their classrooms; they might also inform *each other* about how and why to do so. Thus, this volume relies on short examples, illustrations, and practices from classroom teachers about how to serve children and young people in these increasingly complicated times. These teachers provide the hope and applicable knowledge to address the myriad issues that their peers and students are facing.

> **Box 0.1 Teachers Self-Censor in the Classroom**
>
> A national study reveals that 65% of K-12 teachers surveyed across US schools say they limit instruction on political and social topics, driven by concerns over parental complaints and evolving legislation that restricts discussions on history, race, sex, and gender. The Rand Corp. report highlights teachers' self-censorship, with doubts about the support of school leaders amid political environments that are influencing the restriction of classroom content.
>
> (Najarro, 2024; Natanson, 2024)

This volume aims to amplify the expertise of everyday teachers, expertise which is so often pushed to the margins or silenced because of the vast politicization of schools and classrooms in the United States. In an explicit attempt to counter this external and self-censoring – and instead of preaching to teachers from an ivory tower – our text calls teachers into conversation with each other around issues that have bombarded them in recent years.

What Are the Issues? And What's the *Issue*?

Each chapter in this volume addresses one of the key issues that teachers, youth, our schools, and communities are encountering and examines how teachers from across the United States are grappling with these topics and controversies in their own classrooms, schools, and communities. In addition, each chapter is informed by youths' insights, drawn from the authors' work with the Youth Research Council and the Through Students' Eyes project. While many of these topics, the related pedagogical and practical considerations, and the controversies surrounding these are intertwined, we have organized this volume into ten chapters around these issues.

While these issues are often interrelated – both in content and in the ways that teachers encounter them in their classrooms – this list is also not comprehensive. This is one of the greatest challenges that teachers face: they must keep their ears to the ground and stay attuned in their classrooms to hear what current concern or combination of concerns are most pressing for their students. As much as some administrators, families, and policymakers might resist, the *content* of teachers' instruction goes well beyond their subject area and the latest research in pedagogical methods; the content is *always* the issue of the day, because children and young people bring these issues with them into our classrooms.

For the teachers whose voices and experiences we share in this volume, the real issue, as Matt shares here, is that they simply want to do right by kids, and they long for the day when the barriers to doing so will be removed:

> Teachers are bound by so many structural constraints – standardized testing, the bell system, class sizes. There are just a few things that are shown over and over in education research to be true. One, if we spend more money and we do it wisely, then it leads to better outcomes. Two, lower class sizes are a good thing. And three – and not a single study refutes it: adolescents need sleep…and yet we start middle and high schools at ungodly hours.

Of the more than 30 classroom teachers from across the nation with whom we spoke, not a single one mentioned a political agenda as influencing how or what they taught. Again, caring for kids should not be a political matter. And, yet, as Melanie notes, teachers are aware of and sometimes bombarded by unwarranted reminders about what *not* to address in their instruction:

> We haven't been necessarily told not to discuss issues. We were told not to be political, whatever that means, in our classrooms.

And this was a sentiment that Frankie echoed:

> Working in public schools, it's always "Teach facts. Teach what's objective. What you hear, what can be proven, seen, heard. And don't discuss any affiliations." That's still what they tell every teacher, even

civics teachers. And students, the ones who care, will find out and ask more questions and make connections. But otherwise, it's just this idea that teachers are not people, so they don't have opinions. They just teach you the facts.

So, in each of our ten chapters, we offer stories of what teachers are facing in classrooms today and strategies for how they navigate difficult situations. In addition, in each chapter, we describe "lenses" – what we call "critical concepts" – that can help you view these situations in a new light. These lenses are meant to offer opportunities to challenge assumptions and taken-for-granted beliefs.

Race and Racism

In this chapter, teachers share stories of the many ways in which racism operates in their classrooms and schools. They offer insights into the individual actions of not only students but also their teacher colleagues as well as their administrators. They share how they have witnessed institutional or structural racism and how their racial consciousness has been challenged. But in addition to these challenges, our contributing teachers discuss how they have navigated and disrupted racist practices and policies in ways that are meaningful and often reparative, especially for students.

Immigrants and Immigration

In this chapter, our contributing teachers discuss both the challenges they have witnessed in their schools and the successes they have helped to create related to welcoming students from all over the world to their classrooms. Examples range from how to build meaningful relationships with students who are new to the United States to opportunities to celebrate home cultures without putting students and families into a box of expectations or assumptions.

Civic and Political Engagement

In this chapter, we highlight several experiences from teachers across the United States who use everyday moments to model and teach civic and political engagement. The experiences of these teachers, from Amy in suburban Northern Virginia to Emily in rural Illinois, will help clarify how you and your colleagues might shape your own practices to be more intentional in how you model and teach civic or political engagement – at any level.

LGBTQIA+ Advocacy

Right now in the United States, the equitable treatment of members of the LGBTQIA+ community is being hotly debated, from the Supreme Court to the dining room table. This chapter centers the experiences of our contributing teachers as they grapple with their role in caring for all children in their classrooms. These experiences will help empower you to consider your place in the lives of all your students, especially those who identify as members of the LGBTQIA+ community.

Ability and Disability
Often pushed to the margins in discussions of equity, questions of ability and disability are centered in this chapter, as our contributing teachers reflect on their own experiences balancing legal requirements with caring for each individual child they have in their classrooms. Several examples are offered of how our contributors have pushed back on inequitable practices and policies of exclusion.

Diversity and Equity
This chapter centers broad questions and discussions of equity and diversity across a range of topics, as our contributing teachers offer their experiences teaching about difference, seeking to instill respect and appreciation of all people, cultures, backgrounds, and life experiences. From the elementary music classroom to the high school English classroom, these teachers' perspectives will help you as you seek to instill these same values in your own context.

Social-Emotional Learning
This chapter will offer insights from teachers who see social-emotional learning not as an add-on that teachers and school don't have (or shouldn't make) time for but as a crucial aspect of education. From Matt in a large metropolitan city to Althea and Victoria in Virginia, our teachers share experiences of centering the humanity of students in their pedagogy, recognizing that an English teacher isn't just teaching English and a math teacher isn't just teaching math.

School Safety
News headlines are too often dominated by stories of school violence. This chapter highlights teachers' experiences not only of grappling with these heart-wrenching challenges but also of witnessing the ways in which safety and unsafety are felt by teachers and students alike. Annie shares the difficulty she faced in fighting against institutional intimidation of students of Color. Carleigh discusses biased enforcement of disciplinary measures. And Gabby recalls the trauma of "Code Red" – or lockdown drill – experiences, still unsure whether she supports them or not. This is a chapter to spend time with but also to take self-care measures through. We urge you to consider

engaging in this chapter with others, as this content can be particularly activating.

Environment and Climate Justice

Our final chapter focuses on the ways in which teachers can maneuver to provide quality educational experiences in various contexts. Drawing on years of science education experience in schools across the United States, our contributing teachers share how they have navigated political contexts to have courageous conversations with students to help them understand the nature of environmental justice and how they might help to enact it.

Why Us as Authors, and Teachers and Young People as Experts?

As the authors of this volume, we represent the constituents and audiences with whom we have engaged to develop this text and with whom we hope to engage through others' consideration of the chapters. As we stated at the start of this introductory chapter, our goal is to be honest about all things, including who we are. We are teachers and teacher educators who are attempting to be responsive to who our students are and who they are becoming, in an era when this attempt is increasingly challenging. As teachers and teacher educators, we are embroiled on a day-to-day basis in conflicts that are at best *distracting* from and at worst *detracting* from a progressive educational mission.

We – Meagan, Kristien, and Jeff – *look like* and in many ways *live* in the worlds of the parents, families, community members, and policymakers who are often engaging in less-than-civil manners with teachers, educators, and education leaders. In this age of identity politics, it's necessary that we all be as transparent as possible about our identities and privileges. We bring a pretty considerable set of experiences that orient and inform our work on this volume and our concern for teachers, youths, and schools.

Meagan is a white, heterosexual, cisgender, middle-class woman who grew up seeing her own white, middle-class parents take an active role in their own communities and children's school systems. Some of Meagan's fondest memories are of civic engagement with her family and in the communities where she grew up – from Wisconsin, to California, to Cairo, Egypt. It has been in those moments of engagement that she has built relationships that have informed how she sees herself in the context of and sometimes complicit with systems and structures of oppression and injustice – including white supremacy. As a widely published scholar specializing in community-based approaches to action-oriented research for racial justice, Meagan has worked over the past several years to engage communities in critical conversations about race and the dangerous implications of education policies and practices founded on colorblindness and structural racism.

Kristien is a white, heterosexual, cisgender, middle-class man who understands the frightened and often frightening discourse of our most extreme public school constituents because he was raised in poor, rural Indiana with friends and family members who now support and sometimes spew the racist, xenophobic, heteronormative rhetoric that has become acceptable in political and popular circles. His small-c "Catholic" parents (dedicated to public service) never *preached* about the value of education, but they *taught* their five kids its value. They lived the unAmerican dream of surviving paycheck to paycheck, absolutely the result of their lack of formal schooling beyond the secondary level. A first-generation college student, a long-time classroom teacher, an accomplished scholar, and a committed youth and community advocate, Kristien brings a combination of experiences and personal and professional identities that inform his work on this volume – perhaps most importantly, his award-winning and boundary-spanning teacher education efforts.

Jeffery is a white, heterosexual, cisgender man who teaches in a small school division in rural Virginia and is a first-generation college student. As a classroom teacher for more than 15 years and the 2024 Virginia Teacher of the Year, Jeff has experience working with diverse families and communities. In his role as Teacher of the Year, he has had the opportunity to listen to and engage with many of the very folks this volume most hopes to engage: most often white, often affluent individuals, sometimes school board members, state legislators, or other policymakers who represent them, all who have come to be suspicious of anything that challenges white, heteronormative "standards" in the classroom. A born and raised West Virginian, Jeff has grown increasingly frustrated at witnessing the very tactics and language commonly employed against the poor and working-class people of his hometown now being used to perpetuate racism, sexism, homophobia, and transphobia and hopes the volume might open pathways to meaningful dialogue.

The largest pool of contributors to this volume are classroom practitioners who describe in intimate detail how current – sometimes unnecessarily controversial – issues and narrow administrative, local, and state policy interpretations are negatively impacting PK-12 students' well-being and learning. These teachers offer an "insider" view on this impact and on how they are attempting to address such limitations with their own practices. A third set of contributors to this text are young people who are or recently have been in our nation's classrooms and who offer their own important insights about how teachers and schools might serve them best, particularly around the issues that are the focus of this text's chapters. We introduce these teachers and young people below.

How Might I Use This Book?

We put this book together to honor and amplify the voices of everyday teachers working for change in seemingly small but hugely important ways in their classrooms and with individual students. We hope to reach teachers who may be struggling in their own contexts, wondering how to grapple with a policy or practice that inhibits them from caring for and educating their students in meaningful ways.

Teachers, you may choose to read this book alone, as part of your personal reflection or growth. You may also choose to engage with this book as a workbook of sorts, perhaps reading it chapter by chapter with your grade level or subject team or your community of practice. Consider including your administrators, if you feel comfortable doing so, or reporting to them key insights or reflections you may glean from these pages. Chapters are written to be intentionally short and accessible and to offer meaningful, concrete advice from teachers just like you and young people just like your students.

Each chapter begins with a mini case about the highlighted topic. The chapters then include several experiences from our contributing teachers. You will find a section on "critical concepts" through which we can view the chapter's topic along with reflection questions to help you connect with the experiences shared in each chapter and to consider both the constraints you feel in your own context and the various resources you could leverage toward change. The critical concepts will push your reflections beyond the "easy" answers to potentially uncomfortable – but crucial – ideas for how you might change. Each chapter highlights the voices of young people on these topics and concludes with a list of resources that might be helpful as you consider delving further into learning and change.

Teacher and Youth Introductions

The Youth Research Council (YRC) was formed in 2021 to bring together high school students in the Northern Virginia area to conduct research on topics important to them and related to education and education policy. Now in its fourth year of operation, the YRC has completed two mixed methods studies exploring racial discrimination in schools and the multiple meanings and experiences of school safety – and unsafety. The YRC is dedicating its fourth year to taking action: presenting at school board meetings, conducting teacher professional development workshops, and more.

"Through Students' Eyes" (TSE) was founded by Kristien, high school teacher Jim Harmon, and journalist Piet van Lier as a photovoice high school dropout prevention project in 2004 in Cleveland, Ohio. The project originally asked young people what they thought were the purposes of school, what helped them succeed in school, and what impeded their engagement and success. The project continues to work with middle and high school students, using photography to explore their ideas about school, literacy, citizenship, their communities, and myriad other topics. TSE has also conducted projects with youth in India, Haiti, Sierra Leone, and Iraq.

The names and, in most cases, locations of all of our teacher contributors are pseudonyms. While many, if not all, of them yearn to say (and, in some cases, have said) what they have said in this volume to their colleagues, administrators, and leaders, in this divided and divisive political climate, they would be risking their jobs and often their personal safety.

Bjorn is a current assistant principal in a private Catholic school in northern Virginia. He brings over 22 years of experience working with special education students in both private and public schools and holds a PhD in Special Education Leadership.

Aloe Anastasia spent 11 years as a science educator working with K-8 students. Today, she is an assistant professor of education at a large university in the southeast United States.

Victoria Anderson has spent 24 years teaching high school English, and she was awarded Teacher of the Year in 2018. She also serves as a curriculum developer and mentor for new teachers.

Emily Beechum became a teacher at 30 and is currently in her eighth year teaching high school English in her home state of Illinois. She is currently working toward a degree in English literature.

Melanie Brady has been an English and journalism teacher for 17 years. In addition to inspiring her student journalists, she helped advocate for the New Voices legislation (Senate Bill 121: the Student Journalist Press Freedom Protection Act) in West Virginia that passed in 2023.

John Brown is a National Board-Certified Social Studies teacher in New York City, where he teaches students Social Studies and English. He is also a PhD candidate in history at a New York university.

Brithany Lizbeth Herson is relatively new to public education, but Brithany has been teaching and tutoring English language learners from many parts of the world for years. She currently works in a public high school in the suburbs of Washington, D.C.

Althea James is a career switcher, having left behind the corporate world of IT for the English Language Arts classrooms of secondary school. The American-born daughter of Filipino immigrants, Althea also recognizes the importance of representation and works to ensure that all her students are recognized, loved, and supported.

Matt Jones is a former middle school English teacher and professional development provider on adolescent literacy. After earning his PhD in Education, he had planned on joining academia. Instead, he now works to recruit, develop, and retain new teachers in a large urban public school district.

Petra Matthews is an ESOL (English for Speakers of Other Languages) teacher who won Teacher of the Year in 2023 in her state. She brings her own experience as an English language learner to her classroom where she serves high school students.

Amy Morris has served as an educator for almost two decades. She has taught students of all ages around the world, including in Chicago, South Korea, Germany, Hawai'i, and Virginia. Amy is a National Board-Certified Teacher in English Language Arts with master's degrees in English and education.

Heather Nettle has 11 years of experience as a teacher. She currently works at a high-need school with a vulnerably population, but she pushes back on the school's negative reputation. Instead, she insists that schools are more than their demographics.

Bobbi Page teaches high school English as a National Board-Certified Teacher. She also serves as her school's Writing Center co-director and Equity Lead.

Nathan Parson, who originally finished school for occupational therapy, became a teacher later in life after a variety of jobs and experiences. After three years as a teaching assistant working for a nonprofit with students with disabilities, Nathan finally landed his dream job at an elementary school working with students with autism.

Max Puccio is an assistant principal at a high school in California. He spent 15 years as a teacher and 10 years as an instructional coach and designing curricula for charter schools.

Carleigh Reilly graduated from a well-respected HBCU (Historically Black College and University) with a major in piano performance. Although she dreamed of being a full-time professional musician, she loves working as an elementary school music teacher and serves as department chair at her Title I school.

Frankie Reynolds spent nine years working with students with intellectual and developmental disabilities (IDD) in self-contained classrooms. She left the classroom to pursue her doctorate, which she recently completed, so she can advocate even better for students with disabilities.

Alfonso Roca is in his eighth year of high school English teaching. Born in Peru, he quickly took up the English language, and now he teaches it across various levels of English secondary classes. Additionally, he is involved in college access initiatives for first-generation and historically underrepresented communities.

Diane Sanders has worked in education for over 15 years. She has spent most of her time in Title I schools in the states of Washington, Georgia, and New York and currently teaches as a reading specialist and literacy coach for grades K-3.

Reese Smith is a veteran teacher and doctoral student. In addition to her graduate work, she co-teaches in a multi-age elementary classroom where she works with kindergarten, first-, and second-grade children.

Sabrina Thomas earned her Masters of Science in Special Education with endorsements in Learning Disabilities, Intellectual Disabilities, and Emotional Disabilities while teaching full time. Now in her 24th year in the elementary classroom, she believes classrooms and teachers must be responsive to the needs of children in ways that inspire children to fulfill their potential. She is proud to have a fully inclusive classroom where all are welcome.

Logan Vaughn teaches high school social sciences. He has been teaching history for 16 years with time split between Michigan, South Korea, and Kuwait. In 2023, he was named the National History Teacher of the Year by a renowned American philanthropy group.

Naomi Watkins has a Doctor of Education degree in organizational leadership and certification in administration and supervision. Dr. Watkins has served over 25 years in P-12 education as associate superintendent, director, coordinator, and school counselor. She has been an adjunct professor in higher education and continues to regularly collaborate with community groups and organizations.

Annie Wood is retired after 40 years of teaching high school English. She is now a full-time co-researcher and leader in a well-known research collective about framing conversations around equity and has published numerous peer-reviewed journal articles and book chapters sharing her experiences in participatory action research.

Gabby Wright has taught for 16 years in three different states: Oregon, Georgia, and South Carolina. Gabby has experience teaching biology and environmental science and serves as department chair.

References

Najarro, I. (2024, February 15). Teachers censor themselves on socio-political issues, even without restrictive state laws. *Education Week.* https://www.edweek.org/teaching-learning/teachers-censor-themselves-on-socio-political-issues-even-without-restrictive-state-laws/2024/02

Natanson, H. (2024, February 15). Teachers are limiting lessons on political, social issues, report finds. *The Washington Post.* https://www.washingtonpost.com/education/2024/02/15/teachers-limit-political-social-issues-lessons/

1

Race and Racism

Recently, National Public Radio's (NPR's) Planet Money *(Beras et al., 2023) program featured teacher Mandy Robek, a third-grade teacher at Shale Meadows Elementary School in Ohio. Using the popular Dr. Seuss book,* The Sneetches and Other Stories, *Robek set out to engage her elementary students in an economics lesson about consumer preferences and choices. She explained how as she reads the story to her students, she pauses to engage them in discussion. She asks probing questions about why certain characters are making particular decisions. At various points in the reading, she prompts students to predict what will happen next, and she helps them make connections between elements of the story and key economic concepts.*

In the interview, Robek pauses to recount how in one recent reading of the story, something she didn't anticipate happened: A student raised a question about why some of the Sneetches were treated differently based on their physical characteristics.

At this point in the lesson, the school division's communications liaison, who had been observing and who arranged the interview on the condition that the book and lesson focus only on economic and not cultural or political topics, interjects, "Can I pause this?" she asks. "I just feel like this isn't teaching anything about economics, and this is a little bit more about differences with race and everything like that."

And, with that, the lesson ends. The conversation stops. But – with the division's communications liaison still present – students press Robek for more information, asking what happens next in the book. Ms. Robek prompts them to ask their parents or families to read the book with them at home.

We offer this anecdote about the NPR story because it reminded us that schools are supposed to help students understand the world around them, to help them navigate their lived experiences, and to make sense of how these experiences fit into the broader social landscape. The story of Ms. Robek and her students and the in-the-moment intervention by a district-level administrator illustrate both the promise and the perils of teaching in politicized times and contexts. Students are hungry to understand the world and their places in it. They are also keenly aware of the racialized realities of the classroom, even if sometimes they cannot articulate the nature of and challenges with these realities.

In this example from an elementary classroom, Ms. Robek and her students had an opportunity to engage with the ways that race is inextricably intertwined with economics, politics, and society. It seems clear that Ms. Robek was capable of helping her students grasp and respond to these questions. But the instruction was ended at the behest of an overzealous and overly cautious district administrator, and a learning opportunity was missed because a bureaucrat became uncomfortable with the trajectory of the lesson.

What caused this discomfort? While the Planet Money *story did not reveal the rationale behind the district communication liaison's decision, it seems reasonable to suggest that the current political context was having a chilling effect on this division administrator's leadership choices. And the likely outcome of such a determination would be to curtail Ms. Robek's and other educators' willingness to engage with hot-button issues such as race – even when it is often our students who are identifying these topics and raising questions related to them.*

Laws aimed at preventing children and young people from experiencing feelings of guilt or discomfort when discussing issues of race, at curbing (or at least questioning) the teaching of African American history in states (e.g., in Florida and Virginia), and at attempting to limit access to books or other reading materials on racially sensitive topics have had what we would argue are their intended effects. That is, they are frightening teachers, schools, and school divisions away from even considering engaging students in conversations about race and racism. And that fear isn't just being engendered in our schools and classrooms: it's being fomented at the national level, by individuals vying to be our next president: One leading 2024 Republication presidential candidate struggled to identify race-based slavery as the cause of the American Civil War and another talked about "good bloodlines" and "good genes" when referring to the risks of immigrants crossing the border into the U.S.

We would ask that, as you read this chapter, you consider the myriad ways in which teachers encounter race and racism in their own classrooms, schools, and communities. We would ask you to pay attention to how teachers grapple with and often subtly resist policies and practices that run counter to their desire to care for kids in meaningful ways – by helping them view people of all races respectfully and reject rhetoric that judges others by the color of their skin. And – without ever uttering the words "racial consciousness" or "structural racism" – they help children and young people to understand the histories, causes, and effects of racism in our nation.

Critical Concepts

In this chapter, we share descriptions of the ways in which teachers encounter race and racism in their instruction, the challenges and fears they experience when exploring these issues, and – most importantly – the ways they continue to do this important work even in the face of fear-mongering local and state politicians, policies, and practices. Before you read about the experiences of our contributing teachers, we'd like you to consider two critical concepts that can change how you view some of these experiences, what you take from them, and how you apply your new ideas to your own classroom. As you ponder your own teaching context, instructional practices, and community settings, grab a notebook or start a new file in your phone or computer. Jot down some notes. This is a good way to keep yourself accountable and track your own thought processes.

Racial Consciousness

You may have heard people say, "I don't see race." Although the assumption here seems good – if we don't *see* race, then we can't *be* racist – this "colorblindness" can be discouraging to people who feel their race is a crucial part of their identity, usually people of Color. Adolescents in particular are in the process of discovering their identities, and to deny them a piece of that identity damages the relationship-building they need to do with their teachers. Therefore, it is more productive to acknowledge race and fight against racism when we see it (Wingfield, 2015).

Racial consciousness means you are aware of your own race and the race of others in a non-judgmental way. To consider your own racial consciousness, reflect on these questions:

- When were you first aware of your race?
- What do you remember from childhood about how you made sense of human differences? What were these differences? What confused you about these differences?
- What childhood experiences did you have with friends or adults who were different from you in some way? What still sticks out for you about these experiences – and about the differences of which you were aware?
- How, if ever, did any adult help you think about racial differences?

For those of us who identify as white, our racial consciousness may not be as developed as those who have been "raced" since early in life. Our – this book's authors' – own experiences with race might be useful to you as you consider your own. For Meagan, she remembers being a teenager when her mom praised her "colorblindness." At the time, Meagan felt reassured that that meant she didn't judge people based on skin tone. Yet, 30 years later, Meagan reflects on experiences she has had since then – including marrying a Black man and having children who identify as Black and biracial – that helped her become more racially conscious. Now, as an educator, activist, community member, and family member, Meagan tries to engage with others in ways that acknowledge and honor the many identities people have – including racial identities. This can be tricky. None of us wants to say the wrong thing or be offensive. But by not saying anything at all – or pretending difference does not exist – we can cause harm, erasing important parts of who people – especially children and youth – are.

Structural Racism
Sometimes, biased treatment is what it might appear to be in its simplest, most superficial form: an individual's actions or choices. But sometimes, it's a reflection of something deeper, more ingrained. Sometimes, bias is baked into the system in a way that is particularly difficult to change or even identify. This is called systemic – or structural – racism.

Structural racism is embedded in systems like education, healthcare, or housing (NIH, 2021), and these phenomena are often seen as "the way things are" because of how pervasive they are. Structural racism includes practices, policies, and norms that create barriers to equal educational, economic, and health outcomes. Structural racism is about intentionally – or unwittingly – maintaining white supremacy through mutually reinforcing systems of inequity (Oluo, 2019).

An example is the fact that Black students tend to receive lower scores on standardized math and English tests than their non-Black counterparts. Some may say that this is an "achievement gap" that can be rectified by dedicating more resources to bringing the scores of Black students up to the levels of their non-Black peers. Yet we know that standardized tests are deeply problematic and have clear racist roots, being developed in the early 1900s with the specific goal of excluding children of Color from schools and other opportunities and maintaining the superiority of what was then referred to as "the Nordic race group" (Brigham, 1922).

What we know is that, because of mutually reinforcing segregationist housing, economic, and educational policies, Black students are more likely to attend schools with inexperienced or low-paid teachers (Podolsky et al., 2016). We know that gifted-and-talented programs disproportionately exclude Black students (Flynn, 2023) and that educators often do not recognize the strengths of Black children not measured by standardized tests.

Finally, we know that negative societal messaging about Black students' academic abilities undercut their views of themselves (Wallace, 2023).

Through the lenses of racial consciousness and structural racism, then, we ask that you take some time to consider the following questions. If you feel yourself answering all the questions in ways that foreground individual acts of discrimination, push yourself to think about ways that racism is also present in practices or policies that guide how we act or decisions we make.

- ◆ How does race or racism show up in your classroom? In your school? In your community?
- ◆ Does it show up in really obvious ways or in more subtle ways?
- ◆ Do you see racism appear at a structural or systems level (e.g., in hiring practices, policy decisions, or assumptions about student outcomes) or in more individual actions (e.g., students using racial epithets or teachers using outdated materials)? Both?
- ◆ How do you see yourself as connected to racism? Have you felt targeted by racist comments or acts? Have you been a perpetrator, even in perhaps unwitting ways?
- ◆ If you were to make the case that you are *not* connected to racism, what rationale or argument would you make?

As you read through and make notes in response to these questions, if you find yourself saying something like, "Race is not really an issue here," we would ask that you consider others' perspectives. It might not be an issue for you, but is it an issue for a colleague? For some of your students – or even one? What about for parents or caregivers? Just because *you* don't see or feel the effects of racism doesn't mean it's not a real concern for others. And please note: If a person of Color says it is about race, it *is* about race. Reality is shaped by perception, and race is a crucial part of identity that cannot be erased; people of Color need to be validated in conversations about race and racism and what can be done to address racism (Oluo, 2019).

As you read perspectives from the teachers included in this chapter, and you consider how structural racism might operate in your own school – and, by extension, potentially in your own community – you also may find yourself angry, defensive, anxious, or uncertain. Race *should* be an emotional topic. We're not that far removed from being a nation where slavery was legal, and we're even closer in years to when the U.S. government built Japanese internment – concentration – camps on our own soil.

Talking about how some people are treated unfairly in our world *is* uncomfortable. We invite you to consider the resources included in this chapter to continue learning about this topic no matter your race because we are all shaped by structural racism, and our racial consciousness is never complete – it's always evolving. If you make a mistake, it is important to apologize and keep trying. The alternative is complacency in a system that oppresses people of Color (Oluo, 2019).

Teacher Stories

Now that you've reflected on your own contexts and the assumptions and experiences you bring to this topic, we invite you to read through the experiences of some of our contributing teachers. These are classroom teachers and education professionals who support classroom practitioners, and these individuals are working through these issues of race and racism in everyday ways like so many of today's teachers. We think their stories offer insights that can support you in addressing these issues in your own school and community spaces.

Nathan, elementary school teacher of students with autism: "Honestly, it needs to be talked about."

Nathan identifies as a Black man and is a teacher of students with autism at an elementary school. The school is quite diverse across many lines, including in terms of race and ethnicity. Nathan tells of a recent experience when he stepped up to address an issue with racism head-on. No one had asked him to do it. He was not on an equity or diversity committee in his school or school division. He did not have any formal authority to address this issue, per se. But he had established strong relationships with his students, and they had told him there were problems with students giving each other "permission" to use racial epithets. He spoke with his principal and offered to help:

> I found out that some kid had been going around giving other kids a "pass" to say the N-word. So, I went and talked to the principal, and I said, "This is something that needs to be dealt with and dealt with quick. Because I don't want these kids to *not* realize the severity of this." Because it seemed to be more of an issue among the boys in the 5th grade, I suggested that we pull all the 5th-grade boys into the gym and sit down and just talk to them. So, the principal said that she would call all the boys in and have a talk with them, and I said, "Well, honestly, I think I should be in there, too, because I think something like this would come off a lot better coming from me than, no offense,

coming from you." (The principal identifies as a white woman.) She was like, "Yeah, I think that's a really good idea."

And so, I sat them down and talked to them and at the end just gave them the challenge to come see me if they heard anything or heard a kid say something racist. Just come see me. I took that upon myself because, other than paperwork, nothing was being done for these kids.

Some of these comments, the boys thought they were jokes. Apparently one Middle Eastern boy was told to go back to his country, or he was told that his family was with the Taliban. Now, I didn't want anybody to feel targeted – yet. If it keeps going, I think we need to go to the child and just be like, "Listen, I know it's you. Cut it out." Because that's my approach. I'm direct. Because in a lot of situations, that's the best way to handle it, especially in this type of situation.

I hate to see something like that continue and ruin these kids' lives when it could have easily been avoided. Instead of teaching the proper way, or in a positive environment, it's just something we don't talk about. Even if it causes disruptions in the classroom. Even if it causes disruptions to the learning environment. We're still expected to avoid it. Like, completely. Honestly, it needs to be talked about.

Box 1.1 Your Stories

What connections do you make to what Nathan describes here? Do you see any connections to the idea of racial consciousness? How could you follow Nathan's example to not avoid discussions of racism and to talk about it openly? Is that something you feel equipped to do? If not, what could you do to feel more comfortable or ready?

Carleigh, elementary music teacher: "Be careful raising your voice with kids."

Carleigh is the music teacher at a Title 1 elementary school and has been there for six years. She is the "Encore" lead, meaning that she represents teachers of music, art, physical education, library, and media to the principal. Carleigh identifies as a Black woman, and her principal identifies as a biracial African American man. Carleigh says that most of her issues with education and schools have been related to the administrators she's worked with. And it's about not just how this particular principal treats her but also the ways he talks about being Black: "I've been in several meetings with him where he's referred to himself as a 'nappy-headed, bucktooth little Black boy.' It makes me shudder every time he says it. It's so negative to say that about yourself." Carleigh thinks about the Black students who are in her classes: "How do you think they would feel if they heard you say that? Yeah. Horrifying. If students heard that, they are going to repeat that! They look up to you! You're the principal!"

> **Box 1.2 Your Stories**
>
> In an ideal world, what would your role be as a teacher or administrator in addressing racism at your school? Do you feel like you have what you need to fill that role? What, if anything, is holding you back? Do you have existing relationships with people who can support you? If not, how might you go about building those relationships?

Matt, former high school teacher and current educational leader in a major metropolitan city: "All of our educators of Color have left."

Matt shares how frustrated he is with his own school board in their perpetuation of structural racism:

> I mean, I went to the school board and publicly called them all racists last year. I mean, I said it in academic-y terms. I said that they were engaging in structural racism or something like that. They had pushed out two veteran Black leaders, one of whom was my mentor and friend who had convinced me to come work for [this school system]. I didn't even work a single day under him. Then they didn't pay our first-year teachers their stipends, almost all of whom are Black and Brown educators, and a quarter of whom are multilingual educators. I'm a white man in America. I don't have any kids or family I have to worry about. If I get fired tomorrow, I'll find another job. I have a doctorate from [an Ivy League university]. I'll be okay. My best friend is the head of the [my city's] Teachers Union. And I still lost when I addressed the school board. People are just fed up here. The nonprofit that I work for is a kind of accelerated teacher pipeline program. Eight people used to work here and we are down to two. All of our educators of Color have left. I was going to leave last year, but I'm going to give it one more year. Maybe we can build something on the ashes.

Box 1.3 Your Stories

As you reflect on the ways in which Matt identifies practices of structural racism (i.e., pushing out educators of Color, not paying first-year teachers, most of whom identify as people of Color), you might work with your own grade-level or subject area team or your community of practice to think about how your own school or school district is implicated – or not – in structural racism. Here are some prompts to get you started:

- Take turns briefly sharing your reactions (emotional, physical, psychological) to Matt's experience.
- What stuck out to you? What were you surprised by?
- What connections did you make? How is your context different or the same?
- As you discuss, what comes up as something you might want to learn more about, change, or address in your own context?

As you work with your colleagues to prioritize and strategize for change, you might use a tool called Forcefield Analysis to make sense of the factors at play when working with issues of race. This tool was created for use by community organizers and is also used in community-based research (Chambers, 2002). Such tools can be especially helpful for teachers who are trying to understand and address larger, often political, issues.

Forcefield Analysis can be adapted to fit your style and goals, and it's quite simple to implement. You'll need flipchart paper or an online collaborative tool of your choice (e.g. Google Docs, Microsoft Teams, Canva).

In the center, draw a shape and write in it a word or phrase that represents your goal for a positive outcome to the issue you, your students, your colleagues (teachers and administrators), and/or your community are encountering. Next, draw arrows "pushing" (acting as a positive or helpful force) or "pulling" (acting as a negative or constraining force) toward or against your goal. Use thicker arrows to represent stronger forces and thinner ones to represent forces that are not as strong. This can be a great way to visualize the forces at play and to ensure you have the full picture of your context.

After you have mapped things out, use a different color marker or a different shape to brainstorm opportunities or levers for change. For example, are there new relationships to be formed to help make change? Do you need to understand different perspectives? Perhaps you need to review the policies of your school or the common teaching practices used by teachers in your building. All this can be mapped out using this type of tool.

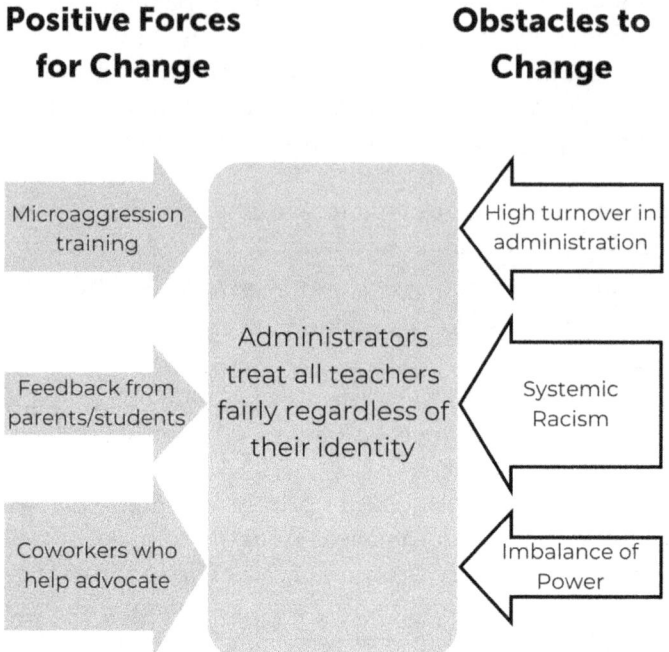

Figure 1.1 An Example of the Forcefield Analysis Based on Carleigh's Experience with Structural Racism.

Teacher Strategies

We know most teachers just want to care for kids and help them learn and find joy in learning. But so much in today's world complicates that. In this section, we offer some straightforward ways that teachers like you have grappled with the complexities of teaching about or in the context of race and racism.

Emily, English teacher in rural Illinois: "So many people want to say, 'Well, this doesn't exist anymore,' because they've never experienced it."

Emily said that a simple thing she does to help her students (most of whom are white) have a broader understanding of race and develop racial consciousness is to choose more recently published books, because students can connect with these and see them as relevant to their lives. Such books almost invariably bring up issues of race and how to work through them:

> I mean, the biggest reason [I choose these books] is because so many of my students are white, and they are going to stay in this community

their entire lives. They're not going to have much of a chance to be exposed to other perspectives on race, and so their understanding is limited. Even for me, as a child, I felt like my parents were very supportive of just generally being kind and respecting all people. But I didn't know anything until I went elsewhere about the realities and history of race and things like that.

And so, I feel like it's important to at least get a small taste of a different perspective on race and a different look into others' experiences. So many people want to say, "Well, this doesn't exist anymore," because they've never experienced it. And so, showing that other people are experiencing these issues right now is really important. That's why I love to get books for my students that are written during my student's lifetime.

Through that lens of teaching literature, Emily discusses how her understanding of race and her teaching practices have evolved over the first almost decade of her teaching career:

As a first-year teacher, I was very like, "We can't ignore history, and it's important to look at it in this book [*To Kill a Mockingbird*] in all its ugly reality, and to face it straight on, and not try to skip over it or ignore it." But I didn't realize that with the students of color in my classroom, maybe they don't want it thrown in their face, especially by me as a white teacher, right? Even just playing the audiobook in front of the class, right? I cringe now. So, yeah, that's one thing.

And another thing, I really like *Monster* [a seminal book by Walter Dean Myers], but I wish the main character wasn't Black and on trial. I wish that there was a different story being told somewhere in there. And that's why I advocated for *Dear Martin* or *All American Boys* or *The Hate U Give*. Just another perspective of not just a Black teenager on trial.

Box 1.4 Your Stories

As you read through Emily's experiences, what resonates with you? How have your perspectives about race and how to address issues of race and racism in the classroom shifted since you've become a teacher? What has been important for you? Are there ways you have been able to subtly resist the status quo in your own classroom or school around such issues? As you look to your colleagues and how they are addressing these issues, what practices might you adopt or adapt? What changes might you suggest to your grade level or subject area team about how – and if – you might collectively take on such issues?

Carleigh: "You have to make education fun and relevant."

Echoing Emily's strategies with integrating more diverse and current literature into her instruction, Carleigh talked about including Black music and musicians in her curriculum. She says that she tries to be inclusive and that even though she gets pushback from parents sometimes, she continues to focus on the music and meet kids where they are:

> I try to be as inclusive as possible in the music I teach. I have had some parents contact me – and even the principal – about how deep I was going into the music. I try to focus on a different artist of the month. So, Michael Jackson and Bob Marley – I've been told by parents they didn't feel like that was appropriate. Just focusing on their music and what they've contributed musically to our world.
>
> As a teacher, you have to meet kids where they are and make education relevant to them. Especially because we're fighting with so many things, with technology, so how can you make school applicable? I try my best to focus on people from all backgrounds and cultures, but I've had complaints because, "Oh, Bob Marley smoked," or the whole investigation of Michael Jackson. I tell parents I'm just focusing on the music, I don't talk about their lifestyle. We're just focusing on their music, we're learning about all genres of music and learning to appreciate all styles. But I have had complaints about that, but not about other artists I may choose to highlight.

Logan, a high school AP History teacher: "Your words are going to have power but not until you have respect for being good at what you do."

Navigating the current climate where even the choice of a book to read, a picture to include in a slideshow, or a story to share with the class can bring about intense scrutiny is a challenge that even the most experienced educators face. Logan, a high school Advanced Placement (AP) history teacher who has been recognized nationally for his work in developing anti-racist AP U.S. History lessons, offers this advice:

> When you're [a new teacher], it's about relationships with kids. It was a strength of mine coming out of college, being young and full of energy. It covered a lot of my sins. But then I grew up. Went

abroad. Got my Masters. Became more confident in advocating for truth where I saw young people we left behind, left to see a false sense of things where these lies were harming students or community. Now I'm older, more experienced, I chose my district carefully…I would say if you're a young teacher, don't put pressure on yourself. You need a long view. Your words are going to have power, but not until you have respect for being good at what you do, right? So that would be my advice to young teachers: Just come in and try to be a really good teacher. To do that really well is hard. That's enough pressure. Master that first. Because you're not in a good position to attack. My whole thing [is usually] "offense, offense, offense" but if you're outnumbered, if you have no real experience yet, attack is a really terrible strategy. Be strategic about it. If I was a young teacher, coming out of college feeling good, feeling passionate about things, I'd keep a slightly lower profile. What until you have some experience. Slowly learn to find that voice.

Naomi, former school counselor and current Family and Community Engagement Director: "Just being aware of who's in the room."

Naomi provides professional development related to equity and diversity across her school district. She shares how important it is when having difficult conversations built to nurture racial consciousness to consider who is in the room and to anticipate any conflict that may arise:

> Every time I do a professional development, I sit and think of as many ways that that could potentially cause a conflict and in a professional development session, I would say that happens every single time because we're in public schools and we do answer to the public, so to speak. People have different perspectives. And so just being aware of who's in the room. where individuals are in their awareness of equity and how it's applied to their lives, and then knowing how deeply to go based upon who may be in a room. For example, if I know people have been doing equity work for a long time, then I'll go deeper and use more challenging resources than if I'm with teachers who may be just being exposed. So, every single time I'm very aware and very conscious of the materials that I'm using for that reason.

> **Box 1.5 Your Strategies**
>
> Taking all the suggestions and examples Nathan, Carleigh, Logan, and Naomi provide here, what do you envision for how you could make small changes in your own classroom or school to develop your own racial consciousness, meet students where they are, and perhaps prompt critical thinking – or the development of racial consciousness – in new ways? How can you push against going "shallow" and instead "go deeper," as Naomi suggests? What would it take to help you feel comfortable modeling that?
>
> We suggest that one of the most important things you can do is build meaningful relationships not only with your students but with their families. In elementary school, this may look like inviting regular participation of family members in your classroom. In upper grades, this may look like reaching out through personalized email check-ins. You'll likely have better ideas based on your own context as well as the needs and particular constraints of your community.
>
> We echo Nathan to stress the importance of talking openly and not shying away from conversations about race and racism. This can be hard, especially in current times of censorship and hostility toward anything related to diversity, equity, and inclusion. You know your context best. If you feel vulnerable where you are, consider reaching out to colleagues and others who could help you create a coalition of sorts as you support each other.

Youth Stories

In addition to teachers, young people understand the complexity and pervasiveness of racism in schools. The Youth Research Council (YRC) was founded in 2021 to gather diverse young people as co-researchers ("YRC Fellows"), alongside university-based researchers, to gather evidence of the mental health effects of racial microaggressions on high school-aged youth in the Northern Virginia/Washington, D.C. metropolitan region. In 2023, the YRC released a report of their findings. One piece of data highlighted in the report is that the majority (60%) of racial microaggressions take place in classrooms, in the full view of teachers. For students who identify as Black or African American, this number jumps to 81%. In addition, YRC survey respondents noted that teachers often dismiss racial microaggressions as "not racist" or as simple misunderstandings, often deepening the wounds caused by the initial discriminatory acts (Box 1.6).

> **Box 1.6 Microaggressions in schools**
>
> While overt acts of racism may be less common today, racial discrimination is a common experience for students in school settings (Hope et al., 2015) through the more subtle, day-to-day acts of racism and discrimination known as microaggressions (Ayón & Philbin, 2017; Steketee et al., 2021; Sue et al., 2007). These microaggressions are "often unconscious and unintentionally hurtful" but nevertheless result in the "'othering' of race, language, and culture" for students of Color (Kohli & Solórzano, 2012, p. 448).
>
> A growing body of research demonstrates that racial microaggressions result in negative academic and mental health outcomes for Black and Brown youth (Benner & Graham, 2011; Hope, Skoog, & Jagers, 2015; Keels et al., 2017). Enduring these acts has been reported to result in students of Color coming to see their culture, names, and other aspects of their identity as inferior to their white peers and has led to feelings of shame and 'othering' as well as increased anxiety (Kohli & Solórzano, 2012). Such negative tolls on mental health have also been connected to increased absenteeism and a drop in grade point average (Benner & Graham, 2011).

But how aware are our students of such acts? What do they suggest teachers and schools might do to address these? Mahmoud, a high school student in Alexandria, Virginia and member of the Through Students' Eyes initiative, shares that, to him, the purpose of school is

> to learn, but most times people think of this as academic. But [what] I mean [is] learning about people's cultures, also social skills. There are a lot of experiences in life – racism, discrimination. Personally, sometimes the influences in your life don't allow you to feel like yourself. Sometimes you just go down and have to get back up.

 Taking Action

So, informed by these notions of racial consciousness and structural racism, how do race and racism affect your classroom? Your students? Your community? Your district? It's different for every teacher, every student, every school, but as we see through the examples provided by our contributing teachers, it is crucial that we consider how we may be complicit in perpetuating both individual acts of racism – even unconsciously – and broader systemic racism.

Teachers, as you consider these ideas alone, with a single colleague, or with a community of practice with a broader group of your peers, you might reflect on individual students you are currently teaching. How do they feel in your classroom? Do they know you care about them, their family, and their community? How can you deepen your relationships with them, so you better understand their perspectives, needs, and goals?

Administrators, are there concerns you have related to race and racism at your school? Do you feel equipped to navigate those concerns, or do you feel at a loss? We urge you to use the reflective questions and tools included in this chapter, get a little uncomfortable, and work for meaningful change.

Perhaps we should reflect on the suggestion made by Bruno in the introduction that

> we need to reimagine the professionalism of teachers, because we are asked to do a lot more than what teachers in the past have been asked to do. We need to go back to basics and provide avenues for students to be able to learn how to talk about their own race and their personal identity.

As you reflect, jot down some notes for yourself. You may consider using the worksheet – or a version of it – found in Appendix A. Whatever you use to aid you in this reflective process, try to focus your thoughts in four areas:

1) What are your current practices, as a teacher, administrator, educator, or advocate?
2) What is your ideal situation in your classroom, school, or professional setting?
3) What are your constraints in achieving your ideal?
4) What or who are your resources in making change?

Once you have some notes or have filled out the worksheet, consider working with a colleague or in your community of practice to note similarities and differences in your perspectives and ideas. How can you work together to prioritize goals, plan, and act for change? We would suggest then checking out at least one of the texts from the library list in the online resources or checking out at least one of the resources listed at the end of the chapter: begin to make your consideration of change *real*.

Resources

Books:

- *Do the Work: The Antiracist Activity Book* by W. Kamau Bell and Kate Schatz. A workbook with guided activities to help people explore their own identities. An interactive way to learn practical social justice strategies. Includes scripts and talking points for difficult conversations. A kinetic way to become more antiracist.
- *So You Want to Talk About Race* by Ijeoma Oluo. The author guides readers of all races through conversations that are both necessary and difficult, from police brutality to the model minority myth.
- *Racial Healing Handbook* by Anneliese A. Singh. In this book, the author guides readers through practical activities to navigate current experiences with racism and heal from past experiences.

Podcast: *Southlake* by NBC (if short on time, Episode 2: Just a Word). Follows the story of the first school district in Texas to begin the fight against Critical Race Theory in schools. Interviews students for their personal stories as well as numerous school board members, local politicians, and families affected by racism in public schools. Episode 2 includes a recorded conversation between a Black student and her white principal after a white student insists everyone should be allowed to say the N-word. The episode highlights the dangerous impact that uninformed educators could make on students of Color, even with the best intentions.

TED Talk: "How Students of Color Confront Imposter Syndrome" (10 minutes). Dena Simmons discusses how being Black and academically motivated fostered an identity crisis as a student. She highlights strategies to make all students feel welcomed and affirmed, navigating hidden biases and stereotypes within both our own identities and the identities of others. Link: https://www.ted.com/talks/dena_simmons_how_students_of_color_confront_impostor_syndrome

Online Resources:

- Essential Partners: Excellent resources on dialogue facilitation, often with a focus on education. Resources are free and include lessons for a school-wide reading of *Just Mercy* by Bryan Stevenson, resisting polarization in an election season, classroom exercise on dialogue, discussion and debate, and more. Trainings are advertised on the website: www.whatisessential.org

◆ Talking About Race: A free online resource from the Smithsonian that helps readers build a sense of identity and celebrate the diversity of humanity while learning how to fight against prejudice and racism. Link: https://nmaahc.si.edu/learn/talking-about-race

References

Ayón, C., & Philbin, S. P. (2017). "Tú No Eres de Aquí": Latino children's experiences of institutional and interpersonal discrimination and microaggressions. *Social Work Research, 41*(1), 19–30. https://doi.org/10.1093/swr/svw028

Benner, A. D., & Graham, S. (2011). Latino adolescents' experiences of discrimination across the first 2 years of high school: Correlates and influences on educational outcomes. *Child development, 82*(2), 508–519.

Beras, E., Romer, K., Peaslee, E. (Hosts). (2023). "The economic lessons in kids books." *Planet money* [Audio podcast]. National Public Radio. https://www.npr.org/2023/01/05/1147069942/kids-books-economics-lessons

Brigham, C. C. (1922). *A study of American intelligence.* Princeton University Press; Oxford University Press.

Chambers, R. (2002). *Relaxed and Participatory Appraisal: Notes on practical approaches and methods for participants in PRA/PLA-related familiarisation workshops* (Vol. 353). Brighton: Participation Group, Institute of Development Studies, University of Sussex.

Flynn, A. S. (2023). Black minds matter: A longitudinal analysis of the persistent underrepresentation of Black students in Gifted education programs. *Journal of Leadership, Equity, and Research, 9*(1), 6–20.

Hope, E. C., Skoog, A. B., & Jagers, R. J. (2015). "It'll never be the white kids, it'll always be us" black high school students' evolving critical analysis of racial discrimination and inequity in schools. *Journal of Adolescent Research, 30*(1), 83–112.

Keels, M., Durkee, M., & Hope, E. (2017). The psychological and academic costs of school-based racial and ethnic microaggressions. *American Educational Research Journal, 54*(6), 1316–1344. https://doi.org/10.3102/0002831217722120

Kohli, R., & Solórzano, D. G. (2012). Teachers, please learn our names!: Racial microaggressions and the K-12 classroom. *Race Ethnicity and Education, 15*(4), 441–462. https://doi.org/10.1080/13613324.2012.674026

National Institute on Minority Health and Health Disparities (NIH). (2021). *Structural racism and discrimination.* U.S. Department of Health and &

Human Services. https://www.nimhd.nih.gov/resources/understanding-health-disparities/srd.html

Oluo, I. (2019). *So you want to talk about race*. Hachette UK.

Podolsky, A., Kini, T., Bishop, J., & Darling-Hammond, L. (2016). *Solving the teacher shortage: How to attract and retain excellent educators*. Learning Policy Institute.

Steketee, A., Williams, M. T., Valencia, B. T., Printz, D., & Hooper, L. M. (2021). Racial and language microaggressions in the school ecology. *Perspectives on Psychological Science 16*(5), 1075–1098. https://doi.org/10.1177/1745691621995740

Sue, D. W., Capodilupo, C. M., Torino, G. C., Bucceri, J. M., Holder, A., Nadal, K. L., & Esquilin, M. (2007). Racial microaggressions in everyday life: Implications for clinical practice. *American psychologist*, *62*(4), 271.

Wallace, D. (2023). *The culture trap: Ethnic expectations and unequal schooling for black youth*. Oxford University Press.

Wingfield, A. H. (2015, September 13). Color blindness is counterproductive. *The Atlantic*. https://www.theatlantic.com/politics/archive/2015/09/color-blindness-is-counterproductive/405037/

2
Immigrants and Immigration

The longer our guest presenter talked, the more visibly uncomfortable Christopher became until he reached the point where he could no longer even listen to the conversation.

"Christopher, are you okay?" Jeff asked.

He shook his head. "Can we talk in the hall?"

They quietly slipped out of the classroom, just as Christopher began to cry. A representative from the community college had come to Jeff's ninth-grade Honors World History class to talk about the process of dual enrollment in World History II for the next academic year; this structure allowed students to earn both high school and college credit for their coursework.

Through his drying tears, Christopher explained his reaction.

> *I can't do this. I am not even a citizen. I can't take these college classes because I don't have the right paperwork. And I can't tell her that because I don't know her. What if she turns me in? I can't take that risk, not with [Donald] Trump as president.*

What should have been a benign presentation had turned into a traumatic experience for Christopher. While many Americans continue to describe public education as the "great equalizer," for so many immigrant students the realities of their experiences make it something entirely different. Christopher was a great student – bright, thoughtful, kind, and compassionate. A quiet leader. Hard-working and inquisitive. In short, the very student every dual enrollment teacher wants to have on their roster.

But instead of feeling proud and hopeful for the next year and the prospect of exciting new academic challenges, he found himself afraid and embarrassed. Instead of celebrating his accomplishments and looking forward to more, he was questioning his claim to the same opportunities his classmates would be pursuing.

As Christopher's experience illustrates, immigration continues to be a highly politicized topic that reaches well beyond the halls of Congress or the campaign trail and into the classroom, but even teachers aren't all on the same side with this issue. For example, in 2018, elementary school teachers in Idaho unintentionally made themselves the center of an immigration controversy when they came to school on Halloween dressed wearing large cardboard segments painted to look like a wall and emblazoned with the words "Make America Great Again." Reasonably, many took offense at the teachers' tone-deaf depiction of former president Trump's border wall and their blatant political proselytizing with the use of Trump's slogan. Yet 15,000 petitioners pledged support for the teachers and pleaded with the school district not to fire them (O'Kane, 2018).

As a sign of just how extreme the rhetoric surrounding immigration has become in the U.S., in 2018 sitting U.S. president Donald Trump described immigrants as being from "shithole" countries. This, of course, was consistent with his campaign speech a few years earlier, when he assessed some Mexican immigrants as – in his words – criminals, rapists, and drug dealers. It's still shocking that his reward for such offensive hyperbole was the highest elected office in our nation. Even as recently as December 2023, Trump used words reminiscent of Adolf Hitler, describing the effects of immigration as "poisoning the blood of our country" (Gibson, 2023). Meanwhile, over the past several years, conservative media have continued to advance the "great replacement theory," a racist conspiracy hypothesis that suggests that non-white immigrants are being brought to the United States to supplant white voters.

Students and teachers have no choice but to operate within this tinderbox of a climate. A case in point: One of the Youth Research Council Fellows with whom Meagan and Jeff have worked described her experiences as a Muslim student in her northern Virginia high school, sharing that a classmate had bluntly told her that they could no longer be friends. She recalled her classmate saying, "Trump told me about your people."

Alarmingly – but not surprisingly, as schools reflect rather than engender the realities outside of them – the rancor common on the national political scene has leeched into local politics, including school board races, and with real effects. For example, in this chapter, contributing teacher Petra Matthews describes the ways in which local political races took on strong anti-immigration fervor and the ways in which these races impacted her school and school division.

We ask that, as you read this chapter, you reflect on how these anti-immigrant sentiments and even policies might impact a young person who is merely trying to get an education and a teacher who is simply attempting to educate young people.

As with issues of racism, teachers like Jeff and Petra are dealing daily with their immigrant students' often-negative experiences.

Critical Concepts

In this chapter, we offer insights into the ways that teachers are attempting to serve their immigrant students, often in the face of the extreme perspectives too many political actors are foisting upon the public under the guise of "protecting our children." As with every such community issue, teachers are just doing their best to care for the kids in their classrooms – regardless of what country they're from or when they arrived in this one. To inform your reading about these teacher stories and strategies, you might explore two critical concepts, which we think will help you consider a new lens on how to be that best teacher for your immigrant students. Please pick up that notebook or re-open that file and keep track of the big ideas and best practices.

Ethnocentrism

Ethnocentrism is the practice of viewing other cultures through your own. While this might seem like a reasonable or even unavoidable – and unwitting – practice, putting the filter of your own culture over the culture of others can distort your view of others, including of the students in your classrooms. To recognize the pitfalls of ethnocentrism and become more culturally responsive to those around you, it's first important to recognize your own culture. "Culture" in itself is a very broad term, but we can begin to skim the surface of an understanding of it by answering three deceptively simple questions about ourselves:

- What foods or drinks are often associated with *your* culture?
- What tools and objects are considered foundational or everyday in your extended family?
- What language or traditions are unique to – and yet "normal" in – your core community?

Everything has or is part of a culture, whether that culture is rooted in a family, friend, historical, geographic, or professional context. For example, if you are a teacher, the food and drinks in your culture may be coffee, apples, or donuts. Objects in your culture may be your favorite pen, chalk, or the copy maker. For language, not only is it your spoken language, but it's common phrases like "Double check that your name is on your paper" or "Single file line, please." Culture is always a mixture of common stereotypes – the way that others may perceive you – and your own lived realities. And often these overlap.

You can apply these questions to other pieces of your identity to discover your personal, familial, of community culture. Maybe you are from New Orleans. Your food is crawfish, gumbo, and jambalaya. Objects in your culture are jazz music, architecture, and masks. Your language would include creole, and your traditions would include Mardi Gras, second lines, and jazz funerals. Again, this example of a culture is a mixture of stereotypes and reality because culture is shaped by history, lived experience, and outside perceptions.

Of course, these questions just scratch the surface of our understandings of culture, but then we start to realize that these elements of our identity are subjective and that each individual – our colleagues, our students, and their families – would answer these in their own way. As teachers serving so many diverse students (or even those who do not *appear* to be any different from their peers), we have a unique responsibility to be aware of this range of cultures, to know them all to some extent, and to help young people to respect their own and each other's. Beginning with an awareness of your own culture will help you recognize the vibrancy of another's culture and remind you that while stereotypes shape culture, they do not always reflect individual realities. We're sure you already realized that there is much more to culture than food, objects, and language. But these queries can open you up to asking the nonjudgmental questions about young people's lives and cultures outside of your own, ultimately enabling you to build the relationships that are foundational to teaching and to expand your own cultural competency.

Collectivism and Individualism Spectrum

Once you've begun to explore that concept of culture and begun to understand how our focus on our own culture can very easily slip into ethnocentrism, we'd ask you to dive in a bit further. Of course, deeper notions of culture go beyond the physical representations of culture – food, objects, holidays – and include other forms of agreed-upon elements, including values, morals, and beliefs.

One common archetype to help us understand deep culture is the spectrum of collectivism and individualism. In simplest terms, collectivist cultures value cooperation, communication, and relationships, whereas individualist cultures value competition, achievement, and independence. In this spectrum, about 20% of the world – mostly European countries – have more individualistic cultures, while the other 80% tend toward more collectivist societies (Hammond, 2015). In an individualist society,

- Individual achievement is honored more often than group success
- Emphasis on self-reliance over depending on others
- Learning and achievement are believed to occur through individual study and independent hard work rather than group interactions and dialogue
- Individual contributions and status are more important than group harmony
- Competition – rather than collaboration – is more often used to motivate individuals

We're sure you can see the potential for conflict when these two cultures attempt to coexist – in a community or in a school. In a society that is increasingly filled with immigrants, such tensions are inevitable, but they often play out in everyday ways in classrooms. One example of these culture clashes with which many of us – including non-teachers – may be familiar is multigenerational living. In the United States, which is considered a highly individualistic culture, it is traditional for children to move out of their parents' homes for college and become independent.

An adult who moves back in with their parents or family after college is often perceived of as lazy or immature. By contrast, in more collectivist societies, moving back in with parents is just a practical – and expected – move. If multiple generations are living together and contributing to a household, they are all working together to pay bills and support one another. In some cultures, it is not uncommon for children to stay in the home well into adulthood.

These archetypes are not to be used as sweeping oversimplifications of people's identities. Instead, they are meant to highlight how one person's understanding of what is "right" might clash deeply with another's. Additionally, many students immigrating to America likely have a more collectivist culture and find the many individualistic elements in American culture jarring. These archetypes offer a starting point for helping teachers to meet students where they are in their orientation.

As with all of the chapters in this volume, before you read, we invite you to take a moment to reflect on your own context, experiences, and current or evolving teaching practices. Keep track of these responses in that journal or in that notes file on your computer; we'd also invite you to keep returning to that journal as you read this chapter, to consider how your thinking might shift, what questions are raised for you, and what practices seem relevant for your own instruction. With this topic we'd also suggest that you begin to talk with not only your colleagues (e.g., other teachers) but also members of your friend and family circles and even members of your community.

- Is your classroom, school, or community more homogenous or more diverse? In what ways?
- What is your connection with immigration? For example, are you an immigrant yourself? Have you ever experienced being a newcomer? Perhaps someone in your family or community has experienced this? How have they felt? Who welcomed them? How were they treated?
- Do you have someone in your classroom who was not born in the United States? Try to take their perspective for a moment. How do you think they feel in your class? How might they feel as they walk into school? As they sit at lunch or on the bus? As they participate in activities or cultural celebrations? As current events are discussed or debated?

Box 2.1 The Numbers

As of October 2023, there were 4.7 million foreign-born individuals enrolled in Pre-K through postsecondary education, which represents 6% of the student population. About 20 million students have foreign-born parents.

(U.S. Department of Education, 2023)

Teacher Stories

As you consider your relationship to and assumptions about immigration and immigrants, read through some of the experiences that teachers shared with us. As you read, you might take notes about how you're feeling and how you are responding to their experiences. Do you recognize them as similar to your own? Vastly different? What are the salient issues in your context?

Petra, 2023 Teacher of the Year in her state: "I just thought we let them age out of the system."

When we talked with Petra, she described the heart-wrenching decision of moving to another school district because of what she saw as a "bigoted" environment in her prior school.

I had some conversations with the superintendent and school board members where they truly were not supportive of [multilingual] students. There were some conversations where they mentioned, "Oh, you know, when students come in and they are 17 [years old], what do we do?" And I said, "Oh, we should really try hard for them to graduate," and the response was, "I just thought we let them age out of the system."

So, there were those conversations that for me really put me in a position where, here I am, the [state] teacher of the year, and I'm all for equity and diversity and doing the best for students no matter where they come from or who they are, or no matter their situation. And the conversations in the district were such a bigoted view of the school system and the people that work there. That was not something that I appreciated. So, I looked for a district that would be more consistent with my core beliefs and landed on [a small public school district], which is very diverse. We are 90% Latino.

A lot of our students are bilingual. I mean, you walk the corridors, and students are speaking different languages. So, I felt that that was a better place and a better fit for me. And not only that, but there was so much opportunity, and so many options for students to build a better future for themselves. So, it was a good change for me.

I still feel guilty for leaving [the other district]. Especially my school. [It] was amazing. I had such wonderful colleagues. They are still there. The overall school was a very good fit for me, but I felt like the political climate was very heavy, and they were putting a lot of emphasis, not on students, but on the political climate and on changing the political sphere rather than on the student population.

If I could pick that school up and move it somewhere else, that would have been my ideal situation. But I think overall looking at how the system was being run, I just could not morally continue to work for that system. I'm not the only one that left from the ESOL [English for Speakers of Other Languages] department. We had 35 ESOL teachers and about 16 left, including me and the head of the ESOL department.

Most teachers cannot – and should not – have to leave a school they love due to the ways that political pressures around immigration are contradicting core human values and compromising services to students. But these are sometimes the moves that professionals must make in order to maintain their personal integrity or to uphold the ideals of equity to which all educators should be committed.

> **Box 2.2 Your Stories**
>
> Who are the students in your classroom or school on whom you see some teachers, administrators, or even school board members or local politicians "giving up"? What are the demographic profiles of these individuals? What makes it acceptable – in the eyes of some adults – to assess some kids and their cultures as unworthy of our highest standards and very best efforts? How might you approach these adults – who with you share the responsibility for helping all young people, regardless of their country of birth – to help them appreciate the assumptions they are making about these students and their cultures?

Petra: "I honestly stopped teaching the book."

But it's not just these ideals that are being jeopardized as a result of these anti-immigrant rhetoric and pressures. As Petra notes, it's also their daily teaching practices:

> There is a book that I think a lot of middle school teachers and high school teachers know. It's called *The Absolutely True Diary of a Part-Time Indian* [by Sherman Alexie]. It's a book about a student who lives on a reservation and attends school on the reservation, and then he decides to go to what we might call a white school. He describes the changes, how he lives, how he compares his old school to the white school. It talks a lot about their feelings coming to a different country and comparing and contrasting their lives with their new schools and different things. But once certain policies were passed in my previous school, I honestly stopped teaching the book. I was afraid that there would be some complaints. I was worried that maybe I would get into trouble for teaching a book that has never caused any issues for me in the past.

While it might seem extreme, too many teachers who have that intentionally empathetic perspective on children and young people are choosing to leave the schools serving young people who are dealing with what is likely the most upsetting reality any of us could ever face: a desperate move out of their home, community, and country.

Aloe, elementary school STEM teacher: "I don't know what I could do about it."

Like Petra, Aloe, a STEM (science, technology, engineering, and mathematics) teacher at an under-resourced elementary school, struggled with the fact that her school lacked many of the resources to adequately support refugee students. In fact, she said the school had begun to resemble a prison in many ways. Ultimately, Aloe left K-12 teaching to pursue a position training preservice science teachers so that she could implement, in her words, a "more holistic and humanizing approach to education." She reflected on what she would have done differently had she stayed a classroom teacher:

> If I had stayed at that school, I would have really advocated a lot more holistically for the students. So that school, I think, is the poorest elementary school in that county. In 2021–2022, they received over 100 Afghan refugee students throughout the year. Now their numbers are at about 960 students. It's ridiculous, and they just keep adding modular buildings to accommodate all the additional students. They have this beautiful field they could use for outdoor learning or recreation, and they just keep adding modular buildings. The year I came they added a quad, and then I went back there in November, and they had had to add two more quads and a bathroom building, all outside the main school. So the space that these 960 kids have to play is now so small and ridiculous.
>
> That was really frustrating for me. I don't know what I could do about it. But if I had stayed, I would want to advocate for access to more places to play, or the ability to maybe even just walk two blocks and go to a park, or brainstorming solutions with administration. It just felt like prison, like the students were just so confined and fenced in, and they had to rotate recess. Three days a week, second graders would just have no playground, and all they had was a really small field, for 150 kids per grade or more.
>
> You think in this area, you think this county is all about equity. But you look at that school compared to others. The teachers who work there are incredible, but they just don't have the resources.
>
> So many of these students come to the United States, and some have gone through a lot of traumatic experiences to get here. A lot of our Afghan female students had never been to school, so there was a lot of trauma and fear. For the most part the teachers in that community were incredible, but outside of that school it was hard for people to understand what it was like.

> **Box 2.3 Your Stories**
> What connections do you make to what Aloe and Petra describe here? Can you imagine making the decision to move out of your home, community, and country – feeling like you have no choice but to leave, for your own and your family's safety and basic opportunities? If you were a teacher or administrator at one of the schools that Aloe and Petra describe, what would you have done? What constraints might you have felt? Whom might you have connected with to address these issues? To what policies might you have looked to address ethnocentric views of curriculum and books or deficit views of immigrant students' cultures?

Teacher Strategies

As you wonder to yourself or with your colleagues what you could do to make a change in your classroom or at your school, we understand you might feel unsure of where to start – or even *if* to start, depending on the political context in your area. In this section, we highlight several of the ways that teachers we spoke with are doing small things with big impact. Perhaps one of these examples may speak to you.

Aloe: "My job is to teach this kid."

Aloe described how she and her colleagues just reminded themselves and each other that at the very core their jobs were just to love their students, to do their best by every young person, and to meet them where they were. They needed to take an assets-based approach to teaching, remembering that their students brought rich cultural experiences and home languages with them. And they needed to actively *forget* what these kids did not have: legal documentation and school fluency in English.

> So, I was a specialist. I saw 20 different classes every week. So, I really got to know the students and the teachers. When a new student would come, sometimes we get a little background knowledge. Sometimes we'd get a lot. And it was never judgmental. It was always just like, "Okay, they're here now and we are going to love them. We are going to teach them to the best of our ability." Just loving that student and not really caring about all the logistics, or whether they are "legal" or

"documented," and just focusing on the fact that my job is to teach this kid. A lot of teachers in that school were working to learn other languages like Spanish and Arabic – languages that were commonly spoken by these students. Teachers would even put words up on their word walls that were translated into other languages.

It may feel hard to try to learn another language: we completely understand that. Sabrina, an elementary teacher working in an inclusive classroom, told us that was not something she could do, but she highlighted how she worked to be intentional in developing the community in classrooms filled with children and young people who are immigrants.

Sabrina, an elementary school teacher: "Most of it is done in the classroom."

Sabrina described that community needs not only to be developed but to be protected – even shielded – from too many external stimuli and pressures, as "safety" for these young people takes on an entirely different meaning than for most students. Sabrina suggested that, if at all possible, resources need to be brought *in* to these classrooms so that students do not have to venture *out* to receive support services.

> Recently our school population has changed quite a bit. Just two days ago we got a brand-new student, new to the United States. A "level one" English Language Learner (ELL). She speaks very little English. With these families coming to our county, we need to be able to provide the resources for these students. One thing that this school does a fantastic job with is their ELL department. They impress me, and for me to be impressed, it takes a lot. Most of the work with ELL students is done in the classroom. Even for level one students it's done in the classroom. A teacher comes in during our language arts block and takes what we're working on and provides more vocabulary for the kids, more pictures, clues. And even though he doesn't speak Spanish, he's able to provide a high level of support collaboratively with me.

Sabrina: "I just opened up the door and I said, 'Can you explain?'."

Sabrina also illustrated how teachers working with students who are immigrants have to be more resilient and creative in order to serve their students, often looking to their colleagues for "in the moment" teaching strategies.

And it's also helpful when your next-door neighbor and good friend speaks Spanish. Her classroom looks a lot different than mine. She is bilingual in her class. So, her students benefit from that. They don't get that in here. I only have my vacation Spanish, you know, and it's embarrassing. I would never use it in front of kids. So, yesterday we were doing an activity. I could not explain to her what we were talking about – even Google was having a hard time translating. So, I just opened up the door and I said, "Can you explain?" And she just did it and now understands.

> **Box 2.4 Your Strategies**
>
> How is this thinking about these issues and serving these students feeling for you? Does it feel overwhelming? Totally manageable? Somewhere in the middle? One of the messages that these teachers continually shared was that building trusting, authentic relationships is key; of course, the nature of these relationships will depend on your school and community contexts. But the authenticity of these relationships depends on our looking past our own, often seemingly "invisible" notions of culture and honoring our students' cultures, in our classrooms.

Sabrina showed how her relationship with her next-door teacher was crucial in providing in-class support to her students, and Aloe talked about how her relationships with students and their communities were central for her. What peer, student, family, and community relationships are most effective in your context? Which ones need work? What can you do today to move your own relationships forward? How might these relationships be strengthened if they even more actively honored your students' cultures, histories, and realities?

Diane, elementary teacher: "Families are our students' first teachers."

Diane was an elementary teacher at a school with a particularly large percentage of ELL students, and she reflected on how building relationships with families was key to supporting her students:

> Language may be a barrier to fostering relationships with families, but we invite them into the building to build relationships – just like you're building community with your students. When you build

relationships with your families, I think it helps that school experience feel really strong for students. Families are our students' first teachers, so we talk about what are some things they can foster at home to support what we're doing here in school? What can they do at home?

We are really careful to not say things like, "We want to empower our families," but we do want to foster relationships that offer ways that they can understand how things work, how the school works. School looks a lot different than it does in, say, Honduras or El Salvador, and you know it is a different environment. So, coming in and being treated as if you are a partner with your child's teacher, I think that feels really important.

Brithany, high school English teacher: "You can't do that without that relationship with him."

Brithany was a high school English teacher working in a SIOP (Sheltered Instruction Observation Protocol) classroom, which gave her and her students the designated classroom space and time to develop the safety to which Sabrina referred. For her students, this physical, intellectual, and emotional security was rooted in the same sort of relationship-building that Diane named:

> So, I'm considering this teacher workday, signing up for a training because I want to reach my kids. And when they tell you relationships are everything: they are. I had a student in my last class. I just called to him in the back of the room, and I used Google Translate to make sure he was clear about what I was saying. I said, "You have an F in my class. Do you want to have an F in my class?" He says, "No." And I said, "Okay, here is the packet of work. You have to write this story. You plan it on this page. You write and draw it on this page. You turn it in. You don't have an F anymore. It's amazing." But I can't do that without that relationship with him, because he's already standoffish, and he's not going to see the good intent and what you're trying to do.

Brithany: "When we're done, we're done."

Brithany reminded us that "building relationships" with immigrant students could often be a very different process than with students who had not experienced so many shifts in their lives or for whom English was their first language. Brithany was teaching young people who were almost always new to U.S. schools and sometimes new to school – period. Developing relationships with her students required a give-and-take and a unique form of pedagogical pragmatism:

So, you just keep trying. You talk to them in Spanish. You slide them on some rules, things that aren't very important. One of the things that I have done this year that has improved relationships in my class is I plan a lesson and when we're done, we're done. Because a lot of times they come in saying, "No work, Miss, no work. No work today, Miss." Today was Halloween, and they said, "No work today on Halloween." I say, "If you get through A to B, we're done. You can have your phone."

Brithany: "To just be kids."

While Brithany doesn't often know the full extent of her students' life circumstances, she's aware that they often are expected to contribute financially to their families' households – and she must use her teaching time wisely to keep building the connections that might keep them in school:

> Then I will come around and talk to them and counsel them and check their work. But for the most part that gives them time. Because a lot of my kids are working. They're doing hotel jobs or they work construction every weekend. They don't get time after school and on the weekends to just be kids.

Aloe, STEM teacher at a Title 1 elementary school: "If you need…"

Aloe shared that one of the ways teachers at her school worked to welcome immigrant students and families – every day and into the culture of school – was via what seemed like obvious acts of kindness:

> There were a lot of care closets for students who had either just come to the country or were going through something at home. A lot of teachers offered basic things, no questions asked. If you need a snack, if you need a hairbrush, if you need deodorant – a lot of things and actions like that.

The families of these students often need guidance with everyday cultural phenomena: they want to understand, but they are often reluctant to ask. But if those cultural nuances are going to get in the way of parents, families, and students engaging with and ultimately being successful with school, then teachers need to be proactive with providing explanations.

Aloe: "Some parents were panicking."

Aloe shared an example of how she and colleagues would help families navigate these traditions, through still simple but more grand demonstrations of awareness.

> The school also had a family liaison who spoke four languages and she would offer how-to's for parents. For example, Valentine's Day is such an American thing, right? Some parents were panicking because their student came home and said, "I have to buy a card for everyone for Valentine's Day." You look at the cards at Hallmark and they're like $6, $7. So, the liaison did a whole thing about Valentine's Day cards and pushed out multiple translations, explaining that you can buy a whole pack of little cards for $2.99, if you want to participate.

Aloe: "It almost puts people in a box."

Many schools in the United States hold a multicultural or international night once per year. They consider this an inclusive and welcoming practice, but these are not events that immigrant families necessarily understand. And there can be a lot of unintended consequences of such events, including, as Aloe says, reinforcing assumptions and generating stress:

> Sometimes those international nights can be super stereotypical, and it almost puts people in a box: You're from Russia, so you better bring Russian food and dance Russian. And for students who are multi-ethnic, it could be really stressful!

Aloe: "Whatever your family wants to celebrate."

Teachers encouraged us to consider other ways to celebrate together, to build those larger family/school relationships, and to appreciate each other's traditions. Aloe shared how her school welcomed everyone in a non-traditional way, with echoes of the "international night" but with much more accessible elements:

> They had a family night because they didn't want to make it just like stereotypical international night. So, it's like whatever your family wants to celebrate. So, some families came all in Packers jerseys because that was important to their family. Some families brought their favorite treat, and it didn't have to be from their country. It was very inclusive and open and then we had a chance for students and

families to put on poetry readings or dance, or music, and we made it really clear: it doesn't have to be from your country, it could just be anything you want to share. Some girls got up and sang pop songs that were American. One family showed up in matching pajamas.

Aloe: "And then we called it a picnic."

This structure was not only sensitive about avoiding ethnic and cultural stereotypes but also responsive to the economic realities of their immigrant families:

> And we had an exhibit hall, a room where they could bring something that meant a lot to their family to share. A lot of them brought things from their country but some of them just brought heirlooms. At another station there was a heart and you'd write what's in your heart, what's important to you? So again, super open ended. And then we had a photo station. And we had what we called the "Performance Hall," where a lot of people did dances, singing, poetry, some cartwheels. I really think they did an incredible job planning it. We didn't say "Bring a food," because with the cost of food, that can get really expensive! So they just brought food for their families. And then we called it a picnic.

Box 2.5 Your Strategies

Aloe, Brithany, and Diane all offer several ways in which they or their schools have approached the meaningful inclusion of immigrant students and families in their classrooms and school communities. From where we sit, one of the common denominators seems to be a simple dedication to building relationships with these students and their families and, because of or through those relationships, doing what they can to reduce barriers to participation – whether that participation is in passing out Valentine's Day cards or succeeding on an assignment.

How do you build relationships with students who are immigrants – relationships that serve as bridges to their participation in your class and in other school venues? Does it look any different than how you scaffold participation and build relationships with all your students? Are there different needs, expectations, or goals you consider? How are these forms of participation and the scaffolding you provide uniquely responsive to your students' cultures, including to young people whose cultures might have more collectivist orientations? As you have read through the suggestions made by our contributing teachers, has something come to your mind that might need to be changed, either in your own practice or at the school or district level? How could you start that process?

> **Box 2.6 Useful Resource**
>
> The National Education Association (NEA) offers regularly updated resources for educators working with ELL students and their families. These include best practices for working with interpreters, creating inclusive celebrations within the school community, and ten strategies for communicating with ELL families (https://www.nea.org/weta/resources-for-english-language-learners).
>
> For example, there are strategies for keeping family contact information updated which can sometimes be a challenge when working alongside transient families and language barriers. Ideas include leaning on educators who know the family well, reaching out to teachers who work with siblings in the family, networking with community and faith-based organizations, and understanding how individual families prefer to receive communication (phone calls, emails, letters, or even social media). Plus, there are a variety of translation services such as hotlines and apps to make communicating beyond language barriers possible.
>
> Additionally, one resource explains how to create "literacy celebrations" in schools, such as book fairs and field trips, that involve whole families. Educators can nest celebrations within holidays or special events (like National Poetry Month, Read Across America, or Banned Books Week) and incorporate literature and themes from a variety of languages and cultures.

Youth Stories

Melvin was a junior in high school and a participant in the Through Students' Eyes project – with that recent iteration of the project that worked with young people in an "advisory" class (what many of us would call a "study hall"). As the son of immigrants who will be the first in his family to earn a high school diploma, he was very conscious of the "advising" he was receiving about what classes to take and about his motivations for doing well in school:

> **"I felt like an imposter."**
>
> In high school, I had to learn about school from my friends, what classes they took. Watching other people, I felt like an imposter in middle school, and at the start of high school, I started taking STEM

classes, because others were taking them. These classes turned out pretty well. After 10th grade, I just did what my friends did…I have two friend groups. They have different demographics. The group that looks like me thinks about school as a place to have fun before adulthood…

My dad is a great guy, but he can't help me much with school. One of my motivations is to become a father who can help his kids academically. My mom provides emotional support. My mom feeds me, so that helps my brain; she's the most caring, she's the pillar of our entire family. I have some advice for my future self: Spoil your mom and take more AP [Advanced Placement] classes.

Do you know what motivates your students who are immigrants? How are these motivations tied to and respectful of their cultures? How might you be able to learn what motivates them and then tailor your approach to speak to those motivations? What are the ways that your school or district honors the cultural diversity of your students and their families? What resources exist in your school, district, or community to serve immigrant students and their families? How do such resources consider the multi- and cross-generational needs of immigrant families?

 Taking Action

It can be challenging to know what to do when the choices seem impossible. It might be easy to ask why Petra chose not to teach a book in the face of political pressure at her school when she knew that her students would connect to it. Finding ways to protect yourself as a teacher while doing right by students and families can sometimes feel like an impossible task, especially when the politics of so many communities run counter to assuming the best about immigrant students and families. One way to do this is to remember the advice that Brithany emphasized: getting to know students and families as unique individuals.

Something that struck us was how Brithany's advice connects to Aloe's words about putting people in a box. We seem to do that in the United States and in schools. Kids get stuck with labels that are hard to shake. Sometimes that might work to a student's advantage, but most of the time probably not. As you review the notes you've taken as you have read through this chapter, we urge you to consider how to challenge yourself – or your school community – to try not to put kids (or families) in boxes or limit their options based on unwitting assumptions we make about what is "normal" or "right." That might look like rethinking your school's multicultural night or doing something different during Black History Month or even just trying harder to see the genius or creativity in a kid whose first language is not English. Whatever that might be to you, try it out.

We'd even suggest trying out one of the exercises that we heard about when talking with these teachers: "Ask first." For example, when an immigrant student makes what seems like a rash or unreasonable decision, approach them and do that "Ask first" thing: *Ask* them what they needed in that moment, *ask* them what had happened earlier in the day or just before or at home that made this choice seem like the most reasonable. *Ask* first. And then we encourage you to share this idea with your grade-level team or community of practice. We know you can do this alone, but how great would it feel to work on this together?!

Resources

Book: *The Newcomers* by Helen Thorpe. This nonfiction book follows 22 immigrant teenagers, many refugees, through the 2015–2016 school year. It features resources and perspectives from their ELL teacher. The narrative reporting style as well as political framings make it a relevant text for empathizing with both students and teachers in the current landscape of multicultural education.

TED Talk: "What It's Like to Be the Child of Immigrants" by Michael Rain (8 minutes). A personal perspective on what it's like to immigrate to the U.S. and carry both cultures. An important perspective for understanding how many students feel. Discusses how to start conversations with immigrants that promotes sharing and relationship-building. Link: https://www.ted.com/talks/michael_rain_what_it_s_like_to_be_the_child_of_immigrants

Online Resource: Teaching English to Speakers of Other Languages (TESOL). You don't have to be an ELL teacher to benefit from TESOL's resources. Their website includes regular professional development and publications with research-backed strategies for working with ELL and multicultural students: https://www.tesol.org/

References

Gibson, G. (2023, December 17). Trump says immigrants are 'poisoning the blood of our country.' Biden campaign likens comments to Hitler. *NBC News*. https://www.nbcnews.com/politics/2024-election/trump-says-immigrants-are-poisoning-blood-country-biden-campaign-liken-rcna130141

Hammond, Z. (2015). *Culturally responsive teaching and the brain*. Corwin.

O'Kane, C. (2018, November 6). Thousands sign competing petitions over teachers who wore border wall costumes. *CBS News*. https://www.cbsnews.com/news/thousands-sign-competing-petitions-over-idaho-teachers-who-wore-border-wall-costumes/

U.S. Department of Education. (2023). Educational resources for immigrants, refugees, asylees, and other new Americans. https://www2.ed.gov/about/overview/focus/immigration-resources.html

3

Civic and Political Engagement

Ask a social studies teacher why students should learn their class content and you are likely to hear some variation on the idea that the purpose of social studies education is to prepare students to become global citizens or to participate in democratic society or to "assume the office of citizen," as Thomas Jefferson put it. For some teachers, that means teaching students the basic structures and functions of the U.S. government. For others, it might mean instilling critical thinking skills. For Mike Neagle, a middle school teacher in Lowell, Massachusetts featured in Season 4 of the popular podcast series Scene on Radio, *it's all of that and more.*

Neagle embraces a project-based approach to teaching eighth-grade civics. Early in the school year, Neagle skillfully facilitates and guides his students through a winnowing process that cuts down more than 50 potential issues to 12, then to five, and then to two. The issues are identified by students. The initial list includes topics such as homelessness, medical financial support, child abuse, drug abuse, and mental health concerns. In the end, there can be only one topic for their project.

However, for Neagle, voting is not a sufficient method to choose the topic. Instead, Neagle has primed his students for understanding the steps of building consensus as a decision-making mechanism. The process is frustrating and messy. They've narrowed the topics to student mental health and medical debt. Students move back and forth from advocating for one of the choices to lobbying for another. The discussions are intense, but Neagle insists that they will continue the process as long as it takes to reach an agreement on their final topic selection.

After several days of intense discussion, Neagle is prepared for more debate and more dialogue. Instead, the students enter his classroom laughing. They're ready to move forward. They've reached a decision. Neagle probes, asking what happened outside of class to move them to this readiness. The students describe crying. Frustration. Debate. And finally, consensus. Neagle asks the students one more time: Are they sure? Are they ready to move forward? "We are," they say. They have settled on an issue: student mental health.

Reaching consensus is only the first step in what Neagle has planned. Students will spend the remainder of the ten-week project gathering data about student mental health in their own school and school district. They conduct surveys of students and parents. They interpret the data and consider what new policies or laws are needed to ensure improved student mental health outcomes. They investigate the process by which bills become laws. They look at pending state legislation and school policy. They create scripts and learn to make phone calls to local officials to gather even more data. They invite guest speakers to help deepen their understanding.

One of those speakers, a social worker, prompts a policy action goal. The students discuss first and then they consult Neagle about their plan to make a case to the school district regarding a need for more bilingual social workers who are fluent in more diverse languages. The students find out that their superintendent has identified more translation services as a goal but has not acted on that intention. They reach out to the superintendent. They take their research, and their actions, and present them at Civics Day. Spoiler alert: Being a good podcast with a feel-good vibe, they win first overall (Biewen, 2020).

By almost any measure, Neagle's approach of first providing his students with the tools and opportunity to co-develop the curriculum of his eighth-grade civics class and then engaging them in the examination and addressing of an issue is excellent teaching that results in tremendous learning. While these processes might be particularly relevant in a social studies class, the authentic researching, reading, writing, and speaking opportunities that he integrates are useful in any content area. And, of course, they lead to the development of life and civic skills to which every young person should have access.

However, were a teacher in Texas to replicate Neagle's instructional approach, they would be in violation of a recent state law that prohibits any classroom assignment that involves "direct communication" between students and their federal, state, or local officials (Lehrer-Small, 2023). In response to this legislation, teachers across subject areas have revised their lessons and moved away from engaging students in active learning and toward rote memorization and testing. The 2022 results of the NAEP (National Assessment of Educational Progress) Report Card for Civics which claims to assess "civics knowledge and skills that are critical to the responsibilities of citizenship in America" through both multiple choice and constructed response questions showed a slight decline in test scores on the civics exam from 2018 to 2022 but no significant difference from the first time civics was tested in 1998.

Such reactive policies – which most everyday citizens would argue fly in the face of the basic goals of public education – are being considered and enacted in many other parts of the U.S. Political leaders in multiple states are attacking any civic education strategy that includes "action civics" – lessons meant to have students actively participate through service learning, letter writing, and other methods meant to actively involve students in the work of citizens – as "woke." Florida Governor and short-lived 2024 presidential candidate Ron DeSantis, for example, pledged to push for the kind of civics education that would rouse patriotism – but that would likely result in the limiting of critical dialogue – by teaching students to accept "responsibility for preserving and defend[ing] the blessings of liberty inherited from prior generations and secured by the United States Constitution" (Alfonseca, 2023).

Critical Concepts

In this chapter, we share not just the "what" of teachers' stories and strategies for helping young people to understand more about the nature of civic and democratic engagement but also many examples of the "how" of such instruction. Of course, this chapter is unique in that the insights that our contributing teachers share are relevant to all of the rest of the chapters in this volume and the topics they address. We introduce the overarching concept of civic action "deficits," which we would ask you to consider as you read about these teachers' experiences and strategies and then reflect on your own. Once again, we urge you to pick up that notebook or re-open that file in your phone or computer and begin to document your thinking and questions.

Civic Action Deficits

Too often, civic action for young people is focused on deficits – educators are tasked with developing students into future voters rather than celebrating their current assets as activists in their community. When we couch civic engagement with "eventually" or "one day," we miss opportunities to value young people as active members of their community now.

Andreana Clay (2012), in *The Hip-Hop Generation Fights Back*, makes the point that idealized images of youth activism circulating in popular culture focus too narrowly on individual activists over grassroots, community organizing. Consider the broad circulation of images of Greta Thunberg, seemingly divorced from years of community organizing and activism around climate change. It is more common to see celebrated individual activists over the communities collectively participating in civic engagement. Plus, because civic engagement is often narrowly measured in political terms – voting and lawmaking – we miss more inclusive ways for young people to participate in citizenship and civic engagement.

Civic engagement means connecting with the people around you in meaningful ways. It is not about you. It is not about helping yourself. It's about helping other people and engaging in their lives and doing what is best for them and helping them. Civic engagement is connecting with people, finding out what they want. What are they struggling with? What change do they want?

And then working to better things in that direction. But in order to really help your community, though, you have to see what is even in your community to begin with. As you read the rest of this chapter, consider how you might become an ally to or co-conspirator with young people to develop them not only as future participants in democracy but current political actors who can contribute to their community with opinions and activism.

Teachers face a daunting task: You must balance traditional, long-accepted forms of civic education that put students in the role of citizen and actively engage them in the basic elements of the political process… with almost paranoid levels of pedagogical caution, to ensure that there is no chance that your instruction appears to engage students in political activism. This balancing act can be a particularly tenuous one for those of us who are politically or civically engaged outside of our classrooms, which every teacher has the right to be.

In this chapter, you will read about how teachers like you walk this tightrope. Before you learn about these teachers' experiences and strategies, we invite you to consider some of the questions below. We encourage you to document your ideas in that notebook or a computer file so that you can clarify and perhaps communicate with others about your thinking.

- What is the difference between *civic* engagement and *political* engagement? Are there similarities?
- What does civic or political engagement have to do with teaching? What do these – and *should* these – look like in school?
- Who is responsible for teaching civic or political engagement? How is it modeled?
- How can citizenship education become asset- and community-based rather than focused on a deficit model?

As with all chapters in this volume, the stories included here come from classroom teachers and education professionals who are wrestling with these very questions. We hope their experiences offer you some insights for your own practice.

Teacher Stories

The most straightforward forms of civic engagement – voting and citizens' rights to vote – have also become among the most controversial and contested in recent years. Multiple states have enacted laws that are thinly veiled attempts at limiting some citizens' abilities to vote, and we have had two presidential elections in the 21st century where the results were disputed – the first in 2000 when the U.S. Supreme Court weighed in on "hanging chads" and the second in 2020 when the campaign of former president Donald Trump attempted to "find" enough votes overturn an election he lost by both the popular tally and the electoral college.

The issues of voting and voting rights are ones that teachers must be prepared to work through, given the significance of these rights to our democratic processes and the fact that almost every high school student is at most a few years – and, in some cases, just a few days – away from being able to vote.

Frankie, high school special education teacher: "We brought it in."

Frankie described how she had recently considered issues around civic and political engagement with her classes of students with special needs at a large suburban public high school.

> Voting and political engagement was part of our junior and senior curriculum leading up to students' 18th birthdays, when they could first vote. We covered the basics on voting and democracy [in our class], but we were also able to partner with other government classes and a state organization to get the vote out and to encourage students to register to vote. A couple of students were really excited about these activities, and they brought the form home and wanted to talk to their families about it.
>
> Some of our students were not yet 18 and some were over 18 but weren't their own guardians, due to a disability. There was that piece of signing forms for which you still need someone else's support or consent just to sign them. So, we had a big conversation around the disability vote. There's an organization called "Rev Up" that is trying to get the disability vote higher because this is such an underrepresented population in voting. A lot of this goes back to people believing that individuals with disabilities have no capacity to vote or to understand the issues and that they're just going to vote based on

what their guardians or parents or social network tells them. Because nobody else does that, right?

That was one of the things we talked about in my class: What makes you decide how you're going to vote? Is it the candidate? Some people truly just decide based on that person. Or do you vote based on an issue? Or is it the history of your family? Is it what Mom says? These issues are not embedded in any curriculum that I have ever had to teach. But by looking to our state standards, we brought it in. There are plenty of high schools that don't incorporate such issues at all, or maybe they have students vote on their favorite lunch. Which is voting but not real civic engagement.

Box 3.1 Your Stories

While Frankie's example focuses on her experience with students who have a disability, the question is applicable to all educators: How do you bring these authentic conversations into your classroom in simple, meaningful ways? What are some access points to these issues offered in your own curriculum? Are there state standards that will allow you to have conversations about voting or civic engagement? Are there organizations you can partner with (like Rev Up from Frankie's example) that may offer resources? And returning to the critical concept that opened this chapter, how do you help your students, your teacher peers, and others to move beyond the civic action deficits with which so many of us view young people – and especially young people with disabilities?

Box 3.2 Voting Among Young People

In the 2022 midterm elections, young people (18–29) voted more often in states where voter registration was easy, such as Michigan, Maine, Minnesota, and Oregon. States with a noted lack of facilitative voting (banning student IDs as valid forms of identification or not offering early, in-person voting), including the states of Tennessee, Alabama, and Oklahoma, had the lowest youth turnout ("State-by-state," 2023).

As with so many "controversial" issues, young people are aware of and curious about how the realities of these issues impact their communities and worlds. Schools should not be places we send kids to help them *escape* these realities. Rather, by the very nature of a school as a social setting where adults intentionally gather youth to keep them safe and support their growth, these issues will and should find their way in. If these issues are part of our students' lived experiences, then the question is not *if* we consider them but *how*. And sometimes those issues hit very close to home, for young people and their teachers.

Amy, high school English teacher: "Sometimes we have real-life spillover."

Amy and her colleagues had recently been engaged in the fight for a fair employment contract:

> Because my classes are for older high school students, we are able to have very mature conversations there. So, sometimes we have real-life spillover. As an example, right now the contract discussions with the school board have been a little rocky. So, teachers have been instituting "work to the rule" starting this week. We are working during contract hours only, not outside of those hours, as a reminder of how much free labor teachers do every day, every week, every month, every year. And I wanted students to know.
>
> Most of them are familiar with the writers' strike in Hollywood, how writers and actors were working together. I so I told them, "You know, we're not striking, but what we are doing is, just like they did, we're trying to make sure that we have a fair contract and that we get paid for what we're doing." Students' reactions have been really positive. They're freaking out a little bit because it's college essay time, but I tell them, "I'm not abandoning you. I promise. We are going to find a time during the day to meet." So, they understand why these things are happening. And teachers are making it clear that this is what we are doing in order to better the circumstances for everyone.
>
> Some students have come to me outside of the classroom and said, "Hey, I'm interested in learning more about this. How can I do that? What is the history of this? Why is this happening?" I let them know that our school board meetings are televised, and they can go back and watch those and even go to a school board meeting if they want to. They can read news articles about contract negotiations and unionization in Virginia and how it's looking for firefighters and police officers and different groups. So, it's this great opening to talk about civic engagement.

Teachers like Amy acknowledged that these are very complex issues to navigate – if, how, and when teachers allow political topics into their classrooms and if, how, and to what extent they engage as advocates for their own profession. Of course, their stances on these issues shift, depending on the situation and their students and their community. But they recognize that, in this era, they needed to be ready to adjust and respond to heightened tensions, misinformation, and even outright attacks on them and what and how they are teaching.

Melanie, English teacher: "I think I have evolved a lot along the way."

Melanie has taught English and journalism at a small rural high school since 2012 – it's also the high school from which she graduated. She acknowledged the ways she had grown and changed as an advocate, for her profession, her curriculum, and her students:

> I think I have evolved a lot along the way. I've been involved in our unions, and I'm our union representative for our building. I've also evolved through teaching journalism and looking at student freedoms and press rights. A lot of my career I've navigated thinking about our rights as teachers and about my students' rights as journalists. I never really thought of these issues when I first started teaching.

Box 3.3 Your Stories

As you read through Amy's and Melanie's experiences and perspectives, did you make connections to your own context? If you were to make the case to a young person, a colleague, an administrator, or a student's adult family member about why it's reasonable to explain the circumstances of these contract negotiations to students, what would you say? Have you ever had a conversation with your students about something that might be considered "political" in nature? How did you feel then? If not, is this the kind of conversation you feel like you could have? If not, what is holding you back? How have the current political climate and heightened political tensions impacted not just youths' but also teachers' senses of their rights regarding having these conversations?

> **Box 3.4 What are teachers' rights to negotiate employment contracts in the U.S.?**
>
> While 95% of K-12 educators have college degrees – with over half of teachers holding a graduate degree – they earn far less on average than other professions with similar levels of education. In addition, teaching wages have declined from 2010 to 2020 and match levels similar to full-time workers without a college degree in the United States (Newburger Cheeseman & Beckhusen, 2022). However, most teachers cannot negotiate for higher pay.
>
> In the U.S., very little about education is mandated by the federal government. Instead, states and districts have the most power in deciding teacher certification, pay, and rights. Therefore, teacher rights and benefits differ from state to state, district to district. In addition to pay, teaching contracts include benefits such as insurance options and retirement pension regulations. Most districts operate a "step and lane" schedule that pays all teachers based on experience (step) and education level (lane). In public education, most teachers cannot negotiate individual salaries and must rely on collective bargaining between unions and school boards (Will & Sawchuck, 2019).
>
> The American Federation of Teachers (AFT) and National Education Association (NEA) are two popular national unions, often with local chapters, but many districts and states have local union options as well. Having a union representative can make pushing back on individual censorship and policies safer for educators. Even with a union, though, many districts do not permit collective bargaining, and there are few ways for teachers to influence their contracts.

Teachers have to make judgment calls about this "how" – if and how they will allow students to discuss the issues through which their communities are working, whether these are topics young people raise or ones that impact the daily operation and the curriculum of the school. Other times, the very traditions of our schools and long-standing accepted instructional content present opportunities for teachers, young people, and even children to examine these issues – and attempt to collectively make decisions that move us all to a better place.

Sabrina, elementary school teacher: "You would have thought the world was coming to an end."

Sabrina shared a recent example of a major shift in curriculum in her school and the ways families responded:

> About five years before I came to this school, there was a big shift in the county from the social studies department. They used to do this thing called Colonial Day across all fourth-grade classes in the county. There were seven different stations through which the kids rotated throughout the day. Students were expected to come dressed in colonial clothes, even though what we think of as everyday colonial clothes were really what was worn by the wealthy, so they were asking kids to represent the 1%. Half the time kids' clothing wasn't even colonial dress, it was more like medieval clothing. It was just so silly.
>
> The day the decision to do away with Colonial Day was shared, you would have thought the world was coming to an end. "My kid's not going to get to churn butter?! My kid's not going to do tin pressing?!". But this decision came from the top down, and as a school, we needed that level of administrative support because we had to defend ourselves with parents to let them know that this is not something that should be celebrated.
>
> The colonial period represented very hard times in our history and especially in this historic area. There are plantations all over our area, and we know what our communities went through during the Civil War and after. I don't think we need to go to Williamsburg to see history. I think we need to go to our own downtown and read through the historic markers to understand our history. But this decision to eliminate Colonial Day really kind of shook the parents. And they asked, "Well, what's going to replace it?" And we said, "High quality teaching."
>
> Last year when I taught 4th grade during my first year of teaching in this county, we did go to Jamestown, and it was okay. We had a young woman as a guide who really understood the types of things that needed to be discussed. In the classroom we investigated primary resources and thought about what questions we needed to ask of these resources. But in my former county, the guiding question for the 4th-grade social studies curriculum was, "How do we resist injustice?". But if we tried to do that here, there's no way.

> **Box 3.5 Your Stories**
>
> Think about your own curriculum – either what is mandated by your school division or district, what you and a team of colleagues determine, or even what you individually develop. Is there any lesson that you have taught for so long that you don't question (or maybe even know or remember) the rationale behind it? Are there alternative perspectives that should be considered? Are there other sources that should be integrated? How is curriculum determined in your context? And how might you get involved in these deliberations? As well, how might your students be involved in these discussions of the curriculum? It's not a stretch to suggest that teachers and young people – the constituents most directly involved with and impacted by the curriculum – should be involved in such conversations and decision-making.

> **Box 3.6 The Zinn Education Project**
>
> The Zinn Education Project is a curriculum foundation based on Howard Zinn's *A People's History of the United States* with the goal of creating free lessons that are authentic and community-focused. Their #TeachTruth unit calls on teachers and students to make classrooms a democratic space for discussion and activism. One activity has students make a political sign and pose in front of a historical site such as a burial site, statue, or museum and then share that photo on social media. For example, one photo shows a student holding a sign that reads "JIM CROW 2.0 HAS GOT TO GO!" in front of a Civil War statue. This is just one of ten lessons included, for free, in the unit (https://www.zinnedproject.org/campaigns/teach-truth/).

Teacher Strategies

So how are teachers professionally, responsibly, and safely engaging students with these issues and helping young people to develop these civic engagement skills? Without putting their students or themselves at risk of being unreasonably criticized for engaging in political activity that's beyond the purview of the classroom and its curriculum? Most often it's not through grand school reforms that turn teaching on its head and transform teachers into full-time political activists. More often, it's through small moments in a unit, treating students with deep respect as human beings, and a few daily practices that lead to young people's deeper understanding of some of these issues and to opportunities for them to practice civil deliberation with their peers and teachers.

Emily, high school teacher: "It's enough structure that they feel like they know what to do."

Teaching in the rural town where she grew up – but after living, studying, and teaching outside Washington, D.C. for several years – Emily had crafted some classroom conversation structures that enabled her students to find a "way in" to examining these issues and developing those vital discussion skills.

> I think it is easier for students to talk in front of just a few people. So [in this literature circles unit] it's just three or four students and me. They're reading books that are really engaging, and they're taking notes as they go. So, they're not just coming up with things to say off the top of their heads. There's a structure to it that we (my co-teacher and I) took a couple of years to develop.
>
> It's just enough structure so that they feel like they know what to do, but not too much structure where they can't break free and go in a different direction if they want to. They have to come up with some questions and some important quotes that they want to discuss, but it is fluid – what order we discuss the questions and quotes in and who says what and at what time.
>
> Those are the best discussions when the students just sort of take over. It usually doesn't happen the first week. During the first week I'm sort of guiding them – "Okay, now it's your turn. And now it's your turn. Now you need to say something about what you just said." But then, by the second week, they just sort of take over and they get the rhythm of it. And they're able to go on their own.

Not all teachers can justify incorporating full lessons or short units of instruction that help young people to learn those day-to-day skills of civility and civic engagement. But they might seek out those opportunities for students to engage in momentary reflections, to briefly consider an issue of the day in the news, and to practice sharing their perspectives on that issue with their peers.

Annie, high school English teacher: "Let them have a voice to say something."

Annie, an English teacher and teacher of English for speakers of other languages at a large public high school, described how she would seek out those moments to interrupt what might become – for her and her students – a rote learning process and shift this it into a brief opportunity to hear her students' voices.

> We would stop to talk about, you know, "This is what happened in the news," or "This is what's happening after our fire drill or a lockdown." And then I would say, "Okay, we're going to do a journal entry about how you feel about a lockdown." Or that was the year that there was the school shooting down in Florida. I brought in the newspaper, and each of them read a small clip based on their reading ability about each of the victims. And then they all wrote letters to the one boy who was seen as the hero for stepping in and saving the lives of a number of his classmates.
>
> They could write to him in English and Spanish to tell him what they thought about what he did and ask him a question and tell him who they were. We packed everything up, and I mailed all the letters down to the school.
>
> We stopped to do these activities that maybe would change how they might respond or feel about something we were learning. I didn't just pretend like things didn't happen. We had to talk about it. We had to address it. "What is it that you're feeling and doing? And how can we respond to it?" These were activities that let them have a voice to say something that they might not ever be able to say anywhere else, whether anybody else read their letters or not.

But when teachers can develop and implement those lessons and units that legitimately and explicitly focus on advocacy issues, it is vital that they make space for all students' perspectives.

Bobbi, English teacher: "I just felt like I had to check in and see if they – all of them – were okay."

Bobbi was a ninth-year English teacher who had recently moved from one of her area's least-resourced schools to one of its wealthiest and fastest-growing school divisions. She shared how she had explicitly asked her students to consider recent protests in their communities – and how to keep each other safe in such tense times:

> When I taught tenth grade two years ago, we were virtual, and I decided to do a unit on protesting and advocacy. We looked at different protests going on around the country at the time, and we

talked about how we communicate when we're angry, how we can be empowered, and things of that nature. We examined protests from all kinds of political opinions. And then I had the kids create their own TED Talks.

I really wanted to see if the kids knew what was going on. It was a very tumultuous year: They could see parents at school board meetings protesting, and they could see the Black Lives Matter protests going on. I wanted them to know that they could have a role and an opinion in all of this. I also was just trying to support them, especially and even the conservative students.

I think the conservative students often feel victimized because they are the minority in my school's population, and so I wanted to make sure they had an outlet to say, "These are the things I'm angry about. These are things I'm passionate about." We have a very vocal contingent of parents and community members who are upset and on the news, and my students know those people, go to church with those people, or they are on the baseball teams with the kids of those parents. I just felt like I had to check in and see if they – all of them – were okay. I'm introducing more current events in my classes so they can share their political beliefs, get more opinions out there, and have more discussions.

Box 3.7 Your Strategies
What are some of the critical reading, speaking, listening, questioning, and presenting skills that you might incorporate into a lesson or unit? What is a single lesson or a shorter unit you might develop and implement that addresses some of those civic engagement skills, even for young students? What are a few of those moments in the course of a lesson that you might use to "interrupt" what might have become a rote flow – and incorporate students' voices? Who is a teacher ally with whom you might work to craft and teach such a lesson or unit so that you have moral and professional support in what might be a significant teaching risk?

In the last several years, some national politicians – and also some local school board members around the country – have engaged in what might have once been unthinkable: they have questioned the very existence of factual information and even suggested there is such a thing as "alternative facts."

Heather, high school science teacher: "'Critical' doesn't mean 'bad'."

Given the ways in which the very nature of truth and facts has come into question in recent years, sometimes teachers must explicitly address the very nature of knowledge, much as Heather has done. She is even explicit about giving students vocabulary to understand the skills and thought processes she is sharing with them:

> Before everything went virtual in 2020, I did a mini-unit on pseudo-science where students analyzed claims about acids and bases. For example, we'd look at claims about alkaline water and the health benefits of it, trying to use a framework for identifying pseudoscience and false science, and trying to decide if this is a selling point – pseudo, false, or real science?
>
> For me, as a science teacher, science shouldn't be scary. Just because something has a formal name that is 35 characters long doesn't mean it's scary or bad. So that part of my class is being able to look at things with a critical eye and decide if I agree or not. Understanding what message people are trying to send. So, general criticality is something I try to embed in everything we do.
>
> I've started to use the word "critical" or "criticize" because I think it's important for students to realize that the word "critical" doesn't mean "bad." You're analyzing it. You're trying to poke the holes in it. You're trying to explain it. You're trying to look at what it means and not taking things at face value.
>
> I'm able to avoid some of the more obvious political issues and I'm finding myself more and more trying to subtly work in some of these skill-building opportunities, building critical thinking skills, and interpretation and analysis skills, which are important in any field and which a lot of people have forgotten how to use. I want my kids to be able to look at data and be critical of it. I want them to be able to look at what's coming through on TikTok and Instagram posts that make claims about, for example, what we eat, and understand what the background is to those claims.
>
> I mean, you can look at a set of data and think, "Is this being spun? Who's presenting this data? What does this data tell me? Is this useful? Does this make sense?" My kids aren't going to read a 20-page research paper. Little snapshots are great, but those are so easily

skewed. So, criticality is about not taking things at face value. It's not saying something is bad. We're just questioning.

> **Box 3.8 Writing a Letter to Policymakers**
>
> One classic way to engage students in real-world activism is by encouraging them to write a letter to policymakers. The Association for Career and Technical Education has an easy guide for writing formal petition emails (https://www.acteonline.org/advocacy/advocacy-resources/letters-and-emails-to-policymakers/), and this can be easily become part of a larger civics or research unit. Students might research an issue that matters to them and find appropriate policymakers to contact. They could submit multiple drafts of their email to the teacher before submission to practice formal, effective writing skills for a professional audience. Even if you do not do this with students, these tools are useful for helping you – teachers – write to your school board members or other policymakers about important issues.

And then, sometimes, teachers' roles, the curriculum, students' voices, and youths' opportunities to practice those civic engagement skills intersect in an extended moment of action. Teachers need to be ready to respond – in and beyond the classroom – when such moments occur.

Melanie, journalism teacher: "We just hammered it hard."

Melanie shared her experience with a moment of action, when her students went all the way to the state legislature to advocate for legislative change:

> I'm our State Director for the Journalism Education Association, and we passed a Student Press Freedom Bill last spring. In March and April of 2023 my students were really involved in contacting their legislators and arguing that they deserved this bill. They explained that legislators needed to pass this bill to protect their freedoms as journalists and to help protect them from being censored at school.
>
> That was really a culminating thing for me to see my students actively get involved in fighting for their own rights. Those experiences have really made me look at that aspect of teaching. The first year in 2022 the bill just died in committee, because nobody really cared about it. And then, when they picked it back up in 2023, we

were pleasantly surprised, and so we just hammered it hard, but it almost died again. The legislature didn't pass it until the very last day.

> **Box 3.9 Your Strategies**
> Whether you're an elementary school teacher in a wealthy suburb or a high school teacher in a rural district, you have a tremendous influence on the ways in which your students consider their involvement in civic life. And it's easy to feel like those "civic action deficits" have "trickled up" to teachers – at a time when our students need us to be ever more courageous, even in small ways. What constraints do you feel in how you model civic engagement for your students? At your school, is there someone you admire? Someone who is particularly effective at modeling civic and political engagement? What do they do that you could emulate? If you don't know anyone at your school who does this well, how could you start a small movement – or even a conversation – about an issue in your school or community with which you're concerned?

Many teachers are aware that they are in precarious positions: individually, as a profession, and via their curriculum and pedagogical practices. But teaching is a public profession, and these teachers recognize that the only way build a new and hopefully stronger sense of trust in the teaching profession is by engaging young people in the often very tense discussions in which schools are currently enveloped – or to which they are being subjected. Youths' development as citizens *must* occur within the walls of that most public of institutions: our schools.

Yet we get to a point where, like Alfonso (a long-time English teacher in another suburban Virginia high school) described, young people express that they "want to live life outside of a discussion in a classroom...enough of this classroom stuff. [We] need to go do something!" The teachers we spoke with across the United States were clear that the primary way to develop the skills necessary for young people to "go and do something" and to lead us back to a place of trust in schools is by being transparent with young people about the very skills we are sharing with them.

Emily, high school teacher: "You can think about these things for yourself"

Emily suggested that we need to be open with our students by centering honest dialogue and by actively teaching self-advocacy:

So even at the beginning of the year, I say, "You know, listen, you're about to go out into the real world where you're going to face a lot of different things that maybe you've never been exposed to. So, we're going to read stuff that's challenging to our opinions, to our perspectives, to our beliefs. And if you ever have an issue with anything that we're reading, I want you to come and talk to me about it, because we can have an adult conversation about it and we can reach some sort of agreement on it."

So, we talk about that at the beginning of the year. And then, before we're reading any of those identity stories, we introduce it again. I say, "Some of this stuff may challenge what you believe, or what you think, or what you thought about the world. And that's okay. That's sort of the point. We can talk about it here and not feel like we all have to have one opinion on the topic. Right? We can come at it from different angles and not just hear what other people have to say about it."

That works for the most part because they like to think of themselves as adults. That's what I try to get them to feel: "You can think about these things for yourself, and not have to agree with me or agree with anyone. Think about it for yourself, and if you're feeling uncomfortable, you can take it upon yourself to discuss it with me, or to do whatever you feel you need to do to advocate for yourself."

Alfonso, English teacher: "For now, it's a hat that you're putting on."

Alfonso shared the deep respect that teachers can – and should – have for students if they are going to be successful with helping young people develop these civic engagement skills.

> I personally teach some of the brightest people on earth, and I could not imagine even convincing them that one fast food place is better than another one, much less convincing them of an idea. But as an exercise in one lesson, I try to make them believe that MLA [Modern Language Association of America] citations are better than APA [American Psychological Association] citations. I always preface everything with, "This is what we're going to do: for now, it's a hat that you're putting on. When you leave this classroom, take off the hat. It's no longer there. Your hair is back to the way it was."
>
> I ran into some issues when I was teaching literary lenses because literary lenses and literary criticism are rooted in social and politi-

cal movements. When you're trying to teach a student to analyze the wealth differences in this piece of writing or in this song, you want to explain the history so that they fully get a grasp of why the theory existed and why the theory may be useful in understanding literature.

You get that conversation of, "Oh, is this political?" or "It's got this keyword that I've been told is used by a certain political party or political ideology." So that's where it gets a little tricky, but I repeat that disclaimer: "This is why we're doing this. You are not believing in it. It's just like using a protractor. You are not going to think in a 360-degree manner when you get out of here. You're *using* it. You're going to throw it away when you're done. That's it."

> **Box 3.10 Your Strategies**
>
> As you consider the experiences of these teachers, what do they make you think about in your own practice? You might get together with some of your school colleagues and discuss how civic engagement is framed at your school. How is it modeled? Do you feel like you are equipped to model civic engagement to your students? What possibilities might there be for encouraging civic engagement among your students? Are there norms or people or situations that might constrain you? Are there rules or relationships in place that could help you? Can you set a goal or make a plan to model or encourage civic engagement in your classroom, to explicitly counter those "civic action deficits"? What are you going to do *now*?

Youth Stories

The young people involved in the Through Students' Eyes project echo and extend many of these teachers' perspectives and experiences, about how the content of school can help them develop citizenship and civic engagement skills and about how school ultimately can contribute to opportunities, democracy, and freedom.

On Writing

Charlie, a high school sophomore in Virginia, shared how writing can be an act of civic engagement: "Young people's opinions are often ignored as a result of being viewed as immature or undeveloped. Writing allows young people to express these opinions regardless of what society thinks."

On Writing, Making Decisions, and Power

Stella, a high school junior, agreed that writing helped her feel powerful and engaged – and she highlighted how teachers' writing assignments could support students to find success:

> I enjoy writing a lot more now than I used to. Recently in my English class we did a 12-15-page research paper. I thought I was going to be stressed out by this. It was very open, and I chose a topic that I was really interested in. I focused on the lack of women in the film industry. It was the least stressed I'd been with a writing project. I wasn't just writing to a specific prompt: I was writing for myself. It can be important to have those assignments, but you need a balance where you can make decisions, and assignments where you are little bit more guided. With writing I can express myself, I can be more creative in my messages, and I've always wanted to be sure I was being authentic. With writing you can create your answers. Writing gives you a sense of power or accomplishment when you are able to create something from your own brain.

On School and Freedom

Rachel, also a high school sophomore, was clear that school could lead to freedom:

> I think [the purpose of school is] to prepare us for the workforce. The world revolves around the economy. I know the history of school has been to prepare people to work in factories. That has evolved and now college has been added, sort of a step up. For me, I stay in school because that is how I will make money. There is a direct relationship between school and the amount of money you will make: School equals money, so school equals freedom. If you only have a high school degree, you can only do certain jobs, but with more degrees you might get to do jobs in which you're interested.

 Taking Action

It feels like now more than ever teachers are constrained in how they can talk in the classroom about current events or topics important to their students. Meagan was in a meeting with her children's elementary school principal during the time we were writing this chapter, and she noted how many times the principal (someone Meagan really admires and respects) said, "These topics are really hard and uncomfortable to discuss." Meagan finally spoke up:

> You know, I think we need to reframe how we think about political topics. They may be difficult or uncomfortable for some of us, as adults, to talk about, but I guarantee you, these are topics that are at the front of many of our students' minds, topics that are discussed at dinner tables and on the way to school.

Meagan's point was that just because the principal or other school adults might be uncomfortable addressing the topics, students – even at elementary school ages – are yearning to better understand the world around them and to be supported in taking action toward making change. Maybe *if* a topic is one with which adults are struggling, we have a *greater* responsibility to help teachers help young people to consider it.

Teachers, as you well know, you are perfectly positioned to be a positive influence in the lives of your students, with the content you share and the behaviors you model. We know you take that responsibility very seriously. We also know that there is real fear about the repercussions of being seen as remotely "political" in today's divided and divisive civic climate. We hope that the strategies our contributing teachers have shared in this chapter give you ideas and inspiration as you consider how you can model civic and political engagement wherever you teach.

We suggest that your first steps might involve two concepts or strategies. The first is about allyship: Begin having even brief moments of conversations with your colleagues about even grade level or subject area or school policies. The greatest enemy of effective citizenship and civic engagement may be the feeling that we are alone in something – when, in fact, more often than not, we're *not*. Do your best to defend against adopting the "civic action deficits" we sometimes mistakenly see in our students.

The second is about normalization: It's healthy and normal, and it is our right and responsibility to consider how policies and practices are supporting or restricting our own and others' well-being and success. And for us teachers – whose job it is to care for kids and guide them toward skills and understandings that will help them be well and successful – that consideration should be a *normal* part of your everyday functioning.

Administrators, you are in key roles to support your teachers in appropriately modeling civic engagement to their students, even via seemingly insignificant momentary conversations in their classrooms. Don't let them down! Engage in dialogue with your community. Consider working with families and community members to envision paths forward. Use some of the resources listed at the end of this chapter to help you.

Resources

Book: *The Listening Leader* by Shane Safir. Though written mostly for administrators, this book has chapters of resources for how to make students and teachers equitable stakeholders in school-based leadership decisions. The ideas, scripts, and infographics will help teachers empower students and could be used to persuade administrators to bring more voices to the table as advocates for themselves and others.

TED Talk: "How Teachers Can Help Kids Find Their Political Voice" (16 minutes). Educator Sydney Chaffee calls on teachers to inspire students to be political activists and find their voice on issues that matter to them. Link: https://www.ted.com/talks/sydney_chaffee_how_teachers_can_help_kids_find_their_political_voices?language=en

Online Resource: "Tips and Outline for Presenting to Your Local School Board." A guide from the American Civil Liberties Union that includes sample language and helpful tips for presenting effectively before the school board. Link: https://www.aclu-wa.org/docs/tips-presenting-school-boards

References

Alfonseca, K. (2023, July 5). Gov. Ron DeSantis' push for "civics" education: What does it look like? *ABC News*. https://abcnews.go.com/US/gov-ron-desantis-push-civics-education/story?id=100709113

Biewen, J. (Host). (2020, May 13). "Schooled for democracy" (No. 10). In *Scene on radio*. Center for Documentary Studies. https://www.sceneonradio.org/s4-e10-schooled-for-democracy/

Clay, A. (2012). *The hip-hop generation fights back: Youth, activism and post-civil rights politics*. NYU Press.

Lehrer-Small, A. (2023, May 1). Texas guts "woke civics." Now kids can't engage in a key democratic process. *The Guardian*. https://www.theguardian.com/us-news/2023/may/01/texas-civics-students-democratic-participation

NAEP Civics: Explore the Results for the 2022 NAEP Civics Assessment. (2022). *The Nation's Report Card*. https://www.nationsreportcard.gov/civics/about/assessment-framework-design/

Newburger Cheeseman, J., & Beckhusen, J. (2022). Average teachers' earnings declining, lower than similarly educated workers. *The United States Census Bureau*. https://www.census.gov/library/stories/2022/07/teachers-among-most-educated-yet-pay-lags.html

State-by-State youth voter turnout data and the impact of election laws in 2022. (2023, April 6). *Tufts University Tisch College-CIRCLE*. https://circle.tufts.edu/latest-research/state-state-youth-voter-turnout-data-and-impact-election-laws-2022

Will, M., & Sawchuck, S. (2019, January 25). Teacher pay: How salaries, pensions, and benefits work in schools. *Education Week*. https://www.edweek.org/teaching-learning/teacher-pay-how-salaries-pensions-and-benefits-work-in-schools/2018/03

4
LGBTQIA+ Advocacy

Rileigh was visibly uncertain as they approached Jeff in class one day. "When you say I can do my research project on anything, do you really mean anything?" Jeff reviewed the parameters of what he considered to be a fairly standard research paper assignment: The topic can be anything so long as it is a world history topic, it fits in the time period of Origins to 1500 CE, and it is something that spans both time and place.

Rileigh quickly got back to work, eventually submitting their proposal for a research project that would explore the experiences of LGBTQ+ individuals in the Ancient and Medieval World. After reading the proposal, Jeff asked Rileigh why they had hesitated to turn in this very well-written and justified proposal. "I don't know," they responded. "I just felt like I would get in trouble with the school. That this wasn't an appropriate topic for school. And I didn't want to get you in trouble either, because I figured you'd let me do it."

Rileigh was in ninth grade when they wrote that research proposal. Jeff felt lucky to work with them again during their senior year in an elective course he teaches. As graduation drew nearer, Jeff asked them to reflect on their growth as a student of history from their time in his ninth-grade course to where they were now, just weeks away from graduation. Rileigh shared with Jeff the impact that ninth-grade research project had played not only on developing research and writing skills but on feeling more comfortable with who they were as a person. Rileigh said that, while they had always known LGBTQ+ people had always been part of history, to read about them and to see their experiences were validating exercises.

As we write this book, it's been more than seven years since Rileigh approached Jeff, nervously, with a topic that they were afraid would be controversial. A topic that was deeply personal. A topic that spoke not only to historical experiences but to Rileigh's own experiences and identity. The years since have seen a rash of legislation claiming to "protect" children from indoctrination into a "deviant" way of life (Villarreal, 2021), painting teaching of LGBTQ+ issues and topics as sexual grooming (Block, 2022), and promising to ensure parental rights to limit their children's exposure to such topics (Amiri, 2023).

Legislation in Florida that sought to limit instruction on gender identity and sexual orientation in Advanced Placement (AP) Psychology courses prompted the College Board to object to such measures and to advise Florida schools that teaching AP Psychology courses that omit these topics would be in violation of College Board policies (Najarro, 2023; "Statement on AP," 2023). Legislation with similar aims has been proposed in dozens of states across the country, including Virginia, where Governor Glenn Youngkin's administration advanced "model" school board policies rolling back protections for transgender students throughout the Commonwealth (Rhoden, 2022) and proposed ambiguously worded legislation around the teaching of "sexually explicit content" that some argue would have a chilling effect on the types of instructional materials used in classrooms (Rankin, 2023).

Would Rileigh's research project have violated the "model" policies and legislation proposed by Virginia's governor? What sanctions might Jeff, as Rileigh's teacher, have faced for such violations? Could Jeff have balanced both complying with the law and honoring Rileigh's identity and research interests? How?

Critical Concepts

This chapter focuses on the ways that teachers are encountering and working through issues of sexual orientation and gender identity with students and in their classrooms and schools. They share how, too often, short-sighted and oppressive policies regarding young people who identify under the umbrella term "LGBTQIA+" are making *all* young people *less* safe rather than more so. And they highlight how teachers might engage as advocates – again, for *all* youth. Once again, before you read, please pick up that notebook or open your computer to track your responses, thinking, ideas, and potential actions.

Heteronormativity

Heteronormativity (or homonegativity) is a term used to name and describe the privileging of heterosexual identities, gender conformity, and nuclear family units. Identities outside of heteronormativity – namely queer identities

– have historically, and still too often today, been categorized as "deviant." The United States is a heteronormative society, and the messages this structure sends are internalized by all of us, regardless of our orientation.

For example, consider for a moment the shows on television which, in the vast majority of cases, depict nuclear family units, heterosexual relationships, and cisgender characters. Such media saturation – where other identities and realities are depicted as uncommon – inevitably leads to young people expecting to grow up and lead heteronormative lives (Pollitt et al., 2022). As a result, people who are members of the LGBTQIA+ community can often experience stigma and self-hatred. Over the past few decades, how we view and discuss these once "deviant" identities has shifted and expanded, but heteronormative biases can still exist within us, shaping our reactions and beliefs in subtle ways, regardless of our sexual orientation or gender identity.

The first step to making LGBTQIA+ young people safe in our schools and society is recognizing these reactions in ourselves when they arise. Homonegativity usually presents itself as a feeling of discomfort. It is important that we sit with, reflect on, or even write about this discomfort. What inspired the discomfort? What root belief is at the source of that feeling?

The next step is to begin to disrupt – both those feelings and any actions, traditions, or structures that support homonegativity. How? Simply by educating yourself more about the topic to see how, in the vast majority of instances, these feelings or opinions are unwarranted. Sometimes, things make us uncomfortable because they are new or unknown. Maybe this is a time to identify an area you should research or read about. There are plenty of resources at the end of this chapter to guide you. Additionally, Gayscape (http://www.jwpublishing.com/gayscape/classic.html) and Rainbowquery.com are search engines curated with reliable information by queer theorists. The next time this discomfort arises, you now have more knowledge to help you process that feeling.

Today, many teachers across the United States face daily difficult decisions regarding how they treat the students in their classrooms who identify with the LGBTQIA+ community. These teachers feel the weight of choosing – often minute-by-minute and facing real young people – whether to comply with ill-informed regulations or to care for the children and adolescents they teach in ways those children find meaningful. In this chapter, our contributing teachers explore the very questions Jeff raised above, offering their own experiences and providing some ideas for how to stand in solidarity with our LGTBQIA+ students (and colleagues) in the face of dehumanizing and oppressive legislation, regulation, and policies that reinforce heteronormativity.

Please consider some of these questions so you can clarify your own thinking and maybe share with colleagues:

- Who are your students? Do you have students who openly identify as part of the LGBTQIA+ community? Who are your students who may not feel safe to openly identify as part of this community?
- What are the policies where you live that may affect your LGBTQIA+ students or their families? How do they align (or not) with your own values? What are the origins of these policies?
- In what ways have you seen heteronormativity operate in your school or school community?
- What guidance have you received from other teachers, administrators, or professional or outside organizations about how you should treat students who are part of the LGBTQIA+ community? How does this guidance relate to your values? Is there a dearth of guidance? If so, what do you need in order to feel like you are in a position to support young people or school community members who identify as LGBTQIA+ or to identify and resist heteronormativity?
- What are you willing to do to support young people who identify as LGBTQIA+? What practices and stances are you willing to uphold? Which policies and practices are you willing to accept? Is there a line you will draw in the sand that you will not cross when it comes to advocating for LGBTQIA+ youth? What principles are you upholding? What traditions are you resisting?

As you think through these questions, remember that all the stories shared in this chapter come from real teachers and educators struggling with the same daily decisions, workload, and goals as you. As you read about how they are grappling with various constraints related to how they are able to care for their students who are part of the LGBTQIA+ community, take notes of insights that are helpful in your own practice.

Teacher Stories

The vast majority of teachers we know pride themselves on curating their curriculum and resources provided in their classrooms to the individual identities and life experiences represented by their students. As you get to know your students, families, and communities, you might find new books to have on your shelves, or you may tweak an assignment to be more inclusive of varied life experiences. Over the past few years, though, gathering such responsive collections of classroom materials has become more and more difficult to do. As we noted in the introduction to this chapter, governors, school board members, and parents across the United States have made it more difficult for teachers to care for students in this way – particularly students who identify as members of the LGBTQIA+ community – and to resist heteronormative practices. In this section, we will highlight some stories that may seem familiar to you.

Amy, high school teacher: "An incredible waste of time."

When asked if she'd had any experiences with the range of social issues addressed in this book, Amy, a high school dual enrollment English teacher at a large public magnet high school, didn't have to think. She described her tremendous frustration at a project she'd been required to complete because of the state's recently enacted laws against "sexually explicit content" in books used in schools. She recognized that such initiatives amounted to a new normal that no longer centers the needs of *all* students.

> At the end of last school year, we were given information about our county's adoption of a ban against books that include "sexually explicit content." So, I was tasked with going through every book on our bookshelves looking for anything that might be considered "sexually explicit content," and then helping the administration draw up ideas for how we were going to provide notification for anything that would be used or that would be available on the bookshelves.
>
> So, there were three texts that were challenged by a parent (yes, *one* parent) at the county level. I sat on a committee to review the challenge for one of the books. We purchased copies of the book for everyone on the committee. We wanted to be sure everyone was represented – teachers, department chairs, parents. There was also an administrator. We shared our thoughts about the book as it pertained to anything that might be considered "sexually explicit" and then we provided our recommendations. Ultimately, we found the book to be of literary merit. It was a memoir and understanding memoir [as a literary genre] is one of our state-mandated standards of learning. So, our decision was sent, and it was appealed in five minutes. So now it goes to the superintendent and school board to ultimately decide. This also happened in another nearby county. It was the same process and as soon as it was challenged the superintendent there just pulled the book permanently, no questions asked. They didn't even go through committees; they just pulled every one of those books.

At first, Amy was cautious when reflecting on the work and time she'd been required to waste because of just one parent's challenge. She used words that seemed carefully crafted – clearly out of fear of professional retribution. And then she seemed to give up.

> I mean, if I'm going to be honest, it was an incredible waste of time. It took hours. I was spending seven hours every day in our book room, flipping through the books, using different resources to help me identify anything that might be considered sexually explicit material. We jumped through the hoops, but it was just a tremendous waste of time. And I anticipate I'll be asked to sit on more of these committees and waste more time. Especially when you know they're just going to appeal any decision anyway. I mean, there's no interest in dialogue.

She reflected on what this kind of censorship – which to her and many of her colleagues was clearly rooted in heteronormativity and homonegativity – means not just for the students who are so clearly harmed but for teachers.

> I think it demonstrates that there is a mindset that teachers should not be trusted as professionals – that teachers are indoctrinating students. I mean, so many teachers just care so deeply about their students, and to have anyone suggest – whether it be a parent or a community member – that we don't have the best interests of students in mind when we make these choices, it's just insulting and hurtful.

Several teachers we spoke with agreed that such politically motivated initiatives were not only hurting their LGBTQIA+ students but also doing damage to them as professionals and to the teaching profession. They shared their emotional resistance to these actions, which at this stage was primarily taking the form of expressing their incredulity with their teacher peers and administrators. They wondered aloud how a small minority of powerful and loud parents could suddenly be entitled to demonstrate such a clear lack of trust and respect for teachers.

Box 4.1 Your Stories

How do you feel when you read about Amy's experience? Has something like this happened in your own school or district? Are there any policies or practices – long-standing traditions or new initiatives – that are not explicitly tied to heteronormativity or homonegativity but that are rooted in such ideas? Have you ever felt like you were not trusted in your role as a teacher, particularly with regard to how you are teaching and advocating for your LGBTQIA+ students? If you feel safe doing so, consider sharing these feelings with a friend or colleague.

Bobbi, high school English teacher: "That would have been devastating."

Bobbi responded to the potentially dangerous effects of another of the current state administration's "model" policies, which pandered to a narrow swath of parents in order to win an election.

> I think some parents aren't fighting for what's best for students – for example, this idea that we should be required to out students to parents. I am gay, and if my teachers had outed me to my family, that would have been devastating. I can't imagine the idea that I would potentially put a student in danger because their family is not accepting of who they are, of what they're going through. Or worse, that we could push a student to suicide because we make a very stressful situation worse. I just don't think parents always know best.

Bobbi says that parents don't always know best. This may be especially true with the very personal, very delicate issues of sexual orientation and gender identity. The truth is, in the United States, we have all been raised in a heteronormative society and so we all struggle to act in ways that resist that socialization. Especially for those of us who are as parents, that can be difficult because we naturally, instinctively, and sometimes blindly want to protect our children from anything that could be seen as making them vulnerable to unjust or biased treatment. Bobbi points out that perhaps some parents struggle with upholding heteronormative systems, practices, and policies and do not realize that such structures may in fact put their children at greater risk.

Reese, elementary school teacher at a private lab school: "It's unfathomable."

Working at a private elementary school in the suburbs definitely has its perks. But for Reese, she still could not escape the ways in which personal relationships were scrutinized and politicized in such a setting. Although Reese "handled" the particular moment she describes below, it highlights the real fear that teachers – especially, *new* teachers – have about bringing anything personal into the classroom because "personal" can be seen as a challenge to established norms that keep some people comfortable with the status quo. Children and young people are naturally curious about the world, particularly when they are deemed to be too young by society to make many decisions for themselves. This curiosity, individuals' lives, and heteronormative and homonegative traditions will inevitably meet.

> My student teacher is gay. She has a background on her computer of her and her girlfriend and she's kissing her girlfriend on the cheek. Some of the students saw the picture and were asking her about it, and she looked at me like, "Am I allowed to say it? Can I tell them?" I was like, "You can tell them. I want you to be able to talk about who you are and your identity." But she was scared for all kinds of reasons.
>
> But we talked about how we could create a safe space, and that by doing this she would model that for the children. So, she just said, "Yes, this is my girlfriend." Some of the kids were like, "That's not allowed. My parents say that you can't do that, or my church says you can't do that. They say that you can't be with a girl. It's one man and one woman." And then we had other kids saying, "My friend has two moms."
>
> And I knew that parents were going hear about it. And it happened. Parents brought in their comments and their questions and their concerns. I think we handled it well, but I think even the fact that it has to be "handled" is just unfathomable – that a person can't say, "This is who I'm in a relationship with."

As a mentor teacher to many student or intern teachers, Reese expressed her dedication and commitment to ensuring that these new teachers feel supported, with regard to how to keep both themselves and all of their students safe – regardless of their sexual orientation or gender identity. But there are real, legitimate concerns about what they will experience when they are no longer protected and mentored by people like her:

> I think it shook her a little bit that these are young first graders. She doesn't want to push back on their world view in a way that's confusing to them. But she's sitting in front of them saying, "This is who I'm in a relationship with." And so, there's dissonance there. I think she felt safe and supported, and she told me that. She said, "Thank you for making that a safe space."
>
> But she's curious, though, about what it's going be like when she leaves this school. How do you know the school you're going to is supportive? What will those parents say? How do you have that conversation? Is it allowed? And the "don't say gay" thing is on her mind. Big time. I think it was a healthy and warm and important conversation for her to have with the students. And I just want to keep having those conversations.

For Reese and her student teacher and for so many others, it can be really scary to challenge the status quo because it is seen as right, good, and necessary.

And you can almost see the gut-wrenching way that Reese and her student teacher are wrestling with these issues, in ways that honor their students and their families but that don't compromise their commitment to serving *all* students and maintaining their own personal and professional integrity. That's the challenge with "heteronormativity": it's almost invisible because it's what we've all been conditioned to think is *normal*. As a result, it takes a lot to unlearn that the systems that have structured many of our lives might not allow others to live comfortably.

Heather, science teacher: "What do I do?"

All the teachers we spoke with described impossible decisions and the fear that accompanies rule breaking around what seems like the simple issue of respect for the young adults in their classrooms. Heather shared her story in detail.

> So, [this state] has enacted some laws related to the LGBTQ+ community and we're grappling right now with the fact that our major hospital systems will no longer provide gender affirming care. So that's been a big issue. We have a policy that specifically says we are not allowed to ask students their pronouns. I'm really struggling with that right now. I mean, all the research shows that using a student's preferred pronouns – and using them correctly – is one of the easiest ways to create an inclusive and more welcoming environment. It goes right up there with using their correct names – the names they want to be used. But our policy says that we cannot ask that unless there is a formal gender identity plan documented. We are not allowed to use anything different than what is on their registration in any sort of formal documentation or communication. So, it has to be in an agreement with the parents. For me, that's been really hard.
>
> I had a student several weeks ago who was referred to by a close peer with pronouns that were different than what their profile says on my attendance system. This was one of their good friends. It's the person they choose to sit next to, and they can sit anywhere in my class. So, I know this wasn't an accident. I know this was intentional. But what do I do? How do I make that student feel welcome and included in my classroom when I'm legally not allowed to ask for the information?
>
> So, on a day when things were kind of busy in the classroom, I just sat down near them and said, "Here's the deal. Technically, I'm not

supposed to ask you this question." But the student knew, as soon as I said that they were like, "I know where this is going." And I said, "I want you to feel welcome and I want to use the right words. So, this is what I heard your friend say the other day. Is that what you prefer?" And they said, "Yep." And I said, "Cool."

This was something I debated for probably a good week and a half. It's that balance between how do I protect myself and how do I protect this kid? Honestly, I dragged my feet for a couple of days. I mean, I didn't have to use the student's pronouns. I could just not say the pronouns. But I wanted to address it and do it in a way that wasn't going to feel weird or intrusive to the student. I mean, technically what I did wasn't right. Which is weird because I'm typically a rule follower. So, I don't know, I don't feel anxious about having done it, because I do think it was right. And it's nothing formal. If I ever have to write home, I'll still use their given name and documented pronouns.

But it's just another layer. Another layer of stuff. In the world of things to be thinking about, I wish this was one thing I didn't have to think so hard about. I wish this was one thing that it was like, you know what? That's what the kid wants to use, so that's what I'll use. It's hard to have a policy that is so actively against something that I personally feel shouldn't be that big of a deal.

Many teachers spend so much time and almost soul-draining energy before they take risks like Heather describes, in order to make sure their students feel validated and cared for in the ways they prioritize. Yet, for others, like Sabrina, the risk is too great.

Sabrina, elementary school teacher: "I'm not reading that book in here."

Sabrina shared a book she loves that introduces a penguin family with two dads. But she now doesn't use the book in her first-grade class, because she doesn't want to deal with the possible blowback.

> There's this most amazing children's book. It's called *And Tango Makes Three* [by Justin Richardson and Peter Parnell]. It's a true story about a penguin family at the Central Park Zoo. There were

two male penguins that were together during every mating season, and the zookeeper noticed that whenever the eggs were laid, and the penguin moms and dads would share the egg back and forth, these two penguins would use a rock. And yet they never ever got to have their penguin baby. But then, one year, a penguin mom and dad gave birth to twins. So, I guess penguins don't do well with twins, so they took one of the eggs and gave it to this male couple. They would do the thing back and forth, and they hatched this baby penguin named Tango, and they lived, you know, silly as it is, happily ever after.

But the thing is, I'm not reading that book in here. I would love to. But I also know that I don't want to get into that right now. I think I already stretch things a little bit. But my kids, my own children, have never been read a book about a family that's like their own. So, my kids have gone all through elementary school and they're reading a Thanksgiving story about mom and dad. They're reading *Our Table* [by Peter H. Reynolds], which is mom and dad. They're reading a lot of stories about moms and dads, but never moms and moms. Now, there are some newer books that are out that are great. But before there were like two options.

So, I do feel restricted when it comes to sharing books. But I try to work around it in other ways, to focus on books that talk about inclusivity, being who you are, being proud of who you are and accepting who you are. And with the governor thing and the whole library thing, I don't have time for that. I get to school at 7 am and I just barely get my work done. So, I'm not getting involved in all that. I don't want to. Even though I came out when I was 14, I just don't want to be the face of that.

As these teachers' (and student teachers') experiences make painfully clear, the fear of resisting norms and practices that are seen as right and good is real. We believe that it is unfair – indeed, irresponsible – to ask all teachers to resist any and everything that is unjust. Teachers and people who are gay or who identify as LGBTQIA+ should not *have* to "be the face" of resistance against heteronormativity, just like Black teachers should not *have* to "be the face" of resistance against racism. As we all learn about the systems of injustice that pattern our lives in unseen ways, each of us must make our own decisions about what we can and should do (Box 4.2).

> **Box 4.2 Your Stories**
>
> As you have been reading through these different experiences, what connections are you making? If you were one of these teachers, what would you have done? Have you been in a similar situation? What did you do? What do you wish you would (or could) have done? How were you constrained? Did you feel like you were adequately equipped to respond (or resist) in the ways you wanted to? Take a minute to write down some thoughts related to how you can resist heteronormativity in your own classroom or school in ways you feel are reasonable, given your context and your role. While it's easy for an outsider to suggest that all of us, all teachers, should immediately right every wrong and battle every injustice, we offer that undoing heteronormativity can begin with very small steps – a single book that opens up students to inclusivity or one comment to a peer that makes even subtly clear that you are an ally.

As you reflect on the level of risk you are willing to take to identify and disrupt heteronormativity and discrimination, it may be helpful to consider a story from one of our contributors who wished to remain anonymous.

Anonymous: "It's not fake, it's not a fluke."

One of our contributors shared a personal experience about her own son. She asked to remain anonymous because, although she "would like to talk about LGBTQ+ issues," she didn't want to make her son's life more difficult.

> I have a transgender son. My son was born a daughter. When he became a young adult, he came out to us, and told us that he never felt that he was a girl and that he believed he was transgender. So, at first, as parents we were concerned for his mental health, so we looked for help. We looked for a counselor, psychiatrist, psychologist, and then eventually we ended up at a medical facility that specialized in working with transgender youth. He was diagnosed with gender dysphoria, which is the proper name for a child who is transgender. Since then, he has transitioned.
>
> As you can imagine, this has been a major change in the family, not just as he changed his clothing. His name has been officially changed and his birth certificate. But I will tell you right now, I went from having a child who was depressed to a child who has been thriving. I am flabbergasted at times, and just so happy for him, because all those issues that we had year after year finally have resolved, just by him being able to express himself.

And so, I hear a lot of people talk about how "transgender doesn't exist, and you can't become this, that, and the other," and being a Latina myself, it was something that I had to work on. I had to go and seek help from other parents who had transgender children. I had to read books and really educate myself on transgender children. But I will tell you right now. It's not a fake, it's not a fluke.

Having been going through the entire process, having talked to the experts, having my son on testosterone for three or four years now, seeing him thrive and become the person he was always meant to be, has changed our lives. And so, as you can imagine I am the number one LGBTQ+ ally and it's something that I share with people. I don't talk about to a lot of other people, but I wanted to mention it because I think with certain policies, like the bathroom policy for transgender youth. My son goes to a male bathroom. No one knows. He's not there to do anything but to go to the bathroom.

He was also given a private bathroom if he wanted to use it, near the counselors. But imagine if he's forced to go to a girl's bathroom. He doesn't look like a girl anymore. He doesn't identify as a girl. That would have been such a blow to him. He is now thriving and happy, and finally found himself. Imagine the mental anguish to all of a sudden not only out yourself, but go to a bathroom that you do not identify with? I saw that you have to have parental consent to have a different name at school. Thankfully we are very supportive of my son. He now has an official new name. But not everyone is lucky to have supportive parents or parents who understand. I feel that would put a lot of students into a very dangerous situation.

I feel that that is such a harsh policy, something that would really put some students in the situation where they could be harmed at home by their own parents or by the people they live with and so that is something that I am against. And I think, as we move forward as a society, you will see, and I see this with my students more and more, when you talk to students now, everyone will tell you, love is love. We don't care. You're a good person. We are more worried about how you are treated and how we treat you. We're seeing that kind of mentality developing into the new generation. And I think that we are just moving more and more towards that.

For this contributor – a teacher and parent – it was crucial to educate herself and to unlearn some of the assumptions and stereotypes she grew up with (Box 4.3).

> **Box 4.3 Your Stories**
>
> As you reflect on the experiences of these teachers on your own, with others in your life, and, ideally, with your own colleagues, take turns briefly sharing your reactions (emotional, physical, and psychological) to these experiences. As you reflect together, you might consider something Amy said: "I understand what could happen to me if I deliberately chose to defy what parents ask me to do. I understand I could be stripped of my teaching license. But if I'm not seeing and acknowledging the students for who they are, then why am I even in this profession? Why am I even doing this? It weighs heavily on me." What weighs on you? How can you and your colleagues work together to relieve some of the stress you feel related to how your students who identify with the LGBTQIA+ community are treated?

Teacher Strategies

While many teachers are actively lobbying their state and local legislators to rescind harmful laws, others are finding everyday ways to resist while still being careful that they will be able to stay in the classroom, caring for kids. Many of our contributors shared the small things they do to skirt these policies, in the name of keeping young people safe.

Amy: "Whatever I have to do to help them navigate, I'm going to do."

Amy described how she continued to establish her classroom as a safe space for all young people even in the face of policies that are hurtful.

> I have had students, even students at this school, who have been homeless because their parents kicked them out of their homes before they were 18 years old, and they have nowhere to go. We make sure they have food and that they can figure out where they're going to be and clothing and all of those things. It's just heartbreaking. So, I try to be sure my students know my classroom is a safe space. Whatever I have to do to help them navigate, I'm going to do.
>
> A lot of the work they do in my class is writing, so I try to have open prompts but also allow students to explore challenging issues in their lives. So, I'll ask questions like, "My life would be so much easier if…" and then they get to write about that for 10 minutes.

Or "One thing I wish adults knew is…" and they go from there. They never have to write on the prompt as long as they're writing. Many students will take that opportunity. They'll say, "I'm not going to write on the prompt today. I just need to vent." And students know they can. That's their place to write. So, I just try to give them the space to be heard and seen.

Reese, mentor teacher at a private elementary school: "We read."

Reese described her main tools for establishing her classroom as a safe space for her young students: they read and they have conversations. She said this should be happening in every classroom, but it isn't.

> We read. We read the book *Julián at the Wedding* by Jessica Love. The students love the pictures. It's two women getting married, and it pushes back on all these gender stereotypes in the context of weddings. So, Julián is a flower girl. Can boys be flower girls? We have this whole conversation about that. And then the two women getting married. So, they make all these connections.
>
> And again, I don't know how certain parents will handle this, but the most important thing is that we are have the conversation about who can get married? Well, lots of people can get married. What is love? It's complex and beautiful, in all these different ways. My student teachers ask, "Are we allowed to read that book?" And it's like, "Yes, we are allowed to read that book."
>
> It's the conversations. We are showcasing that love is beautiful and relationships are beautiful. I think that what was so amazing is the children loved the book. They loved the connections. It gave them a space to talk about a lesbian wedding, and had they seen that before or not, what would that be like? And that's what [the student teacher] would have if she married her girlfriend. It felt simple. It felt beautiful. It felt like what should be happening in every classroom. and it makes me sad that it's not.
>
> I think that lays a foundation without explicitly saying, "Okay, today, we're going to talk about LGBTQ issues." You can still talk about the inherent value of people and the rights that they should have. I think, in very broad, expansive ways that are still foundational. Now, I would still say, I think you can absolutely still read a book like *Julián at the Wedding*.
>
> But I think it's how you couch it, how you set it up, how you end it. I don't think that it has to be a big "Oh, my gosh, huge reveal!"

Let the children talk about it. Let them say what they think. It doesn't necessarily have to be your big agenda saying, "Today we're going read a book about a Lesbian wedding." But it's, "We're going to read Julián went to a wedding, and what happened at that wedding."

We read books that show all kinds of things all the time. So, I think dropping books into your curriculum just to show how love and human relationships and family relationships work because there are kids who have two moms and two dads and so this validates that child's experience and validates the experience of love being expansive and beautiful. It can be as simple as reading a book, letting the kids talk, highlighting a person's right is to be able to love who they love. Now I know that's maybe more than most teachers would be comfortable doing, but I think those are simple, everyday ways that your tone can be set every single day in your classroom.

> **Box 4.4 Your Strategies**
> Reese teaches at a private school, and many of you reading her experience might be thinking, "Well, we can't do that at *my* school in *this* state!" And you may be absolutely right. But consider her final statements about pulling back a bit from the specifics and focusing on the larger issue of "letting the kids talk," highlighting the rights of all people, and validating the lived experiences of students. What is something simple you could do in your own classroom to create a safe space and set a tone of inclusion for your students? What is a topic, an event, or a tradition that you could use as the entrée into discussing how what is "normal" is created?

Carleigh, elementary school music teacher: "You don't want students to feel excluded."

Carleigh believes that changing small things that are within the purview of one teacher can have a big impact on the extent to which students feel included and valued. Even having one-to-one conversations with colleagues and administrators:

> We have two students in fourth grade who identify as non-binary. So, oftentimes when our principal is giving announcements, he'll say, "Good morning, boys and girls," and I've talked to the assistant principal saying, "We do have these two kids who have told us that

they identify as non-binary" and to be careful about saying "boys and girls" because that excludes kids who don't identify that way.

Even in my classroom, I used to do review games as boys versus girls. I don't do that anymore. With bathroom passes, I used to have a boys pass and a girls pass, but now I just have two passes that say, "Bathroom pass" because you have to adjust things for the student population. You don't want students to feel excluded.

Sabrina, elementary teacher of an inclusive first-grade classroom: "We do have an impact."

Sabrina identifies as a member of the LGBTQIA+ community, and she agrees that small things, like the language that teachers use, are crucial for students feeling included and cared for. She shared a letter she received from a former student who thanked her for being authentic and helping her feel comfortable and safe, and Sabrina used this to illustrate how "small tweaks" in the language that teachers use can mean a lot to students – even in first or second grade.

> I've always been true to who I am. The students know [my wife]. They might be young where they don't quite fully get it, but I've always been true to who I am. I've never hid who I was. If you don't want me to work at your school because of this, then I don't want to work at your school. It's weird. I've never in my life felt like anybody's displayed homophobia toward me, which is a good thing to have being 46 years old.
>
> So, it was a few years ago, before COVID. I get this letter in the inter-office mail and it's a letter from one of my students, Jenna, that I taught in second grade, and she was now a senior. And part of their senior project was to write a letter to one of their former teachers who influenced them, kind of like who you remember, and why. And she wrote about how I was always true to who I was, and she saw that as a second grader, and she said, "Now that I identify as part of the LGBTQ community, I feel comfortable and safe, knowing that it's okay for me to be who I am."
>
> To hear that from a senior? We do have an impact in first or second grade. You know, in first or second grade, they don't know if they're gay or not. They may have never heard the word transgender, or you know, or non-binary, but soon they will, and there's going to come a time when those kids are old enough to identify with a certain group, and often it comes in middle and high school. I'll always keep that let-

Figure 4.1 The handmade thank-you card a student sent Sabrina. Photograph provided by author with consent of Sabrina Thomas.

> impacted my life as my teacher. ... was definitely nerve wracking for me because I had just moved back from Southern VA. However, your warm smile and character instantly made me feel welcomed and prepared for the year. I remember always being so excited to participate in your fun classroom activities, like Fruit Friday and writing on the SMARTboard with your "magic" wand. I always felt loved and comfortable being who I was in your classroom. I even remember writing my own "chapter" book about a chihuahua which you placed on your bookshelf for all the other students to read. In addition, I met some of my best friends in your class, and I'm still in touch with many more. We all seem to recall the classroom "connection" hand sign and the crazy costumes we wore to Mrs. Norris's Paris party (I still have the pictures on my computer!) However, the biggest way you impacted me occured many years after 2nd grade. As an individual who now identifies as part of the LGBTQ+ community, it is very inspiring to have someone to look up to as a successful individual who is also unapologetically herself. Although I didn't know it at the time, I was being taught lessons that exceed basic math, reading, and writing. I was being taught about love and how it comes in many forms. As part of Teachers for Tomorrow this year, we are given the opportunity to participate in an Internship in one class in our area. Since I love to cook, I want to engage my students by working with food because everyone loves it and it teaches many lessons beyond just the lesson. I also want to make sure I am as supportive and welcoming with my students as you were with me...

Figure 4.2 Text from the handmade thank-you card a student sent Sabrina. Photograph provided by author with consent of Sabrina Thomas.

ter from Jenna because it's a reminder for me that how I act and what I say and what I do is really important in the classroom.

I think we sometimes forget that we have students who identify as part of this community whose families are highly supportive. We have parents who identify as part of this community. Therefore, their kids are also a part of this community whether they know it or not. And I think about my own kids. I think about it every time I hear someone say, "Go ask your mom and dad." And then the questions start coming. The language we use is very important. And sometimes it's just a few tweaks, like, I never say boys and girls, ever. I always say students or crew, or some type of group. So sometimes it's just small tweaks and language.

Beyond the changes in the language we use in our classrooms, several of our contributing teachers shared ways they build classrooms that are inclusive and that push students who may identify as part of dominant groups to think critically about their own assumptions and life experiences.

Emily, high school teacher: "It's okay if you're not perfect as long as you're trying to do what's best for the people around you."

Emily describes one of the readings she used to start conversations about trying to do better in simple ways, even if we might fail sometimes.

With the senior identity unit, we tried to pull in a lot of different short stories from a lot of different sources, to try to get as many different identities and different perspectives and different experiences as we can to these seniors, so they see that there's a wider world out there. We probably read 15 different stories.

But there's one in particular that always comes up and makes for some dramatic moments at times. It's a nonfiction piece about how a woman's sibling transitioned – she's now a transgender woman – and her adjustment to using the correct pronouns. She writes about how it was so ingrained in her to use the old pronouns, and she wasn't trying to hurt her sibling, but it was a struggle for her. She was just trying to adapt, right? And so, it's told from her perspective and her journey.

It's great because it's a struggle that some of my students have where they're just like, "I don't always remember." I really like the perspective of this piece, because it's a woman who is earnestly trying to do better, and she's failing some of the time. She's really trying and working through what it means to her, and how it's changed her life, and how she can do better to support her sister. So the message is that it's okay if you're not perfect as long as you're trying to do what's best for the people around you.

Althea, high school teacher: "We don't give them a chance to talk."

In addition to choosing readings and other resources to spur critical thinking, Althea, a ninth-grade teacher in a suburban public high school, described how a literal, physical tour of the school can lead to observations about the environment, safety, indications that everyone is safe, and issues of identity – a gateway activity into considering larger issues of identity.

> We were doing a little tour around the school, because it's first-year high school students, and they were just like, "Hey, so, I noticed that you've got a pride flag. Do you know what my pronouns are? I want you to know what my preferred name is." And I said, "Thank you for telling me. Have you told your other teachers?" And they said, "No, I feel like I couldn't."
>
> I was just heartbroken because I know their other teachers, and they would love to know that information. So, I got their permission to share that information with the other teachers. It feels like we go a couple of steps forward, a couple of steps back, in terms of just being able to have open conversations, and to shift the dialogue and the vocabulary, the words that are being used by students so that it is more inclusive and equitable.
>
> To have that baseline level of respect just for others as human beings, right? I feel like that's a huge part of what we have to do here, especially as secondary teachers, because they're at such a critical age. They have all these questions about their identity and who they are and how they matter in the world. It all comes to a head here where they're exposed to all these different perspectives, and we don't give them a chance to talk about them in a safe space and feel like they can be open and ask questions without judgment or be able to share information without judgment and continue the conversation in a way that progresses positively.

The idea of "resistance" might conjure up mental images of large groups of people marching in public places, going on the news, or standing at a podium. This can be daunting for teachers like you who are just trying to care for kids, changing lives one at a time.

So, what if "resistance" was just what these teachers are talking about – shifting the language we use, having open conversations, and changing our lesson plans or assignments to be more inclusive? What if resistance involved just helping students to understand that norms and traditions are just the choices of fallible human beings – and that they can and sometimes should be challenge and modified. As you consider what you can do to push back against heteronormative practices, remember resistance means just that you're challenging your own assumptions, you're open to new ideas, and you're trying to be comfortable with the fact that you might be wrong.

Youth Stories

Diana, who recently graduated from a large public magnet school, remembered a time during her first year of high school (before COVID) when she was playing on her school's volleyball team. For one game, they played against a school in a different school district. The team was well known as one of the best female volleyball teams in the area. Diana remembered that there was a major issue because one of the players on the other team identified as transgender:

> I remember a lot of the students were like, "Oh, that's not fair. They shouldn't be allowed to play on the team. They already have a lot of other advantages." They were just saying how it was really unfair and it shouldn't be allowed. They just kept saying they shouldn't be on the team. It was a whole thing. A lot of parents from our team were freaking out saying that it was unfair. They were really mad. They wanted to talk to the school board to get the girl removed from the team. Even the next day there were a bunch of older kids saying they should talk to the board, that it shouldn't be allowed. But nothing changed. It was still just the same thing. Even COVID year, they still played against the same team. The girl was still there. It was just the same.

As Diana remembered experiences she had had during her high school career, she ultimately shared that, while questions around students who identified as LGBTQIA+ might have been an issue when she was younger, it seemed like a lot had really calmed down, and she said she didn't remember any of her friends or acquaintances having any problems in the past few years, especially as it related to some of the most politicized questions we so often hear about on the news and in media.

> Honestly, the whole thing with trans kids using the bathroom, it's not even a big deal at my school. I mean, maybe before COVID it was more of an issue. Like, people might have been like, 'Is that a boy or a girl,' or whatever, but now, it's just more normalized. It's not really even an issue. If that's how they want to do it, then that's fine. No one really cares.

For Diana, vocal parent groups and divisive political rhetoric didn't affect her everyday school experience. But for others, like Finn, a Fellow in the Youth Research Council, the everyday of school was filled with fear and anxiety:

> I'm a trans student. I'm white, and I am privileged with that, but then, like, people will comment on my body. At school you have to find people you can be comfortable with. And it's really hard to talk to teachers and be like, "Hey, I'm trans." There are so many teachers who I feel so uncomfortable correcting and so I don't do it, but that means I also feel uncomfortable when they refer to me in class because that's, like, outing me in a way…I don't feel safe because there are kids who threaten trans people. I'm fine if they say mean stuff to me, but I'm worried about the non-mean stuff, like the violent stuff.

For some students, especially those who, like Diana, do not identify as part of the LGBTQIA+ community, schools are often experienced as inclusive places. Yet for others, schools can be very scary, and it's only the teachers they see every day, whose primary professional responsibility is to keep them safe, who can offer them a lifeline.

Taking Action

The educators who contributed to this chapter have all grappled with impossible decisions weighing the protection of self against the protection of students. While they made different choices – from Heather, who quietly preserved the dignity of her student by confirming and using their preferred pronouns, to Sabrina, who declined to introduce a book she knew would cause problems – they all agreed that their primary goal is to help students feel safe and cared for.

One of the through lines we noticed in these stories was that these teachers took the time to really know – and notice – their students. How do you get to know your students? What do you notice about them? Are there tools you use? Are there things you do to help you create relationships of trust?

Perhaps you need to rethink what you do, or maybe you need to share what has been successful with others. Ultimately, we believe that as you take the time and care to build meaningful and appropriate relationships with your students, you will be in a position to not only understand but also advocate for them in ways that are meaningful to them. And maybe that's the key – prioritizing what is important to students, not to powerful families or the media or even government officials.

We would be remiss if we did not note that in the midst of writing this chapter, news broke nationally about the death of a nonbinary student, Nex Benedict, in Owasso, Oklahoma. At the time of our writing, the exact cause of Nex's death remains under investigation. What is clear, however, is that Oklahoma's newly adopted policy for bathroom use by transgender students forced Nex into a situation that resulted in bullying and in a physical altercation in the girls' bathroom (Cann et al., 2024). It is not hyperbole to say that the matters discussed in this chapter, for some students, are matters of life and death.

Resources

In addition to the classroom books we suggest in the Appendix, check out these resources related to supporting LGBTQIA+ students and families:

- **Book**: *The Educator's Guide to LGBTQ+ Inclusion* by Kryss Shane. This book lays out best practices for supporting LGBTQ+ youth with a variety of identities and intersectionalities to create a safe environment and, therefore, better learning for all students. It includes narratives from children across the country, and it is appropriate for educators in a variety of roles, not just classroom teachers.
- **Podcast**: *UnErasing LGBTQ History* by History UnErased. With each episode under 30 minutes, this humorous podcast has real K-12 educators presenting on different inclusive, LGBTQ+ lessons from their classrooms along with a variety of surprising stories from history and pop culture with the goal of putting LGBTQ+ history in the classroom.
- **TED Talk**: "A Short History of Trans People's Long Fight for Equality" by Samy Nour Younes (15 minutes). Exactly as the title states, this walks the audience through a history of notable trans folks who have been fighting for equal rights since the beginning of recorded history. It's an important reminder that this is not a "new" identity, and it has reach far beyond the Western world/culture. Link: https://www.youtube.com/watch?v=qRJJR6bGyL4

Online Resource: "Being an Ally to Transgender and Nonbinary Young People". A basic primer for understanding gender identity and respecting others. Includes what to do if you accidentally misgender someone. Not only is this a helpful guide for you, but it is a nice link to share with others when they have questions about gender. Link: https://www.thetrevorproject.org/resources/guide/a-guide-to-being-an-ally-to-transgender-and-nonbinary-youth/

References

Amiri, F. (2023, March 1). *McCarthy, GOP introduce measure to protect 'parents' rights'*. AP News. https://apnews.com/article/parents-rights-schools-woke-mccarthy-congress-f4643fa74dc4d82067c339fe950c3080

Block, M. (2022, May 11). Accusations of "grooming" are the latest political attack—With homophobic origins. *NPR*. https://www.npr.org/2022/05/11/1096623939/accusations-grooming-political-attack-homophobic-origins

Cann, C., Young, M., & Osterman-Mayes, C. (2024, February 22). Death of Nex Benedict did not result from trauma, police say; many questions remain. *USA Today*. https://www.usatoday.com/story/news/nation/2024/02/22/nex-benedict-case-oklahoma/72695904007/

Najarro, I. (2023, August 22). The Florida ap psychology controversy, explained. *Education Week*. https://www.edweek.org/teaching-learning/the-florida-ap-psychology-controversy-explained/2023/08

Pollitt, A.M., Mernitz, S.E., Russell, S.T., Curran, M.A., & Toomey, R.B. (2022). Heteronormativity in the lives of lesbian, gay, bisexual, and queer young people. *Journal of Homosexuality*, *68*(3), 522–544. https://doi.org/10.1080/00918369.2019.1656032

Rankin, S. (2023, July 18). Virginia finalizes guidance on transgender students, including rolling back some accommodations. *Associated Press*. https://apnews.com/article/virginia-transgender-students-schools-youngkin-ba073a1e8a9286456a7509688f40115b

Rhoden, G. (29 March 2022). Florida isn't the only state pushing legislation that could be harmful to LGBTQ students. *CNN*. https://www.cnn.com/2022/03/10/us/states-anti-lgbtq-legislation-florida/index.html

Statement on AP Psychology and Florida. (2023, August 3). *Newsroom: College Board*. https://newsroom.collegeboard.org/statement-ap-psychology-and-florida

Villarreal, D. (2021, August 25). Teachers "abusing" positions to indoctrinate kids, NC Lt. Governor says of report. *Newsweek*. https://www.newsweek.com/teachers-abusing-positions-indoctrinate-kids-nc-lt-governor-says-report-1622762

5

Ability and Disability

Jeff really wasn't sure how to help her. He'd read the Individualized Education Plan (IEP) and had reviewed the goals related to organization and self-regulation. What he didn't find were goals related to his class. He went to her special education case manager to ask for help. "Kayla is really struggling," he said.

> *We just took our second quiz. I read it to her and tried to modify it as we went, but she still didn't get any of the questions correct. I've done what the IEP says, but I'm struggling with what to do next.*

"Yes, she's a tough case," her case manager replied.

> *Look. I'm just going to say it. Nobody expects her to pass your class. Nobody expects her to pass the SOL (Standards of Learning exam given at the end of a course). The state says she has to take the class. She's so sweet and she'll do anything you ask her. Just give her some coloring sheets and let her do her thing. She won't be any problem.*

Jeff was livid. How could this be the best answer from a professional responsible for helping Kayla get a high school education? He'd worked with students like Kayla, students whose disabilities made accessing the traditional curriculum very challenging. In the past, though, he'd worked with a co-teacher who helped him figure out the student's strengths and consider how they could use those strengths to help the student learn the course content, develop important skills, and be successful in their class. Now, though, he was on his own. Kayla needed to have her materials read to her. She needed the curriculum to be modified. And she was in a class with other students who had unique needs, including two students with limited English proficiency, several with chronic absenteeism, and a brand-new student who had just arrived as a refugee from Afghanistan. How could Jeff possibly help all of these students on his own?

Later that week, as Jeff continued to think about what his next steps would be, he received an email from the school counselor. Kayla's family was moving, and she would be transferring to a new school. Now, several years later, as Jeff thought back to this situation, he wondered what happened to Kayla. In her new school, did she find a case manager who was more helpful? Was she finally put in a co-taught class where both she and the content area teacher would have the support they needed to help her be successful? Or was she sitting in the back of somebody else's classroom with a coloring sheet?

Critical Concepts

In this chapter, we share stories and strategies from teachers who have encountered issues of ability and disability in their classrooms and schools. We also highlight their pedagogical and professional decisions that have allowed them to serve and advocate for children and young people with disabilities. Before reading about these contributing teachers' experiences, we will share another critical concept – the notion of "ableism" – and we will ask you to consider this as you think about your own beliefs and practices. Once again, please grab that notebook or open your computer and keep some notes about your observations, ideas, and potential actions.

Ableism

Having disabilities is a facet of the human experience. Most of us will have a disability at some point in our lives. However, too often we think of people with disabilities as having "special" needs rather than as part of our community. This is certainly true in schools where special education is separate (or what one of our contributors framed as "segregated") from general education.

Our understanding of what "able-bodied" looks like is a social construct. Our world is designed for able-bodied people, and often our language around disability is too focused on what disabled people *lack* rather than what they *need* to be fully present, fully participating members of our community. This is ableism: giving preference to those without disabilities. One problem with ableism is that it serves a narrow portion of the community when accommodations might help everyone.

For example, imagine you are building a school. Out front, you construct a set of stairs. Only able-bodied people can use these stairs. However, if you construct a ramp, both able-bodied and disabled people can use the ramp, thus impacting who can access and attend this school. Such responsive design features, including a ramp or a curb cut (the cut along sidewalks that allow people with wheelchairs, strollers, or carts to enter and exit the sidewalk) often are no more, and sometimes can be *less*, expensive than architectural elements that used to be considered "normal." And these accommodations frequently not only serve people with disabilities but also increase accessibility for everyone.

Consider this list of ableist behaviors, beliefs, and attitudes from the Anti-Defamation League (https://www.adl.org/resources/lesson-plan/understanding-and-challenging-ableism):

- Assuming people with disabilities can't do anything and are helpless
- Feeling pity for people with disabilities
- Using offensive and ableist language and words like "retarded," "lame," "spaz," "psychotic," or "crippled"
- People with disabilities thinking they can't do certain things because of their disability
- Students with disabilities getting bullied in school
- Assuming that you can see whether someone has a disability or that all disabilities are visible
- The lack of people with disabilities in the media (e.g., movies, TV shows, and apps)
- Jobs not providing the necessary accommodations for people with disabilities to perform their work functions
- Public transportation that isn't accessible for people with disabilities (mobility, sight, etc.)
- People with disabilities being isolated from and/or invisible to the general population

Can you think of examples of ableism you have seen in your own community or in your school? If you can't think of any, consider having a conversation about ableism with a colleague or even your students. What examples can they think of? Make a list. Next, sort these into three categories: interpersonal (bullying, threats, stereotypes), institutional (legal, discrimination, education), and internalized (thoughts or beliefs about people's worth and abilities). When you are finished, reflect or journal on these questions:

- What did you notice as you were doing this activity?
- Did any of the examples fit into more than one category? How so?

- Do you think some of these examples are more serious than others? Explain.
- Do you think some of these examples are more easily addressed than others? How so?
- How do other aspects of people's identities (e.g., race, gender, sexual orientation, and religion) impact the discrimination they may experience as a result of having a disability?

According to a recent report from the National Center for Education Statistics, more than 75% of public schools in the United States have reported challenges in hiring special education teachers (NCES, 2022). Additionally, 65% of schools report being understaffed in special education, resulting in intense fatigue, burnout, and mental health struggles for those special education staff that remain in the profession (Bodenhamer, 2023). These shortages, coupled with the demands placed on special education staff and content area teachers, can force us to focus on *dis*ability rather than ability, on student deficits rather than on their potential to learn and add to the school community.

As you read this chapter, consider the role you might play in pushing back against deficit orientations of students with disabilities:

- What is your connection with ideas about and forms of disability? For example, do you identify as someone with a disability?
- Even if you do not have a formal assessment as having a disability, have you experienced school, professional, home, or community contexts where you felt differently "abled"?
- Or perhaps someone in your family or community is a person with a disability? How have they been treated, in school, at home, in the community?
- Do you have someone in your own classroom who is an individual with a disability? Or someone in your school whom you might not teach but whom you know fairly well? Try to take their perspective for a moment: How do you think they feel in your class? How might they feel as they enter (not necessarily walk into) school? As they sit at lunch or on the bus? As they participate in activities or celebrations? As current events are discussed or debated?
- In other teachers' classrooms, your school, or your community, how are students and individuals with disabilities involved in everyday activities? In the life of your classroom, school, and community? What is done to ensure that every student is included and has access to all materials and activities?

- ♦ How has the level and nature of inclusion of students (and teachers) with disabilities changed in recent years? What do you speculate or know are the reasons behind these changes?

These questions are intended to provoke critical and even uncomfortable reflection on your part – a central goal of this book. As educators, each of us has had to do the work of looking in the mirror. In fact, you've likely realized that for a teacher that's a process that pretty much never ends. As we share the experiences of our teacher contributors in this chapter, keep that idea of uncomfortable reflection with you. Know that we are all in a process of becoming. As we approach these questions with humility, an eagerness to learn and be better, and an ethic of care, we are convinced we will learn ways to be better, more inclusive educators.

Teacher Stories

We spoke with several teachers about their experiences with and advice for working with and advocating for students with disabilities. They reflected on what has changed in our schools and classrooms in recent years with regard to this work and on what has remained – and should remain – the same.

Bjorn, an administrator in a private school: "The wonder and the joy and the passion."

For Bjorn, who has spent almost twenty years as a special education teacher (recently turned special education administrator), what we should always remember when working with students with disabilities are the "small things" and the "moments."

> I think what's stayed the same is the wonder and the joy and the passion for small things that are gigantic in terms of sitting across the table from someone else. You know, whether you're a teacher or you're an educational leader, you can still have these moments. That's something that I had to figure out as an administrator: how to continue to have these moments. Sitting across the table from someone with an intellectual disability and having them come to a realization, whether it's a concept, or a connection, or just their space in my life.

Those small moments of connection are important for both teachers and students. But it can be hard at times to enjoy those small moments when teachers feel that they lack the resources to serve students, feel or actually are isolated, or feel or actually are constrained by the political climate. For Nathan, that isolation is apparent.

Nathan, teacher of students with autism: "We're all on an island –together, but alone."

Nathan shared that at the elementary school where he teaches, teachers who work with students with autism often do not receive the same level of support from or communication with colleagues and administrators as those teachers who are in inclusive classrooms.

> Our district recently developed a policy so that instead of snow days where students and teachers don't come to school, now that all students have a device, students are expected to be learning online, with teachers providing their lessons online. Our school has sent all this information to parents about what to do on these days, where and when to login, what to have at home in terms of supplies, etc. But there has been absolutely no guidance for teachers of students with autism, and no guidance for parents and caregivers. There's just not much that comes from the top in terms of assistance. A lot of times with SPED [Special Education], we're all on an island. Together, but alone. Like, all the SPED teachers, we're all in this group, this bubble in the school.

According to our contributing teachers, this feeling of being alone extends to how they are treated by parents and families. While parent and family assumptions and demands are often leveled at any teacher, teachers of students with disabilities who already feel isolated in a building and because of a lack of communication from administrators can feel the effects of those parent demands more acutely.

Nathan: "I'm being attacked for what they assume I'm not doing."

Nathan shared how the inaction or oversights of administrators with such communications can mean that special education teachers are left unable to effectively serve their students, with parents and families assuming the worst about these teachers' practices. Like so many teachers, he appreciates so many aspects of his job but is often put in untenable professional situations.

> For the most part, it's very rewarding. A lot of the kids are really great, and a lot of the parents are really receptive, understanding we are really trying to help their kids. But there are a few parents who do give us a lot of pushback. Specifically, I had a situation earlier this year. I began getting emails from a parent within the first week of school. I hadn't learned anything about this kid, this kid was categorized completely differently previously so I didn't know anything at all yet.
>
> So, I began to get angry emails right at the beginning of school this year. Talking about how they don't feel like he's getting the services he needs, he's not being given the attention he needs, we told you we wanted this, we told you we wanted that. All of this is happening within the first week. I mean, I haven't even had time to learn this kid. I'm still trying to get to know this kid, figure out movements, service minutes, and how we were going to serve them and stuff like that. It felt like they cared more about what they wanted than what might have been best for the kid.
>
> That's something that I've encountered a lot. I mean, I'm here to help the kids figure out who they are and what they can do. There's also the flip side where I'm trying to help a kid advance and parents come to me and say, "No, that makes them unhappy." or "They have too much work." So, they're limiting the kids but at the same time I'm being attacked for what they assume I'm not doing. So, it's this contradiction, and I'm just sitting on this island wondering how I'm supposed to be doing both things?

Complicating these competing feelings of isolation and being under attack are the very real and constant concerns about liability, as special education is highly politicized and regulated, more so than other areas of education. All of these factors result in an intensification of the isolation that's already just a part of the job of working with a very special population.

Nathan: "It's created this stress."

These myriad pressures – exacerbated by sometimes excessive and misguided legislation and policies and coupled with an increasingly litigious society – mean that the very nature of his job and how he spends his time have shifted. As we talked with Nathan, he shared his concern that much of his work boils down to checking boxes to avoid liability rather than focusing on his students, their needs, and their goals.

> Overall, a lot of the legislation or changes to legislation that have come down recently are holding teachers more liable for anything. It's created this stress coming down from central office. So, it's like, "You need to make sure and check these boxes, so we don't get a lawsuit," without them actually saying, "You need to make sure and check these boxes, so we don't get a lawsuit." Everything that we do is out of fear of getting a lawsuit as opposed to for the betterment of students.

Bjorn: "Teaching joy."

For Bjorn, who has been in schools for over 20 years, first as a teacher, then as an administrator, and then as a special education teacher, it's all about doing whatever you can to not lose sight of the joy that is in teaching. He recognizes – like we all do – that there are so many pressures on teachers – especially special education teachers – but that, at the end of the day, the most important thing is teaching joy and teaching passion.

> What's changed, I think, is what seems to be the complexity and all the things that we have to negotiate, to get to those moments where we can focus on the power of the moment. There's just this constant adding on of pressure and complexity. I see a lot of people forgetting the power and joy of the moment because they get wrapped up in the complexity of all that they're required to do. In special education, in particular. Not only are you a special education teacher, you're a case manager. So, you're walking in two different worlds. You're a social worker, and also you're a teacher, and the more you get pulled out from the teaching joy and passion by other things, the greater the risk is for you to lose sight of that joy, and therefore not want to continue to do it, or continue to do it but lose the passion. And then you just have a job as opposed to a calling. I think all teachers at some level are called to do something that is difficult, that is meaningful. It's hard to sustain, because I really believe that the things that are the most joyful in the world, things you love the most, also require the most work.

Ability and Disability ◆ 111

> **Box 5.1 Your Stories**
>
> Have you ever felt the fear and stress that Nathan referred to? Are you able to focus on the everyday needs of your students with special needs, on their abilities and the challenges they are facing? Does it seem – or is it actually the case – that you are having to consider more and different issues as part of your job? How do you cope? Have you ever considered leaving the teaching profession because of the stress or isolation you feel? How do you manage those feelings? Are there ways you see to push back? Does pushing back feel possible? Are you able to focus on the joy, even in small ways, like Bjorn encourages? Consider recording some of those small moments of joy in a journal. It can be helpful to read through these memories when you are feeling particularly stressed.

Teachers who work with students with special needs also feel pressure as they advocate for the services to which these students are entitled, help them develop an awareness of their abilities and disabilities, and fight for them to be treated with the dignity they deserve – each of which creates additional stress. But even if they are expected to engage their students with these lessons and even if they do so exactly "right" or with the best of intentions, parents and families can react negatively.

Frankie: "If he wanted to learn more, could he have?"

Frankie, a former teacher of students with intellectual disabilities, started her teaching career feeling optimistic about the ways she could make change for and with her students. She shared with us a time when she taught a "mini history lesson" on the use of the word "retarded" because she wanted to empower her students with knowledge and let them know that they are in charge of how they identify. But it backfired, and she worried about how being less open with students with disabilities reduces their abilities to learn and grow.

> There's a huge campaign in the spring that's called *Spread the Word to End the Word*. So, it's pushing back on the word "retard," and saying that it is no longer used socially. Spreading information that it was a medical term and stuff. And in my very first year of teaching, I headed the campaign. Some of my students had never heard the word before and so they were asking me, "What word? What is the bad word? What's the R word? I don't know it." And these are students who have always been a part of the advocacy organizations that promote this campaign, too, but still they said they've never heard the word. So, I did a mini history lesson about how it started with the term "mental retardation," as a medical term and then people said

> other things related to that and now you are in charge of how you want to identify. Maybe you just talk about your strengths and needs, and things like that. What I thought was very cool and forward thinking. This was in like 2013.
>
> But a parent emailed and told me, "He has never been told he has a disability. He's never heard that word. And you really just wrecked his self-confidence. You really should have gotten approval before you talked about this word." It was my first year of teaching ever, and I felt horrible. And even with time, I still do, because I still recognize I didn't have a disability. I don't have a disability. And I did take that away from him and his family. But I also just wonder when and where, if he wanted to learn more, could he have? And where could he have? If it's not the segregated (because that's what I call it because that's what it is – segregated) "safe" room with me, and it's not at home with his family, what's going to happen outside of the classroom? If the classroom is supposed to be preparing him for life?

Frankie recognized that she may have made a mistake, as we all do sometimes. Yet she identified a tension that is particularly salient for teachers of students with disabilities: we want to protect our students and keep them safe, but at the same time we want to equip them with information and knowledge to help them be as independent as they can in how they control their own lives.

Frankie, "It was even more poignant in my classroom…because of these assumptions about their capacity."

Frankie continued to explore the extra tensions and pressures inherent in the work of a teacher of students with disabilities when she touched on the unwritten rule of teachers not discussing their own political opinions. Frankie suggested that this rule is even more of an absolute in classrooms like hers because of an assumption that students with intellectual disabilities lack the capacity to make their own decisions.

> I think in my classroom, and all of the classrooms like mine, I always found that you followed that "no political talk" rule, even more so than in the classrooms I grew up being in, where there was civic discourse and debates, and talking about both sides of any issue. One, I think probably it has to do with the assumption that those learners with IDD (intellectual or developmental disabilities) didn't care or couldn't master concepts like social justice and politics. And two, the

fear of brainwashing students. "They're so impressionable, they'll just regurgitate what you say," so you can't let them know your thoughts and feelings or your affiliations. The latter was definitely my experience. And I know this happens in all classrooms more in the past several years, but it was my experience that it was even more poignant in my classroom with students with IDD because of these assumptions about their capacity. And so that really limited the kinds of conversations we could have – even more than in the general education classrooms.

> **Box 5.2 Your Stories**
>
> If you are a teacher of students with disabilities, how do you push back against this ableist assumption that your students lack the capacity to consider big ideas or to master concepts like social justice? Or even to begin to understand their own disabilities? When have you seen that assumption be challenged in your classroom or in your school? Do you feel like there are ways for you to counter that narrative?

Frankie: "We are potentially taking that away or picking the identity that gets highlighted or included."

Frankie helped clarify that when teachers do take even very small risks – like having unsettling conversations or using curriculum that might make students or families slightly uncomfortable – administrators need to step up and at the very least support teachers' decisions, especially when they are in line with approved practices. She shared how if administrators are more supportive of their teachers, their students will benefit.

> It was May of 2020, so everyone was home because of COVID, and the Black Lives Matter movement was really taking off. And so, the teachers I used to work with were trying to weave current events into some of their studies. There's a curriculum that's specifically for students with IDD that the county approves and uses and pays a lot of money for called "News to You," and it brings current events at the right reading level with visuals and everything. And there was a George Floyd story – very, very, very basic, not graphic. A mom wrote a scathing email to the teachers in school: "How dare you indoctrinate my daughter! She will not read about this and be told she's a horrible person just because she's white." And it really hurt the teacher I was

working with. It really, really hurt this teacher who gives her life for these students and who as the case manager of the students has taught the students for three years already and used approved curriculum, approved resources. She didn't go, you know, "rogue" teaching some random curriculum. This was approved for use in the classroom. But she gets treated with such vitriol from the family.

The school didn't support my friend, the teacher. No kind words like, "No, you weren't wrong." It was like, "Well, you know, make sure you just give an alternate assignment, offer something else." I think that piece, especially with disability, the giving something else, or something special or different, it feels like a lot of uncomfortable conversations that could lead to learning and could lead to new knowledge and could lead to perspective-taking, are being missed. Already the students in those classrooms need to be working on these skills anyway because that is a deficit. There is an executive functioning and social skills, perspective-taking need that needs to be practiced way more. A lot of the time teachers are faced with this. A lot of it has to do with disability identity and my role as a teacher teaching self-advocacy and speaking up. And we are potentially taking that away or picking the identity that gets highlighted or included. Picking the learning that happens and taking that choice away from the students or taking it away from the families who wanted to do that.

> **Box 5.3 Your Stories**
>
> Teaching is full of tensions. Frankie recognizes one of those tensions here – the need to urge students out of their comfort zones a bit as they learn about people who may be different from them. And the need to challenge the ableist assumption that students with disabilities should not be nudged in this way. Yet, as we see now more than ever, there are such constraints placed on teachers in terms of how, when, and where that can be done. How do you feel about this idea Frankie introduces of picking the learning that happens? How else might you approach a similar scenario?

Teacher Strategies

As with so many aspects of the professional lives of teachers of students with disabilities, even pushing back takes on a more complicated and intensified form: These teachers have to be even more circumspect when they are considering how they might best advocate for themselves and their students. While we, as the authors of this book, are asking you to reflect on how you might take steps to push back, disrupt, or counter dominant narratives (e.g., ableist assumptions), taken-for-granted practices, or outdated policies related to the students you teach and your role, the truth is that we are not in your classrooms. We are hundreds or even thousands of miles away, sitting in the safety of academic freedom (although even that has been challenged recently!). We know there is real, valid fear around the risks we are suggesting you take.

Bjorn, an administrator in a private school: "I knew how to reach kids."

Sometimes, even if we don't feel like we know what we're doing – like at the beginning of COVID when all of a sudden we were thrust onto Zoom and Canvas or some other learning management system – what really matters is that we know how to reach kids. Sometimes, like with Bjorn, especially with his students with special needs, at the end of the day, that's all that really matters.

> I've gone back and forth between public and Catholic schools, and I think it's been a really great perspective, because there's good that goes on at all of them. I feel like I'm becoming more of a whole educator by those experiences. I was at a new public school during the pandemic: I got hired two months before COVID hit. So not only am I returning to the classroom, having been an assistant principal for seven years, but I'm returning to the classroom in a virtual environment and I was never trained to do any of it. All of a sudden, I go from being a nineteen- or twenty-year veteran teacher, with all these experiences, to 100% relying upon brand-new teachers to help me teach me how to do my job.
>
> Teaching is teaching, right? And good teaching is good teaching – with accommodations. All of a sudden, I've got students with varying degrees of learning disabilities or students with intellectual disabilities. How the heck am I going to incorporate the support structures these students need into technology-based teaching? I learned how through the 23-year-olds telling me how to do my job. I thought, "Here we go again. I'm being humbled. I have no clue what I'm doing." I didn't, but I knew how to be a case manager. I knew how to reach kids. I knew how to build relationships. So, I taught the young teachers those things.

Frankie: "I don't know if I ever would have been protected."

One of the lessons from the teachers who contributed to this volume was about the nature and level of this awareness and this caution. But they were also clear that because of their roles and who their students were, they had a greater opportunity and a greater responsibility to engage with their students around their rights – again, to challenge the ableist assumption that they were not capable of understanding these rights. Frankie reflected on the deep relationships that she built with her students and suggested that because of those relationships, she felt like she connected with her students differently than perhaps teachers and students may have connected in a general education classroom. Yet she recognized that she likely would not have been protected had she been challenged legally.

> I think with IDD teachers and students with IDD, they do kind of have more power than maybe the average general education teacher, because there is a lot of care taking: nursing, feeding, toileting, changing, a lot of intimate things that we are doing. And so, we really do build relationships that are deeper than ones that I had with my teachers in a general education classroom. And so, I would hope that my opinions, or my anecdotes, or whatever I brought in, would be viewed as like, "That's just another part of Frankie, working with my child," but legally I don't know if I ever would have been protected. I don't know.

> **Box 5.4 Your Strategies**
>
> How do you feel about what Frankie says here – that she's not sure she would have been protected if an opinion she offered had been challenged? Looking back on the ways you guide and advise your own students, are you concerned about not being protected? With whom in your professional circle might you discuss this concern or reality? It's best to identify and connect with those allies now, so that you all feel better supported to do this challenging work.

Nathan, teacher of students with autism: "Even though parents and students are so grateful."

For Nathan, and probably for the majority of those who read this book, this consideration about being protected from legal liability and legal challenges is less of a concern than putting the needs of students first.

> I've been getting demands to use research-based programs and interventions with students – even to make goals based on "the research."

And sometimes these are great, but sometimes the "research base" will not work for a particular student. They're just not made to fit every student's needs. But I feel like it kind of falls on deaf ears when I bring that up and say, "Hey, this isn't working for this kid." So, I've just been writing my goals based on what I see fit based on that kid. Last year, I was told any reading or math goals, the wording had to be, "…using a research-based program…" and I just don't do that. Because I know for some of the kids it just doesn't work for them. So, I've just stopped. Same with social skills – that's a big part of my job, teaching kids how to behave in social environments. Research doesn't cover all the bases that kids are going to need to know.

So, I teach my kids in real world situations. I'll sit kids down and talk to them. Just teacher to student. I've found that that works a lot better than these "research programs" that are based on sort of safe areas, like school environments. Some of these videos, the kids in the videos look like they're really young, no more than second grade, and I teach third through fifth graders, so my kids don't relate to them. I've had parents straight up ask me to talk with their kids about real world topics to prepare them for middle school. And some of these research programs just don't do that. And honestly, I feel like I'm stifled in what I'm able to talk about out of fear of somebody – an administrator – getting upset, even though parents and students are so grateful.

> **Box 5.5 Your Strategies**
>
> Nathan suggests that, as a teacher who works closely with students who have autism and who has strong relationships with these students and their families, he sometimes knows better than an established curriculum or "the research" what the student needs. Have you ever felt that way in your own classroom? Does it feel like ableism can extend from students with disabilities to the teachers of students with disabilities? How do you navigate that? Are you supported by your administrators or peer teachers?

Youth Stories

From 2021 to 2023, the Youth Research Council (YRC) conducted a mixed methods study exploring the mental health effects of racial and ethnic microaggressions on high school students. As they conducted their study, though, and analyzed the quantitative data they gathered through a survey, they realized the survey did not capture all the nuances they knew were tied up in microaggressions and discriminatory behavior. So, during one of the YRC's

Figure 5.1 An example identity map created by a Youth Research Council (YRC) undergraduate research mentor. Photograph by author with consent of artist.

research meetings, they decided to use basic art tools (blank paper, markers, pens, and colored pencils) to draw their own intersectional identities. They didn't get any more direction from facilitators than that. Draw your identity. The drawings that were produced by the YRC Fellows offered just what had been missing – insights into the messiness and complexity of discrimination. For example, Figure 5.1, drawn by the YRC's undergraduate research mentor, shows the ways in which her identities as a low-income, first-generation student who has type 1 diabetes and identifies as neurodivergent all co-mingle and make just one, simple explanation of her life experience impossible.

Taking Action

We recognize this work is hard. It is full of tensions and stress, isolation and frustration, often even more acutely for teachers of students with disabilities. If you are a teacher of students with disabilities, or perhaps an administrator, we urge you to consider how you might act on some of the ideas that may have popped into your head as you have read this chapter and reflected on some of the questions we have raised. What instances of ableism do you see in your context? What type of pushback (or resistance) feels possible for you, in your school or in your classroom? Who are your allies or potential allies with whom you network and connect – even daily – to remind yourselves that you're not alone in this work, in the need to sometimes go "off-script" and beyond the research to do what's best for your students?

In what ways do you feel comfortable prioritizing the needs of your students over misguided or outdated policies or procedures? What do you need in order to feel more equipped? While we can offer ideas (as we have in this chapter), we know that *you* know your context best. Whatever you decide, we urge you to do *something*. Something to counter taken-for-granted assumptions about students' capacity, unfair curricular practices, or unjust policies. This could look like creating that affinity group of allies in your school to learn more. Or you might set a date to talk with your administrator about making a change – perhaps even with at least one other member of that affinity group. It could also be talking with parents and caregivers differently – proactively rather waiting to do so when a challenging situation arises.

In an effort to practice what we preach, we end this chapter with the words of Bjorn, one of our contributing teachers. We agree with him – no matter what you do or what you decide to work on, at the end of the day, it's all about love:

> One of the things I try to remind myself and tell people all the time is love is a word. Love can have feelings associated with it, but love is also an act. It's an act of will. Some people say about a relationship, "Well, I fell out of love." You can't fall out of love. That's not what love is. Love always wants the greatest good for the other person, not what's best for me. And so, when I think about that in an educational sense, if I love my job, if I love my students, I'll want what's best for them, even if it means me sacrificing something or doing something I don't like. Now as educators and as leaders, we are also just human beings. We have to take care of ourselves, too. It can't be all self-sacrificial stuff, or else we fall. We get sick physically, we burn out. So, you have to protect yourself, and that also is an act of love.

Resources

Book: *The Inclusive Classroom: A New Approach to Differentiation* by Daniel Sobel and Sara Alston. This guidebook highlights strategies that help all students while reducing stress from teachers. Each chapter is broken into a strategy that is inclusive and effective for student growth including backup plans for when things do not go according to plan. Appropriate for all levels.

Podcast: *Creating a More Equitable World for ALL Learners* by the Learning Disabilities Association of America. Each episode is about 30 minutes as experts cover areas of interest for educators hoping to be more equitable for their students with disabilities. Topics include teaching students self-advocacy and supporting nonverbal students.

TED Talk: "Disabling Ableism: The Modern Pathway to Inclusion" (17 minutes). Alycia Anderson breaks down what ableism actually is and how it presents itself in our language, schools, and beliefs. This is ingrained in our culture, but Anderson discusses how we can take steps to shift our thinking to recognize and dismantle ableism to be more inclusive. Link: https://www.youtube.com/watch?v=ah_NWrE291o&ab_channel=TEDxTalks

Online Resource: "Unified Sports Resources from the Special Olympics". Unified Sports is when students with intellectual disabilities are paired with students without intellectual disabilities to play together on the same team. Many schools have Unified extracurriculars and elective classes, including sports, PE, theater, band, and family and consumer science. These programs benefit both groups of students immensely in social-emotional learning and leadership development. The Special Olympics has created a resource page to help coaches plan and implement a Unified team. Link: https://www.specialolympics.org/what-we-do/sports/unified-sports

References

Bodenhamer, S. (2023). Special educator shortage: Examining teacher burnout and mental health. *Institute of Education Science*. https://ies.ed.gov/blogs/research/post/special-educator-shortage-examining-teacher-burnout-and-mental-health

National Center for Education Statistics (NCES). (2022). *Too few candidates applying for teaching jobs the primary hiring challenge for more than two-thirds of public schools entering the 2022-23 school year*. U.S. Department of Education, Institute of Education Sciences. https://nces.ed.gov/whatsnew/press_releases/09_27_2022.asp

6

Diversity and Equity

Sanya had become one of Jeff's favorite students. He had been fortunate to work with her in a previous class, so he was thrilled when she signed up to take a new elective his school was offering: African American History. In the summer of 2020 in the wake of the murder of George Floyd, Virginia Governor Ralph Northam decided to fast-track an already-in-the-works program to offer state-designed online modules on African American History to schools. When the opportunity came to apply to pilot one of those courses at our school, for Jeff it was a no-brainer.

As class started the first week, Jeff talked a little with his students about what they were expecting from the course, why they signed up for it, and whether they had any questions. Sanya, one of a few African American students who took the course that year, put it bluntly. "Well. My aunt wants to know why we have a white guy teaching this class." Jeff just smiled. "What did you tell her?" he asked. Sanya smiled her infamous mischievous smile and started to giggle. "I told her you were alright. Not to worry. That you were a spicy white guy and it'd be okay."

Jeff laughed and told the class the truth: "I'm teaching this class because I think it's an important class to have at our school. However, the state requires anyone who teaches this class to have a license in Social Studies Education and our social studies department is 100% white."

A few years later, in that same elective class during a seminar on school integration, the students read several perspectives on the Brown v Board of Education of Topeka case and its legacy. They discussed the ways in which racial segregation continues to play a role in public schools and how that can take new forms, including segregated

Advanced Placement (AP) classes, disciplinary disparities, and even in the makeup of the school faculty.

One student, Helen, became emotional. She struggled to speak. But finally she opened up. She shared with her classmates how she had gone most of her school career never seeing a teacher who looked like or spoke like her at the head of a classroom and the impact that this void had had on her. Her contribution helped open a new lane of discussion in Jeff's class.

Later, toward the end of the year, Helen stopped by Jeff's classroom after school one day. She said, "Mr. Keller, I wanted to tell you something. I want you to know that the discussion in class that day has really stuck with me. It's made me realize that I want to be a part of the solution. I never want a student to go through school without a person who looks like them. So, I've decided to become a teacher. And not just any teacher – a history teacher. And I want to come back here to do it. I want to help students in my community know that they matter."

These two stories scratch the surface of the range of needs in schools with regard to diversity. On the one hand, teachers need to diversify our course offerings, our readings, and our curriculum so that our classes better represent and engage the students we are teaching. At the same time, the need to recruit and retain teachers who look and sound like our students is both real and pressing.

Critical Concepts

Students are acutely aware of the lack of diversity in U.S. teaching ranks, even as the student body becomes increasingly diverse. It wouldn't be overstating the situation to say that teachers continue to look *less and less* like the students in their classes. A 2023 report from the National Center for Education Statistics estimates that 80% of the teaching force is white, while only 47% of the student body identifies as white (NCES, 2023). Even as some teachers move to address the disconnect between their lived experiences and those of their students, the current political climate of book bans and legislation against the explicit inclusion of diverse topics and viewpoints (see Chapters 1 and 2 for a discussion of the legislative and political contexts) has had a chilling effect on initiatives that very recently were deemed vibrant and exciting. So the issue isn't just that teachers *look* less and less like their students; it's that teachers are being made to fear and made to avoid considerations of issues of which *they* may not be very knowledgeable but with which *their students* are very familiar.

In this chapter, we hear from teachers about the ways in which they try to bridge these gaps between what they *look* like and what their students *look* like, between what *they* know and have experienced and what their *students* know and have experienced, and, ultimately, between who they *are* and who their students *are*. All of this can likely be summed up in a single, all-important word: identity. The teachers who contributed to this chapter describe how they have navigated – and at times pushed back against – explicitly hostile as well as subtly tense environments. They highlight the intentional curricular choices they have made to both diversify the curriculum *and* prevent parental, family, administrative, and community pushback. Before you read, go back to where you are taking notes and consider these questions:

- ◆ How do you define "diversity'? And how do you define "identity"? Is some aspect of diversity more or less salient in your context or to your identity? Do you consider one aspect of diversity more important to foreground than another? Do you feel less or more knowledgeable about certain areas of diversity than others?
- ◆ Do you enjoy being in a situation, environment, or group characterized by diversity, or does that make you uncomfortable? Have you ever been in a situation where you felt like you were in the majority? What aspect of your identity made you feel this way or aware of this reality? How about when you were in the minority? How did you feel in each of those moments?
- ◆ Have you ever attended a diversity training or professional development? What did you take away? Did your practice change in any way after that? What stayed the same? What do you feel like you still need to learn or change?
- ◆ Have you ever felt like there was something wrong or lacking about your state-mandated curriculum? What have you done to change or circumvent those requirements? Do you feel like you can make change, given your specific context? Are there relationships you can build or leverage to help you feel more confident in pushing for change?
- ◆ On the flip side, what is something you really appreciate about your curriculum, if anything?

Intersectionality

The beginning of all equity work is understanding your own identity and its implications. In Chapter 1, we talked about racial consciousness and the importance of recognizing and celebrating identities. However, identity goes beyond race. All of us have intersecting identities, experiences, and values that make up how we perceive and experience the world. However, let's start with just eight. On a piece of paper in that journal or on a page in that computer file, answer how you identify for each of these categories:

1) Race
2) Home language
3) Gender
4) Spirituality or religion
5) Ability/Disability
6) Socio-economic status
7) Nationality
8) Sexual orientation

After you finish your list, cross off one identity from the list – the one that matters the least or is the least salient to how you move through the world. You might make a note next to this identity about why it is least relevant to you, in comparison with the others. Then return to the list and find the next least pertinent to you – again, perhaps making a note about why this is less important to you. Continue with this analysis, removing an identity, one at a time, until you are left with only one identity.

As you move through this activity, you will likely find it difficult to discard pieces of your identity. Choosing which identity is "more important" or "less important" than another is difficult. However, people are asked to hide or discard their identities on a daily basis, and some of us and our students are asked to do so more often than others. Understanding our own identities, and how deeply personal they are in all of their intersecting, complex ways, can help us value the diversity within others who naturally feel just as deeply about their own identities as we do.

As this simple activity illustrates, identity is not just *one* part of us. We have many identities, some apparent and many more subtle. The term "intersectionality" describes how our identities intersect in different ways to offer us different privileges as well as to cause us to face forms of discrimination. For instance, a white woman has privilege as a white person but may face discrimination for being a woman. However, a Black woman could face discrimination for being both Black and a woman.

But please note: Intersectionality is not the oppression Olympics. When we use this term or engage this as a tool to understand the complexity of how the world works, we are not comparing individuals to see who has it "worse." Instead, this concept works as a kind of lens to help us see how intersecting identities might affect one's experience in certain situations. For example, in schools, exclusionary discipline (i.e., being removed from an educational setting – a classroom – for perceived misbehavior) affects Black and Latinx students at higher rates than white students. This is a structural inequity. However, Black or Latino boys who are disabled have the highest levels of exclusionary discipline (U.S. Department of Education, 2023).

When considering a disproportionate effect of treatment or punishment on a particular subgroup, ask yourself this question: Why is this inequity occurring? If your answer blames the group, you are engaging in prejudice. For example, if you think, "Well, boys just struggle to behave," you are blaming an identity for a behavior rather than accepting the fact there must be something about the system that is preventing many individuals with that particular identity from succeeding.

Teacher Stories

Several of our contributing teachers described a growing tension across the United States – in blue and red states, urban, suburban, and rural communities, public and even private schools – that has overflowed from the political sphere and has seeped into classrooms, affecting not just how students and teachers *feel* but what is *taught* and what is *learned* about who we are as a country and who we are as individuals. The question of whether words, topics, or curricula are deemed "too political," while always parts of a teacher's consideration, have become central, even consuming for many teachers. Parents and families – typically those who already enjoy a great deal of privilege and power in this country – have been even more empowered and emboldened to demand curricula that make their entitled children feel comfortable, secure, and unchallenged. Teachers like Carleigh have chosen to push back with gentle but important nudges toward inclusivity, respect, and appreciation for difference.

Carleigh, music teacher at Title 1 elementary school: "I want them to grow up with a respect and appreciation for other cultures."

It's not uncommon for teachers to receive complaints and concerns from families related to being inclusive around cultural holidays. Carleigh, an elementary school music teacher, is clear in her responses to parents that her goal is to allow students to learn about music from all over the world.

> I have had some complaints, for instance, with Christmas. I don't teach about Christmas, but I do incorporate music from lots of different cultural celebrations, especially in the wintertime. And I've gotten

emails from parents with, "My child doesn't celebrate Christmas," or "My child doesn't celebrate Hannukah." I did a concert where we focused on Christmas, Hannukah, and Kwanzaa, and I had some students who couldn't participate because they didn't celebrate those holidays and I told them, "I don't celebrate Hannukah, and I have just started to celebrate Kwanzaa, but it's more about learning about these different cultures, learning where these celebrations come from, where they originated, we learn about the different dances, the different types of music. And so, I have had issues where I felt like I was limited on how much I could teach and what I could teach. So, I usually just explain to the parents what I'm doing and that's been fine, overall. It hasn't escalated.

I try to give my students what I didn't get growing up. Growing up we really just focused on Christian music and then Chopin and Mozart and Beethoven. That was my music education growing up. That's not really representative of all the incredible music all over the world. There's so much rich culture and music. I just want to include that in my education to my students because I want them to grow up with a respect and appreciation for other cultures and other holidays even if it's not what they celebrate, just to have a respect for it. I think it will help students to view each other as more equal by learning to appreciate other cultures. I just feel like there wasn't enough of that growing up.

While not naming this objective, Carleigh was hoping to help her students – and, perhaps by extension, their families – appreciate that while they may view themselves through the lens of one identity, they and the whole world are comprised of many. And while Carleigh described a school and community context that she managed to maintain constructive through careful communication, Petra told us of the fear that teachers in her former school district had of retaliation if they spoke out against certain policies.

Petra, 2023 Teacher of the Year in her state: "There was a lot of fear of retaliation for just speaking out."

Petra described the chilling effect of recent educational policies and political rhetoric and how they impacted her curriculum choices as well as her comfort level in her own classroom. She described (in Chapter 2) how she stopped teaching a book called *The Absolutely True Diary of a Part-Time Indian* by Sherman Alexie because she felt the content might spark controversy. She continued:

> I love to do lessons around equity and diversity. I think it's so important when you have students coming from different cultures. But I was reluctant to do them in my previous district. In fact, a lot of teachers there were watching what they said, what they did, what they taught, the books they had in their classrooms. I wouldn't say we were afraid, but we were very aware that there are certain things that we were not allowed to do, and we were just not sure. I think there was a lot of fear of retaliation just for speaking out. I think that was something that a lot of the teachers were feeling. They were afraid of saying certain things in fear of retaliation.
>
> And I believe there *was* some retaliation. One of my friends from my previous district, because she was so vocal at the School Board meetings, and because she was so vocal with the state, she was assigned to a different school less than a week before school started, which was seen as retaliation. It was her and two other teachers. They were just suddenly reassigned. No reason why. So obviously, I think when you work at a district where politics have taken over, you start to question what books are you going to read? What are you going to say? Can you do the same lessons that you did before? I think everyone, not just me, we were all watching ourselves and being very cognizant of what we used in the classroom, and what we said in the corridors.

Petra, you may recall, made a choice to leave that school district because of the fear that she and others felt.

Frankie, teacher of students with intellectual disabilities: "Not everyone is allowed."

Frankie, on the other hand, embraced the opportunity to engage her students in open conversations about who gets what they want or what they need. While the conversation was in the context of her students with intellectual disabilities, the broader applications were apparent.

> I think a lot of what I noticed – and it wasn't an issue on any ballot – but it came down to education is for everyone. And what it boiled down to was placement. What class you're in and who you take classes with. And it got very murky because it did overlap with disability identity. And IEPs [Individualized Education Plans] and rules and what test you take means what room you go in. But just the concept that not everyone is allowed and there are actual rules and laws written that not everyone gets to come to this school with us and be in

our classroom and go visit government classes – because we literally have to go upstairs to visit the inclusive government class. But, there are students who are not allowed to go into that inclusive classroom upstairs.

And we would talk about why a particular student doesn't get to go. Maybe someone doesn't walk. Or maybe someone doesn't talk with her voice, she uses an iPad. So, I would ask, "Well, do you think she should get to go to the field trip?" or whatever. And they would say, "Yeah, it would be fair if everyone can go."

And so, these equity discussions really showed me that [students with intellectual or developmental disabilities] do have the capacity to understand and grapple with concepts around equity and fairness. On the flip side, there were conversations like, "Yeah, I don't want to go to that class (the inclusive class upstairs). I like this class. This is where I'm comfortable." Or "I think we should all pick what classes we want, like my brother got to pick his elective. I want to pick."

Box 6.1 Your Stories

How do you feel as you read through these experiences? Have you felt more like Carleigh – able to maneuver and feel fairly comfortable with your curricular choices? Perhaps you've felt more like Petra – ready to move to a new school because of the oppressive fear around possible retaliation? Or maybe, like Frankie, you're somewhere in the middle – engaging your students in "real talk," sort of crossing your fingers behind your back that no one gets a whiff of what's going on in your classroom? Have you felt ways in which your intersecting identities have played a role in choices you have made? What about the intersecting identities of your students? However you feel, how are you coping? What – or whom – do you rely on? Do you feel like you are managing fairly well, or do you feel like you might need to do something different? We hope to offer you some sparks of inspiration as you read the next section.

Teacher Strategies

These teachers – like you – are dedicated to caring for their students in ways that challenge the status quo. The political rhetoric of the past few years has made so many of us hunker down, finding safety in one of our primary identities – too often race – rather than acknowledging that we have many such identities, including ones that we share with individuals with whom we might not otherwise seem to have much in common. Our contributing teachers were full of ideas and examples for how teachers can not only cope but thrive in today's complicated political environment.

Emily, high school teacher: "Eventually they do share."

Emily shared with us that she has learned to give her students time to open up. She said that, when she taught in Washington, D.C., opening up happened more quickly because diversity was part of everyday life. But in the rural United States, often a much more homogenous environment, students need time to feel comfortable sharing their experiences and questions.

> There's not as strong of a diversity of opinion or experience here [compared with the D.C. area]. And that doesn't just happen organically here. In other places, like where I was outside of D.C., it just happened organically because there were a lot of different people with different experiences and different viewpoints and different perspectives and different knowledge like putting together a puzzle. But here I've got one giant piece of the puzzle, and I might have some other pieces. But I can't just put them on the spot to represent their entire perspective. If there are just one or two kids in the class, I'm not going to put it on them to try to educate us.
>
> So, I'm put in the position where I'm trying to educate them, and that's fairly uncomfortable because I'm white, and so I can read up a lot, but I haven't had the experience myself. So, then I'm trying to just point to the literature for the experience. But then most of my freshmen can't read and analyze and comprehend the deeper levels of literature without my help. So, I'm still having to explain it. But it's a hard process. I pull in outside sources. Obviously, like we do a lot of just reading historical articles or reading like articles from today and discuss them as a class. Instead of reading one big book we just read like 20 different short stories, and then they really have a wide scope of perspectives. I just try to foster that community where it is an open space where people can share if they want and try to give them a bunch of opportunities, so that eventually they do share.

Emily: "A lot of kids are happy to talk about how they've been discriminated against."

She continued that one way she starts conversations is to use ideas her students can relate to, like being discriminated against because of their age – age is, of course, one of those identities that they share with their classmates.

> When I used to teach the entire book of [*To Kill a Mockingbird* by Harper Lee], I did it from an "-isms" approach. I would start with ageism because they all had a lot to say about how they felt discriminated against because of their age. Everyone could picture that so then we went to either sexism or classism classes. And a lot of kids are happy to talk about how they've been discriminated against because of their lack of money or their family.

Emily: "They're just super profound and thoughtful."

Another way Emily gets her students to open up is by choosing books and other materials that students can relate to, not just in terms of the demographics of the main characters but also in the substance of the challenges they face – and overcome.

> We go into a literature circles unit where there are six different books to choose from. They all are books about teenagers who are struggling with different things – mental illness, suicide, rape, racial prejudice. There is one where the narrator is a transgender teenager. But because they get to choose, we have less pushback. Because there's a wide variety of stories, and the students can pick for themselves. We go out into the hallway once a week, and I discuss with each group the part of the book they've read that week, and they've prepared some material and stuff. And those discussions are the best discussions we have the entire year. They're just super profound and thoughtful stuff that the students have to say.
>
> There are so many reasons this works. There's the fact that they get to choose. There's the fact that all the main characters are teenagers. And then they're all modern stories, so they're super relatable to them. And it's because all the issues are relevant, they are happening to them as well, and so they always are bringing in things like, "My friend went through this same thing," or "My cousin had this thing happen to them." Or themselves: "I was dealing with this issue." I think that's why the kids are really more respectful or more understanding or more compassionate, because it's things that they've seen and experienced for themselves. We have an online discussion component, so they're reading one day, and then they're filling out some notes for the discussion, and then the next day they have a discussion with me. It's all of our senior classes in the same discussion. It's really cool.

Carleigh, elementary music teacher: "The kids love it."

Like Emily, Carleigh makes intentional choices in her curriculum with the express purpose of engaging her students in new – and sometimes unexpected – ways.

> I try to have it where we're not just singing but we're singing and then we're playing instruments and then we're learning folk dances. I've also been introducing some producing where they get to make their own music. I just feel like that's important, too, because kids don't have to feel like they're not a good singer so therefore they're not good at music. There are so many different areas of music that they could be talented in. So that also needs to be encouraged as well. Making sure your musical education encompasses different areas of music. It's been going well. The kids love it.

Sabrina, elementary teacher: "Kind of a top down."

While several of the teachers we spoke with described a kind of bottom-up approach to navigating hostile political environments, for Sabrina, it was important that leadership come from the top as well.

> I was the equity lead at my school for three years. It was very streamlined. The Equity department had these modules, more like professional development, that were very scripted and they pushed them out to all staff throughout the county. But they pushed it down through equity leads, and then we would facilitate that to our schools. So, kind of a top down. So, we would start by taking self-assessments and then move into subgroups of equity, like special education, race, religion, LGBTQ.

And still, several of our contributing teachers said they have stopped doing even the small things they used to do related to helping young people consider their own and each other's diversity and identities – out of fear.

Petra, 2023 Teacher of the Year in her state: "These feelings that students have are valid."

Petra described how she talked to her students – newcomers to the United States – about their feelings related to coming to a new country. She said that they often start out in a "honeymoon" period, when they think everything is amazing, but then they slowly realize their new life comes with new challenges.

> A lot of times, when students come to this country, they'll have a honeymoon period where they are like, "Wow! This country is amazing! Look at all these beautiful things!" We even have drive-through banks, or things that we don't see in their home countries. But after four or five months you'll notice they're getting depressed, and it's because the honeymoon phase has faded. It's a very difficult phase for the student. They realize that this is not as great as they thought it was, and they miss home, and they miss the language. "I miss my parents. I miss my friends." A lot of students will have their heads down or they don't want to interact.
>
> It's very important for students that are coming from another country to realize that there are a lot of times when they feel, after a few months or a year in the United States, that they are losing their culture. Sometimes this transforms itself into, "I don't want to learn English. I don't like the English language. I don't like being here." And you start seeing that kind of pushback against not just the language, but the culture, local customs, or the food.
>
> So some of the lessons I have with students are about, "Hey, let's look at this from another perspective. You're not losing your culture, you're gaining another culture. You're not losing your language, you're becoming bilingual." And we have to look at it from that perspective because you know, these feelings that students have are valid. You came from a different country, and all of a sudden you are hearing English all day. None of the foods, the customs, the dances, none of what you see daily represents you anymore. So, it's a valid feeling that they have. So, some of the lessons that I do is, "Hey, let's stop and think. We're not losing ourselves. We're still who we are. We still have the foods that we eat and the beliefs that we have. We're just adding and becoming more culturally aware. And we are also working with the culture that we are in, so that we understand. And we can work with it."

Petra: "I have stopped."

Petra explained that through these types of lessons she worked to create relationships of trust between her and her students. (If there's one theme to the strategies our contributing teachers have shared, this is it: Take the time to build and maintain relationships.) Yet because of the political environment in her area, she stopped having these conversations.

> These feelings that they have will not resolve themselves overnight, but just by having that conversation and making them aware of these changes and these things that they are going through make the classroom so much easier to manage, creates that connection between myself and the students, and lets them know, "Hey, my teacher has gone through this. I am going through this, too, and I can get through it." So, I think those lessons are very important, and these are things that I usually do but have stopped.

Such growth in cross-cultural awareness of and appreciation for diversity can happen – needs to happen – not just with newly arrived immigrants but also with *all* students. Young people need to recognize the intersectionality not only of their own identities but also of their peers' and their teachers' identities. The teachers who contributed to this volume highlighted how their instruction focused on key ideas, to move students toward this awareness and appreciation.

John Brown, high school social studies teacher: "Humans make decisions."

John acknowledged that these are often the types of lessons that students don't appreciate until years later. This meant that he had to be even more intentional about highlighting those key ideas and repeatedly emphasizing them in his instruction.

> On one side, it's just the basic human level. If I want them to be open to other humans, engaging and connecting with them, in terms of their views of the world and their political engagement, I always emphasize that humans make decisions. And those decisions matter and individual decisions collectively can make a difference. And, on the other side is just some humility to be sure you go back to different historians and different interpretations, to appreciate that we might find new evidence in the future that forces us to change our views. And so, no matter how strongly you believe something to just always be open to the idea that that can change, so we're not so stuck in black and white.

John: "She was able to recognize the humanity and diversity."

John shared an example of how this orientation played out with one of his former students, who visited him about a decade after graduating from high school.

> She talked about how for her growing up in New York City she was used to very diverse environments. This is a young woman with a white mother with a black father. She went to school in upstate New York, and she had never engaged with suburban kids, but she was able to recognize the humanity and diversity in a sense that that these peers had value in ways that many of her peers coming from New York City couldn't see. She was able to make friends with both groups, whereas other people could not, and then she was also able to then influence those people in positive ways.

Like John and Petra and several other teachers we spoke with, many of our contributing teachers shared with us that these types of conversations are crucial to establishing a sense of trust between students and teachers and that that trust is necessary for a positive learning environment.

Althea, high school teacher: "If you don't model that for students, then you're setting yourself up for failure."

Althea echoed John's insight, adding that teachers not only have to have trust but also have to be clear on what their values are and then model their values for their students. If you value openness and honesty in conversation, then, according to Althea, you need to model that.

> I think it's really important to know what your values are and what you believe is true, and to really do that deep reflection of who you are and what you're willing to stand up for and make sure that if you decide to go into education, if you decide to go into teaching, that you're going to stay true to those values. I think this is true particularly for high school teachers because teenagers are very, very perceptive and they will call you out on your shit. They'll say, "Wait! You said this, but then you did this thing so that doesn't make sense." So having that sense of who you are and what you stand for before you come into the classroom is going to help tremendously, so that you are willing to be vulnerable and have those conversations with students.
>
> It's uncomfortable for young people to say, "Hey, my name is so and so, and I identify as blah blah blah, and these are my pronouns." Especially if that's not something that you've been used to doing your entire life. But if you don't model that for the students, then you're setting yourself up for failure. But if you have this vision of what your classroom is going to be like, lively and full of conversations, where students can come to you for advice, that won't happen unless you

model that by saying, "I'm here. This is who I am. And I invite you to be true to who you are in this classroom."

> **Box 6.2 Your Strategies**
>
> Consider, what do you model for your students? In terms of what you *really* believe is important, in terms of big ideas and your own openness to diversity? In terms of who you are and what identities matter to you? Go back to our critical concept for this chapter – intersectionality. How do your own intersecting identities play a role in what you model? Are you intentional in this practice? Remember that your students are always learning more than just what you are trying to teach them out of books or worksheets. They watch you. They emulate you. Or they may reject what they see you stand for. But no matter what, they're paying attention. Take some time to think about what students learn from you. Is it the tone with which you speak to them? The way you pay attention to and respect their opinions? The identities to which you expose them in the literature and curricula that you choose? Can you do anything differently to make sure your values align with your practice?

Youth Stories

Nardos, a high school junior and a participant in the most recent iteration of the Through Students' Eyes project, highlighted what teachers who are open to diversity – of ideas, of who their students are, of how to serve all of their students – do.

> The best teacher is someone who can break down the content in the way you want them to. Someone who is available for each student. A lot of teachers are 'my way or the highway' but students need it to be their way. Some teachers don't want to provide students what they need, which is time… Not everyone has a quiet space at home. Why don't teachers/school provide some of these tools? Some teachers are tired of having to repeat themselves, when students have not taken advantage of the resource. Be there for students.

Students at Sabrina's elementary school struggled with using racial epithets, often in ways they didn't fully understand. The school's Equity Taskforce, which Sabrina chairs, suggested to the principal that they do a school-wide photovoice project similar to the Through Students' Eyes project. Everyone in the school was invited to participate: students, teachers, and staff. With a student population of around 800, over 400 people participated.

The questions that formed the basis of submissions was "Who are you? Who are we?" The idea was that students and school community members could submit a picture that represented some important part of who they are and that, when taken together, the community could recognize their differences and similarities, conversations about diversity could be started in developmentally appropriate ways, and teachers could use these pictures, which were framed and put up all over the school, in their teaching.

At the exhibit, over 700 guests walked through the school. They saw lots of pictures of Legos and soccer and stuffed animals. They also saw pictures of medical devices, families, and holidays. Some submissions included no words, and others were written in languages other than English. Students from kindergarten through fifth grade had an opportunity to make connections, tell their stories, and be heard. While Sabrina, her teacher peers, and their administrator never mentioned the word "intersectionality," it was clear that kids and their families were witnessing – maybe for the first time – a richer range of their own and each other's identities.

Taking Action

Diversity has become a dirty word in a lot of areas in the United States. Equity and inclusion are dismissed as liberal tropes for making those in positions of power feel bad for what they claim is their own luck or what they characterize as their own hard work. The fear is palpable. And so is the resignation by so many teachers. What can we really do when we're faced with this orientation to diverse ideas? I am one teacher, one person, one community member. There are so many people in power, in office, with money, who control the narrative. And it turns out it's so much easier to go with the narrative rather than fight it.

Our country is at a crossroads, politically for sure, but perhaps primarily in terms of the values we *espouse* versus those we *live*. There is no room to debate that much of the rhetoric of the Donald Trump presidential administration generated fear amongst certain – mostly white – segments of our population that they were losing control of "their" country. But this rhetoric was also deeply, profoundly undemocratic and flew in the face of our grandest ideals.

What can you do? Whether you are actively engaging your students in political debate or are just trying to survive and keeping your head down, we see you as a powerful force in the lives of your students. When we started this project – over three years ago – we thought we wanted to talk with teachers who, in our minds and according to our definitions, were activists. People who were on the streets, calling out social wrongs, demanding change, leading unions, speaking to school boards, and joining picket lines. What we've learned, though, is that each one of you is creating change every day, with every student. As you choose which books to read, which questions to ask, which moments to highlight, or which current events to discuss, you are changing the world, one student at a time. It turns out that when it comes to that idea of "intersectionality," we're not just talking about the range of identities that exist in each one of us: we're thinking about intersections that you are forging between your students. Let's keep doing that.

Resources

Book: *Say the Right Thing: How to Talk About Identity, Diversity, and Justice* by Kenji Yoshino and David Glasgow. This book offers practical, shame-free advice on how to speak out and ask the right questions about sensitive issues. Written to address allyship and intersectionality, it's a research-based but conversational guide to sidestep microaggressions and help others.

Podcast: *Unlocking Us* by Brené Brown. This podcast by well-known researcher and motivational speaker Brown features a variety of diverse guests who talk about important social issues. Particularly moving episodes include "Laverne Cox on Transgender Representation" (June 17, 2020) and "Austin Channing Brown on *I'm Still Here: Black Dignity in a World Made for Whiteness*" (June 10, 2020).

TED Talks:
- "The Urgency of Intersectionality" from Kimberlé Crenshaw, who coined the term intersectionality. Link: https://www.ted.com/talks/kimberle_crenshaw_the_urgency_of_intersectionality/transcript
- "Why I Keep Speaking Up, Even When People Mock My Accent" by Safwat Saleem (11 minutes). A humorous story by an animator who wanted to voice his own characters, but he struggled because of his stutter and his Pakistani accent. An important examination of intersecting identities and how to foster self-confidence and representation for students. Link: https://www.ted.com/talks/safwat_saleem_why_i_keep_speaking_up_even_when_people_mock_my_accent

Online Resource: American Civil Liberties Union (ACLU) Talking Points for Pushing Back on Censorship. A bulleted list of talking points to use when there is pushback about a lesson, book, or material being used in class. Link: https://www.aclu.org/rtl-resources/talking-points

References

National Center for Education Statistics (NCES). (2023). *Characteristics of public school teachers*. U.S. Department of Education, Institute of Education Sciences. https://nces.ed.gov/programs/coe/indicator/clr/public-school-teachers

U.S. Department of Education. (2023). Creating and sustaining discipline policies that support students' social, emotional, behavioral, and academic well-being and success: Strategies for school and district leaders. Title IV-A Technical Assistance Center (T4PA Center). https://t4pacenter.ed.gov/Docs/Fact-Sheets/Supporting_Students_School_and_District_Leaders_508.pdf

7

Social-Emotional Learning

Brainwashing. Trampling parental rights. Indoctrination. Actively promoting teenage suicide. These are just some of the allegations leveled against social-emotional learning (SEL) by Moms for Liberty and other conservative-backed advocacy groups (Kingkade & Hixenbaugh, 2021). SEL has been an integral part of school curricula for decades. The American Psychological Association (APA) notes that SEL "teaches students interpersonal skills and how to understand, control, and express their emotions" and has identified SEL as "essential for student learning, mental health, and well-being" (Abrams, 2023 p. 28).

Over the past several years, however, SEL has been conflated with Critical Race Theory (CRT), an academic theory that explores systemic racism in laws, policies, schools, and other institutions. A 2023 Washington Examiner *article, for example, described how SEL is a disguise for teaching CRT and gender diversity ideologies (Eden, 2023). In Montana, Yellowstone County Moms for Liberty chapter president Alba Pimentel put it this way: "When we think of social-emotional learning as parents, we are not thinking our children are being pushed into gender ideologies, talks of oppression, or social justice. Children should be taught skills safely without agendas or ideologies" (Stanford & Meisner, 2023). The confusion of SEL with CRT, gender diversity awareness, or other diversity issues has resulted in a growing set of laws meant to curb or ban SEL in schools. A September 2023 report from the APA identified bills in eight states supporting such a move (Abrams), while a National Public Radio (NPR) report from 2022 identified 25 states taking action against SEL that year (Anderson, 2022).*

The logic in these moves is baffling: Parents, families, and legislators are seeking to limit the ability of education experts to help young people cope with trauma while we continue to contend with what might be described as a national age of anguish. The list of these distressing events is long – the COVID-19 pandemic, the racial reckoning following the murder of George Floyd, the ongoing debates surrounding immigration, anti-LGTBQ+ rhetoric and legislation, curbing of women's rights, and the continued debate and fallout from the January 6 insurrection. And all of these issues intensify the already challenging reality of just being a teenager in the United States.

Students know that things aren't alright. Teachers know that things aren't alright. And both understand that schools need to do more to support students' mental and emotional well-being, if only because young people spend a minimum of six hours per day together and in the presence of teachers.

Back in Montana, state Representative Lola Sheldon-Galloway is a great example of what happens when teachers and elected leaders listen to one another. The sponsor of a bill that would ban SEL due to her belief that it violated parental rights, Sheldon-Galloway tuned in carefully as parents, students, and educators explained to her why her stance was detrimental for students. After paying attention to their perspectives, she changed her mind and pulled her support for her own bill. She said, "The teachers have spoken loud and clear that they believe that this program is an excellent program…Maybe I did not have a clear vision of that…You have taught me well" (Stanford & Meisner, 2023).

We would advocate for more of this listening to teachers.

Critical Concepts

Like so many of the big ideas addressed in this book, "social-emotional learning" is challenging to define. But because of its centrality to the very nature of school as a place where teachers care for kids, it's vital that we understand its meaning and related concepts. In this chapter, we share descriptions of the ways in which teachers are doing just that – caring for children and young people and paying attention to their well-being while teaching them about all manner of subjects. As throughout this volume, before you read about the experiences of our contributing teachers, we'd like you to consider a few critical concepts, to inform your own pedagogical practices. Once more, please grab that notebook or open that computer file.

Trauma-Informed Practices

Trauma-Informed Practices (TIPs) are practices that create safe, caring environments for students by creating predictable routines, building relationships, and supporting student self-efficacy. However, teachers have a lot on their plates, and often TIPs can feel like just one more thing in a growing list of emphases and objectives. Here are some common TIPs from the National Education Association (https://www.nea.org/professional-excellence/student-engagement/tools-tips/trauma-informed-practices), many of which you may already be doing if you are a teacher:

- Awareness of triggers in your community, such as tasks or activities that might impact students or staff negatively
- Relying on compassion over judgment when students act out or demonstrate behavior problems
- Give students space to share and express their feelings
- Foster a growth mindset with authentic, positive feedback
- Build positive relationships with students and families
- Take care of yourself and your own needs and triggers, so you can be there for others

Relationality and Holding Space

Relationality is a sociological term that measures how connected people or members of a community are to one another. When school communities emphasize empathy to build relationships and connections, they give students the tools for sustainability and resilience (Kan & Lejano, 2023). If students feel connected to their school community and teachers, they are more likely to try difficult things when you ask. This is because they trust you.

One way to prioritize empathy and build relationships is by holding space. Holding space means to sit near someone and listen without judgment or distraction. You may ask follow-up questions, but you do not make the conversation about you or push unrequested advice. Instead, you create a container for them to vent and express themselves safely.

Consider the people in your life who hold space for you. What emotions do you associate with that relationship? Consider times when you have held space for others. How did it make you feel to hold that space for them?

In this chapter, you will learn about some of the issues that teachers are helping young people to navigate and the strategies that teachers are employing to help children and youth make sense of these concerns. As with all other chapters in this volume, we ask you to begin by considering some core questions, to help you connect with this topic. Please continue to track your own thinking, in part so that you can share and reflect with others about your ideas.

- What were the issues in your life, your community, and our nation that you were dealing with when you were in elementary and high school?

- Still thinking about your own school experience, what were any of the issues that you noticed your peers struggling with and with which they needed emotional support?
- What did teachers and your school do to help you and/or your peers make sense of, respond to, or deal with these issues?
- What are the issues with which you are dealing today? Who are the people and what are the tools that help you to respond to these in a healthy way?
- What do you think should be teachers' and schools' responsibilities for helping young people work through their individual, our communities', or even our nation's challenges and traumas?

We hope you appreciate the stories and strategies below, offered by teachers who, like you, are wrestling with these questions on a daily basis.

Teacher Stories

Teachers have always paid attention to youths' feelings and well-being. Even if their job descriptions didn't require them to consider young people's emotional states, they have done so as a result of their sense of shared humanity and the awareness that they are collectively attending to our country's present and future psyche. Although integrating SEL structures into classrooms did not begin during the COVID-19 pandemic, it is this monumental and ongoing event that has galvanized teachers around the recognition that we need to help the children and young people in our schools with making sense of emotional ups and downs, big and small, mundane and historic (Box 7.1).

Box 7.1 Impact of COVID on kids' learning

A 2022 study of student learning during the pandemic found that 20% of students who attended school in person from 2020 to 2021 saw their grades decline. Thirty percent of hybrid students – those who spent part of the year virtual and part of the year in-person – saw a decline. Thirty-four percent who remained virtual for the entire school year saw a decline. The report also noted that teachers felt their grading was more lenient during this school year than in years prior (Fisher et al., 2022).

Matt, a former English teacher: "The kids haven't changed at all"

Matt provides us with the contexts that we should be considering – and the corrections that our schools and society need.

> Too many people are saying, "The kids have changed. They're just different. We can't expect them to have any social skills or coping mechanisms because of COVID." But the kids haven't changed at all. We've gone through a multiyear traumatic event, and we're trying to pretend it's over. Nobody is talking about it. Nobody says the word COVID in schools anymore.
>
> We're moving "forward." We're going to get those test scores back up! We forced kids to get back into schools, and the main reason we did it is because of standardized testing. But guess what happened when we didn't have this testing? The sky didn't fall! People were able to teach without that "super important data"! Adults in schools are forcing these tests on kids, pretending COVID is no longer an issue. Not even talking about the fact that we've lost grandparents and parents, aunties and uncles. And, of course, kids are acting out at the absurdity of it all. And they're right! They are 100% right! It's the adults in the building who are acting completely irrationally and who don't understand what's going on.

Box 7.2 SEL strategies from CASEL

CASEL – the Collaborative for Academic, Social, and Emotional Learning – produces trainings, webinars, and full lesson plans to implement (CASEL, 2024). One strategy details teaching learners self-calming skills such as breathing and grounding techniques. The trick is to model these behaviors for students, so they see that adults can get worked up, too, and need to calm down. Another lesson shows how teachers might start classes with daily dedications that have students – and teachers – reflecting and showing gratitude to begin class on a positive note with an attendance question. Finally, there is a breakdown of the "kindness jar" activity which has students translating acts of kindness in a tangible, explicit way that encourages both gratitude and community building.

> **Box 7.3 Your Stories**
>
> As you read Matt's frustrations, we encourage you to reflect on how your own life has changed as a result of the pandemic – maybe in a way that you're reluctant to admit to anyone else or even to yourself? What do your social interactions look like now as compared with before March 2020? Who has fallen out of your social network that was in it before the COVID-19 pandemic began?
>
> After reflecting in private, you might consider working with colleagues to reflect on how the institutions with which you regularly engage have changed since the pandemic began. Who has been most impacted by these changes – in particular, who might not be able to count on that institution or those institutions as much? How are we as a society helping individuals to deal with losses that result from the pandemic – of people, routines, jobs, and these institutions?

The issues with which students are dealing and which teachers necessarily must help them process – if only to provide them with the mental and emotional space to focus on the classroom content – are myriad. These are so numerous that it's impossible for teachers to have training in understanding all of them: but if a young person arrives with the concern, then it's a teacher's duty to help them make sense of it.

Amy, a dual enrollment high school English teacher: "You have five-year-olds dealing with burnout."

Amy reflected on the cultural nature of trauma, how even historical anguish can manifest itself in everyday ways in the classroom:

> You know, everywhere I've been I've encountered students who have had different types of trauma. Even when I was teaching in Korea, you have five-year-olds dealing with burnout. That's really hard to see. In Hawaii, the overthrow of the Hawaiian Kingdom had a long-term, systemic impact on native Hawaiian students and others who were brought as slaves to run the plantations. So that's had an impact on communities and generations since then.

Amy: "They came home, and their family was gone."

Where Amy taught, the issues and traumas were often more immediate and often related to policies that seemed beyond her own and her students' control:

> I mean, there's nothing I can do for students whose parents are undocumented and they don't know how or if they will be able to get papers, or if they're just going to come home one day and their family isn't going to be there. That happened to one of my students! They came home, and their family was gone. They were deported. Of course, I want to try and help every student as much as I can. But it's really hard having so many students and there's nothing I can do because these are such big systemic issues.

What does SEL look like in such circumstances? While SEL skeptics might worry that in these contexts a teacher would employ some manipulative strategy that smacks of a government conspiracy, our teachers are just responding with in-the-moment humanity, beginning with small structures – TIPs, versions of "relationality," and forms of "holding space" – that would typically go unnoticed.

Sabrina, elementary school teacher: "You greet the students at the door"

Sabrina noted how she pays attention to her students' emotional states:

> Social-emotional learning is all about keeping a temperature read on your students all throughout the day. Sometimes, even before they come in, I'll get an email from a parent that says something like, "So and so was very clingy this morning," or they're just tired or whatever, but you greet the students at the door, I have a choice board, where students indicate how they want me to greet them. Do you want to give me a high five? Do you want to give me knuckles? Do you want to hug? Do you want to wave?
>
> So, I see the kids coming down the hall. I watch them. Is their head down? Are they kind of moping their way down the hall? Social-emotional learning takes place all day long, and I think we have to be explicit at times in the way that we teach it. It could be through story. It could be through role play. It could be keeping a close eye on

the playground and working through things - social stories. Guidance counselors coming in once a month for 30 minutes is not social-emotional learning.

Amy: "Sometimes all I can do is listen."

Amy's stance mirrors Sabrina's. Her approach to SEL is similarly subtle but intentional but does not involve extended interventions or interruptions in the school day:

> Sometimes all I can do is listen. Even if I couldn't *do* anything…So, at the very least, I just want them to know that someone is listening and that they're not forgotten. And they're not alone. So, in the classroom, I just let the students know, you're not alone. The world can often seem like a big, bad, scary place. But there are good people in the world, and good things can happen, even if it doesn't always seem that way.

Victoria, high school teacher: "People just want to be heard."

Victoria, a high school English teacher who works at a school with a large percentage of English-language learning and immigrant students, echoes this sentiment, that listening to students is key.

> Listen without judgment. Listen. Not every problem is going to be fixed by you. Not every problem has to be fixed by you as the teacher. So often people just want to be heard, and I don't care if you're eight years old or you're 80 years old. We want to be heard. We want to have our feelings validated.

Victoria: "But it's not my job to agree with him."

But Victoria also highlights that such a listening practice matters as an in-class, pedagogical practice and that such respectful attentiveness is even more important if we are to help young people make sense of controversial issues in these often-tense political times:

> I am often asked "Why do students confide in you?". It's because I don't judge, even if what they say I don't agree with. In my last class today, we were having this conversation, and a kid said something that I very much disagreed with. But it's not my job to agree with him.

It's my job to listen to him. My job is not to say you're wrong. That's what he believes, and he has every right to believe.

My job, though, is to make sure when he is stating those things that it's done in a non-offensive, respectful manner. And that it is for the sake of open and honest discourse and learning, and not just because he wants to espouse whatever he wants to espouse. It's my job to listen and say, "Okay. Now, can you support that? Or why do you think that?".

Amy, high school teacher: "Aren't we all just little kids at heart?"

These listening strategies also translate to elementary classrooms. If students are too young to understand or even to have the words to share their realities, teachers like Amy respond with other approaches, which can have both immediately calming effects and provide young people with long-term self-care strategies:

> My school really likes to support socio-emotional learning. They encourage whatever teachers want to do, even providing funding. So, I have the anti-stress zone in my classroom. It has Band-Aids, coloring books, temporary tattoos, bubble wrap, little notebooks, stickers, stuffed animals, tiny squishees. They never have to ask. They can just go there if they need to. Just grab a little sheet of bubble wrap and go outside and just pop it. Or if they just need to squeeze a stuffed animal.
>
> And I try and model that for them. So, at the beginning of the year, while I'm lecturing, I'll just casually go over and carry a stuffed animal around. It's so interesting because different classes love different parts of it. Some of my classes are obsessed with temporary tattoos. They will do arm sleeves and put them on their faces. They love it.
>
> And then some of the students want every squishy stuffed animal. I also have this huge shark – it was a viral thing from IKEA because it was the trans shark because it's blue and white and pink. So, I have a big one. It's up on a shelf. So, if they need something really big, they can grab that. So, I really try for whatever they need. We do brain breaks if they need a moment. I've had parents say, "Wow, I wish I had that at work or in my room." I mean, aren't we all just little kids at heart?

Integrating SEL strategies into instruction has created an additional workload burden for teachers, but it's one they are approaching as professionals and with intentional plans.

Diane, elementary school teacher: "I didn't have to make a plan."

Diane, who works in a school where the majority of students are English language learners, highlighted this stress:

> Something that has changed is the social-emotional learning that teachers now have to intentionally plan for. I didn't have to make a plan for that when I was teaching kindergarten, or first or third grade back in the nineties and early two-thousands. I wasn't having to chunk out time in my day to foster as much of the social-emotional piece as teachers may need to do now.

Diane: "There's less conversation happening among families."

But she also noted that families could be doing more to support their students' SEL needs – as well as their language development – and easing this burden for teachers simply by switching off some of the technology that is now pervasive in almost everyone's life:

> Our children are more technologically literate, and they have more time on screens. But there's a fine line with technology: It can have a real positive side, and it can have a negative side. We have children who come through our kiss-and-ride line, so they're in the car, literally for three minutes and they're on a screen. They're watching a movie in the back of the car, or they're on their parent's phone…. That means that there's less conversation happening among families at home. So, for a school like ours, where building a language is so incredibly important for everyone, conversations are so important for families to have with one another. That means we have to intentionally teach and explicitly model those talk moves and those conversation pieces, while we're also trying to develop the academic vocabulary and working on tier one and tier two vocabulary, too.

Box 7.4 Your Stories

What connections do you make to what teachers are describing? If you were in Victoria's position, what would you have done when a student stated something with which you – personally and/or professionally – disagreed? What are the little, everyday ways with which you deal with stress? How would any of the example TIPs help you or your students to deal with this stress?

Teacher Strategies

Ultimately, the organic, everyday ways in which teachers employ SEL strategies are motivated by the empathy they feel for their students.

Sabrina: "I feel very empathetic."

As Sabrina articulated, that empathy is often driven by teachers' awareness that they share humanity and a community with their students and their families:

> When I get an email from a parent or caregiver, and I sense – because I'm also a parent of kids who have teachers – the urgency, I feel very empathetic toward a lot of what parents say. I prefer to call you right away. You know, there's no need to respond in an email because a lot can get lost in translation and if you call a parent immediately, they know that you care about what they say. And you know it really helps build a stronger team?

Bobbi, high school English teacher: "They don't lack empathy; they just lack experiences."

As Bobbi – still adjusting to working with a very privileged student demographic after spending much of her career in an under-resourced community – noted, teachers are simultaneously motivated by their sense of responsibility for developing that empathy in their students.

> For many of my students the only thing we're ever focused on is getting into a good college. So, I've focused them on current events, invited them to consider that inequalities exist, and highlighted how people can have different upbringings than them. They don't lack empathy; they just lack experiences. When you're looking at students who are this wealthy, who are all going to go to really good schools and who have great SAT scores, you're looking at future leaders. A lot of these kids are going to be very influential one day.
>
> I wanted to make sure that we were talking about some form of empathy and considering the perspectives of others. When I was teaching in a Title I school pre-COVID, our focus was "Let's teach you that you're valuable and let's get you some life skills." In my current much wealthier school, our focus has been "Let's teach you that there

are more important things than your ACT scores and that people need you to be kind."

Sabrina: "What my first job is."

The teachers with whom we worked for this book emphasized that SEL is also about safety – about keeping our kids safe and about teaching them how to keep themselves and their peers and families safe but not from existential, international threats.

> It takes time to do when you're new to a community. And so, I collaborate and communicate with the parents. I ask things like, "Where do we come together on this? And what steps can we do to make a child feel comfortable, safe, and secure at school?" Because if you ask the first graders in our class what my first job is, they know that my first job is to keep them safe and secure, and that can mean a number of different things for their emotional well-being. I will stop instruction if somebody is having a little bit of an emotional need. I'll touch base, and we have our take-a-break station here where it's not a punishment, but it's a strategy that I use. And the kids know that if they ask, "Can I take a break for a few minutes?" they can absolutely go there.

Althea, high school teacher: "No, I messed up on this."

The most profound of the SEL moves that teachers are making often involve simply admitting when they make a mistake. Althea, who was working in a very diverse high school, spoke to the power of such acknowledgements:

> Being able to reflect and being able to own up to things and admit, "No, I messed up on this thing." This goes a really long way, not just for yourself, as a person, but also as a teacher, to the students. They're thinking, "Oh, here's an adult who says all these different things, but they also messed up, and they're taking accountability for it." Because I'm not just going to teach you all the rules of grammar or everything by Shakespeare. It has to go beyond that, because you can't have students reach their potential, unlock those higher levels of learning and processing, and expand their thinking without also addressing the other things that are going on in their lives that impact like their ability to take in that information. It's Maslov before Bloom: You have to make sure all those things are met.

Brithany, high school teacher: "It falls under giving grace."

Brithany echoed the importance of a stance of humility:

> Last period I had a kid who just got up and walked out like he wanted to go to the office. He couldn't tell me why he wanted to go to the office – I was teaching when he asked. So, he got mad because I wouldn't write him a pass to the office, and he walked out. Today he was back in class, and he said that he was sorry that he had left, and that he'd had some trouble at home. I said, "I'm sorry you had trouble at home. I'm sorry I had to email your parents and let them know."
>
> I try never to use parents with my kids because I never know who they're with. So I said to this student, "Why don't we work on getting better at this together? Why don't we work on talking to each other more and just doing it together." And he said, "Yeah, okay."
>
> When you can say "I'm sorry" to a teenager, they get that because a lot of adults don't say that. I think it falls under giving grace. All of us, every human being on this earth, deserves to just have some time where they're not accountable. And if I want them to take agency for their learning – which is a huge issue in my population – I need to make them independent people. So, I tell them I'm sorry, and I give them that space.

Bobbi, high school English teacher: "You're going to see that it's fine."

The most radical of the SEL strategies that teachers are employing involve simply talking students through how to handle stress and respecting them enough to admit how challenging this can be. One of the ways Bobbi does this is by being transparent about her pedagogies:

> I think students have found language to advocate for themselves in a way they didn't have before. They're much quicker to challenge me, which is sometimes really annoying to be totally honest, but sometimes I totally get it. It's especially hard when you start a school year, because I don't quite have their trust yet, and I'm trying to get them to be comfortable with chaos. I always explain my teaching orientation to them. I tell them, "In so much of life you are in flight or freeze mode. So let me stress you out in some of our lessons but begin to trust that I'm holding onto you. Yes, I'm going to purposely stress you out, and then you're going to see that it's fine. We're going to

train your brain to understand that you can function even when your amygdala is mad at you."

Victoria, high school teacher: "Who's going to be on my team?"

Victoria does this by explicitly allowing them to consider that most core question – the one only *they* can answer and the one that they are going to explore regardless of what any adult or lesson or policy suggests: the question of their identity. Again, ultimately, as with all things SEL, it's about safety:

> For many older teachers when we were in high school you fit into a box. You fit into a label, and that's who you were. But society is progressing and understanding that not everybody deserves a label, needs a label, has a label, or wants to fit into that label. I think with that there comes a lot of distrust from our students, and that is what poses a safety risk. They ask themselves, "So who do I trust? Who's going to be on my team? Who's going to accept me for who I am? Who I am and might be one way today, and it might be a completely different thing tomorrow. Right?
>
> So that's the really tricky part: they have to feel safe with people around them who, if today, they feel one way, and tomorrow's a different way. That person must say "Okay, I'm still here for you. That's cool. We'll work with that." Or someone who asks, "What does that mean? Are you just discovering who you thought you were?" Because they're maturing because they are children, and their brains are developing.

Matt, former English teacher: "Resist a little bit harder."

For Matt, safety might be more possible if teachers would resist the policies and practices they know are wrong, misguided, or unhelpful:

> I wish teachers would fight back a little bit harder. Resist it a little bit harder. I know that in a lot of places teachers' jobs are on the line because of test scores, but there's just so much deficit thinking about our kids.

Matt: "Space for grieving and healing."

Matt believes, as do many teachers, including many of our contributors, that schools need to center the humanity of young people, acknowledging the trauma that we have collectively experienced and the traumas that are still occurring. For Matt, schools should be places for healing:

> I've lost all hope that we are actually going to ever change anything to make schools humane places that really put the whole essence and humanity of young people at the center, but if schools could change something tomorrow, just one thing, acknowledge that we are still in the pandemic. The trauma that kids are living with and living through didn't go away when everybody got vaccinated. People still have relatives who are sick. They're still dealing with loss. I have a friend who is a teacher in the Midwest who told me she had eleven students who lost family members. Eleven!
>
> Just because kids aren't getting sick anymore doesn't mean they're over the loss of their family member. Where is the space for grieving and for healing in our schools? It's all crowded out because, you know, the kids are so far behind on their reading, or we have to tutor these kids. None of that stuff is going to work when you have a hole where your grandmother used to be. We just don't understand that if you don't have a solid socio-emotional foundation, you can't build academic content on top of that. It was true before COVID hit and it's especially true now.
>
> Really, it's what we are not doing in schools to create that healing, to create that community, that humanity. But even if we didn't have the pandemic, those three things should be at the center of everything we do in schools. What I've tried to do with my first-year teachers is bringing circle practice, restorative work in. Teachers are hungry for this healing and kids are absolutely hungry for restorative practices.

Box 7.5 Your Strategies

As you consider the suggestions and strategies offered by some of our contributing teachers, what connections are you making? Do you see an opportunity for your own classroom or school to integrate any of these practices? How are you naturally paying attention to your students' SEL – maybe without naming it as such? Is there a way to engage in your practice in more trauma-informed ways? Are there simple ways you can "hold space" for your students?

Youth Stories

Conner, a participant in the Through Students' Eyes project, summed up how and why teachers and schools needed to focus on these SEL ideas and lessons. For him, these reasons were about school's very purpose:

"Relate to other people"

The purpose of school is making friends. Finding people you connect to, talking to them. I remember when school just meant having fun. Now it's learning how to experience how to do a lot of things – like being in a relationship. If we have coworkers, school helps us talk to them, relate to them more. Relate to other people, have empathy, communication skills.

Eve, a junior involved in the Through Students' Eyes project, took a black-and-white photograph of a backpack on a bed surrounded by shuffled stacks of papers, which were clearly assignments and homework. This image depicted what she was getting in the way of many youths' success in school – a form of teenage "burnout":

Figure 7.1 Black-and-white photo of a backpack surrounded by school worksheets and notes. Photograph by Eve, a student.

The second reason students don't engage with school is some version of burnout. Although initially willing or eager to 'buy into' school and put effort in (different from the blue-sky students), as school gets harder some can't muster the will to care anymore. The photograph's black-and-white coloring depresses the viewer, similar to the absence of enthusiasm burnt-out students feel. The juxtaposition of the ultimate school symbol, the backpack, and school papers on a bed, the most private and restful of places, symbolizes how all-encompassing and invasive school can be in the thick of exam season and how corrosive that can be to students' physical and mental health.

 Taking Action

We find it difficult to understand how anyone could argue with the current emphasis on SEL integration into schools' curricula. But as we have noted throughout this volume, schools and teachers are never the ringleaders behind these new movements: schools are merely the institutions that are best positioned to implement them, and teachers are just the players who are responsible for attempting to actualize these, in the spirit of, again, simply caring for kids. To be clear, SEL is not necessary *because* teachers deemed it so; SEL is vital because children and young people *arrive* in our schools needing these services.

We believe that schools should be havens. They should be the safest, happiest, most joyous, and even restful places that young people – and their teachers – encounter. And yet they are not. As Matt discussed, in the United States we are so obsessed with testing and placement and narrow notions of "progress" that we have completely lost our focus on what should be schools' and teachers' priorities. Our contributing teachers have clearly and profoundly put their fingers on what matters – or what *should* matter – most: the kids. That's it. There's no magic formula or upcoming research. We all know it. And yet so often teachers feel completely incapable of centering the social and emotional needs of young people in schools.

So, what can we do? What can *you* do – today – to more fully acknowledge and center the humanity and healing of the young people in your classroom? What can you do – *today* – to foster a sense of community at your school? What can you do – *today* – to help your students feel safe and to rediscover joy at school? What would even a momentary interruption in the treadmill-like drudgery of testing and "progress" look like?

We don't want you to feel burdened by these questions – these urges to do something different. Rather, we want you to feel emboldened and empowered. We want you to know that other teachers are grappling with the same things you are, whether you are in Oregon or Ohio, New York or New Mexico. Our contributing teachers have offered their everyday experiences as opportunities for you to consider as possible places to start. But what they've also revealed is that that one tiny interruption in the routines of a school or teaching day, if repeated once more, can quickly become a habit and expectation. And that we will all be healthier for these new routines.

Resources

Book: *Teaching When the World is on Fire*, edited by Lisa Delpit. Each chapter is written by different educators and covers crucial issues facing schools today, such as discussing politics in class to addressing the climate crisis. Ultimately an optimistic take on how to support students who are experiencing trauma while their teachers may be equally traumatized.

Podcast: *School Me* by NEAToday: Episode 88, Social and Emotional Learning 101. *School Me* has a variety of topics presented by genuine educators. Episode 88 (about 30 minutes long) is a primer on the history of SEL and its benefits to students.

TED Talk: "How Social and Emotional Learning Benefits Everyone" by Caige Jambor (10 minutes). Bridging the gap between TIPs and SEL, Jambor shows how SEL has always been implicit but making it explicit through targeted lessons benefits us and the people around us. Includes several specific SEL tools. Link: https://www.ted.com/talks/caige_jambor_how_social_emotional_learning_benefits_everyone

Online Resource: Social & Emotional Learning Ideas from Edutopia. This page is regularly updated with community-building activities and trauma-informed lessons for all grade levels. It can be a quick check-in for resources and ideas. Link: https://www.edutopia.org/social-emotional-learning

References

Abrams, Z. (2023, September 1). Teaching social-emotional learning is under attack. *American Psychological Association*, 54(6), 28. https://www.apa.org/monitor/2023/09/social-emotional-learning-under-fire

Anderson, M. (Host). (2022, September 26). How social-emotional learning became a frontline in the battle against CRT [Audio podcast episode]. In *All Things Considered* [Audio podcast]. National Public Radio. https://www.npr.org/2022/09/26/1124082878/how-social-emotional-learning-became-a-frontline-in-the-battle-against-crt

CASEL. (2024, July 15). Fundamentals of SEL. https://casel.org/fundamentals-of-sel/

Eden, M. (2023, August 30). Does social and emotional learning work? Let's hope not. *Washington Examiner*. https://www.washingtonexaminer.com/opinion/beltway-confidential/2726963/does-social-and-emotional-learning-work-lets-hope-not/

Fisher, H., Hawkins, G., Hertz, M., Silwa, S., Beresovsky, V. (2022). Student and school characteristics associated With covid-19-related learning decline among middle and high school students in k-12 schools. *Journal of School Health*, 92(11). https://doi-org.mutex.gmu.edu/10.1111/josh.13243

Kan, W. S., & Lejano, R. P. (2023). Relationality: The role of connectedness in the social ecology of resilience. *International Journal of Environmental Research and Public Health*, 20(5), 3865.

Kingkade, T. & Hixenbaugh, M. (2021, November 16). Parents protesting "critical race theory" identify another target: Mental health programs. *NBC News*. https://www.nbcnews.com/news/us-news/parents-protesting-critical-race-theory-identify-new-target-mental-hea-rcna4991

Stanford, L. & Meisner, C. (2023, July 7). Social-emotional learning persists despite political backlash. *Education Week*. https://www.edweek.org/leadership/social-emotional-learning-persists-despite-political-backlash/2023/07

8

School Safety

"Mr. Keller, the bathroom stinks like weed again, there are like 35 people crammed in there, the vape detector has been going off since second block, and no administrators have come to check it out," a student proclaimed as she came back to Jeff's class from the restroom. "Which one did you use," her classmate asked. "The secret bathroom. The one close to the conference room," she said. "Why would you go to that one? It's always like that. I never feel safe in there," her friend replied. "Yeah, well, I don't have a choice. It's the orange zone bathroom and I had an orange zone class. The whole thing is stupid."

This was a fairly regular conversation in Jeff's fourth block class. Variations of this same exchange had taken place in all of his classes, in working with students after school, and in our Student Equity Council meetings as well as during small group conversations with Fellows at the Youth Research Council. In the school where he teaches, establishing zones for bathrooms, limiting access to certain bathrooms, and installing vape detectors had come in response to two trends over the previous several years. The first was a post-pandemic shutdown TikTok challenge where students took videos of themselves stealing or destroying school property, usually in bathrooms (Doubek, 2021). The second was a continuing increase in vaping among teenagers (U.S. Food & Drug Administration [FDA], 2023). The results of these new school policies – which included closing bathrooms and more closely monitoring students who were in the school hallways between classes – had not had the intended impact. Instead, many students – like the ones in his fourth block – continue to report feeling unsafe to even enter a school bathroom.

Critical Concepts

School safety is a huge topic and an amorphous, ever-evolving issue. Many of us might think of blatant physical bullying or violence as the primary safety concern facing young people in schools today. Sadly, that stereotypical David vs. Goliath, nerd vs. jock version of intimidation may now be the most obvious, the easiest to address, and the least sinister form of safety concern in schools. It's not even the most common physical threat that kids are encountering today.

Today's young people, teachers, school administrators, and community members must be concerned with not only versions of bullying but also the destruction of property promoted by those TikTok videos, students' use of illicit and sometimes life-threatening substances, fights in the hallways and around school, all manner of threats made between students via social media, and – at its most extreme – gun violence and school shootings. This incomplete list of issues might explain why nearly one-fifth of students report feeling unsafe at school (Mori et al., 2021).

Even more troubling, if we drill down just a little bit into today's school realities and listen to teachers and young people, you will hear about other safety concerns, including harmful and even threatening behavior between and among teachers, the use of intimidation and threats by administrators against students and classroom teachers, and the ways that policies and enforcement practices that are supposedly intended to keep young people safe often disproportionately impact and target students of Color.

Implicit Bias

Our brain is always filling in the blanks and capturing patterns. If I say the word "peanut butter," what word comes to mind? Most likely, it's "jelly." How about "salt"? "Up"? "Left"? "Chips"? These word associations are nearly automatic, and implicit bias happens in much the same way.

Implicit biases are subtle thoughts or feelings that happen outside of our immediate awareness, but they impact our thoughts, feelings, and actions. All of us are subject to implicit bias because all of us have brains that make these patterns, and all of us have grown up in a society with historical and structural inequalities. Here are some common examples of implicit bias that can play out in schools:

- Gender: You ask Joanna to write on the board even though Andrew wants to.
- Cultural: You ask Rodriguez to tell the class about Cinco de Mayo.

- Racial: You are surprised Jada scored so high on the test when Emily scored so low.
- Socio-Economic: You ask Jose if his family does turkey with Thanksgiving.
- Ethnic: You think SongYu will have no problem with the Algebra test, so you don't check in with her.
- Disability: You exempt Danny from a test since he has an Individualized Education Program, and you don't think he will understand it.

Some of these may not seem insidious. In fact, if you have an established relationship with these students, some of these scenarios could be responsive and helpful. However, it is when we make assumptions or do not even realize we are treating students in these ways that implicit bias becomes hurtful.

School discipline and many decisions about what and who are "safe" in a school and who represents a threat are largely based on judgment calls – a single teacher's or a single administrator's interpretation of an incident. Which is, of course, susceptible to bias. One way to try to counter implicit bias is through debiasing:

- Expose yourself to counter-stereotypes and counter-stereotypical individuals in media and life
- Experience intergroup contact with people with different identities than your own
- Consider multiple viewpoints and perspectives in every situation
- Work to develop new associations that contrast with the stereotypical associations you already hold

If you want a better understanding of implicit bias, or to measure your own biases, the Harvard Implicit Association Tests (https://implicit.harvard.edu/implicit/takeatest.html) are great resources to assess your own subconscious biases. For instance, they have tests to evaluate how you view people with different weights, gender, disability, and race. We all have implicit biases, and awareness helps move the bias from subconscious to conscious, which is necessary to begin debiasing our brains.

Consistent with the content of the other chapters in this book, in this chapter you will read about teachers' experiences with safety and security matters, and you will also learn what teachers are doing to address these concerns, inside and outside of their classrooms. Before you continue, we'd suggest you invest again in reflecting on these issues, to clarify your own perspective and frame your consideration of these teachers' experiences and ideas. You know the drill: Pick up your computer or notebook and get ready to summarize some of your thinking, strategies, and questions.

- What were your experiences of safety in/around school when you were in middle and high school? Who or what posed threats to your feelings of safety and security?
- Who were the students who seemed – or actually were – the least safe in your classrooms and schools? Why?
- What is your awareness of how safety and security issues have changed since you were in middle/high school? Why do you think these changes have occurred?
- What roles did teachers, administrators, and other adults in your schools play in actively making you feel safe and intervening when there were threats to your own or others' safety?
- What policies and practices do you believe are most effective at keeping students and teachers safe in school? Which of these policies and practices have you experienced?
- Who might have faced implicit bias in your class or school – and why?

Teacher Stories

Any consideration of teachers' experiences with school safety issues has to begin with the elephant in the room: the COVID-19 pandemic. Health-care experts continue to debate the current status of this once-in-a-century event, and federal, state, and local policymakers are still discussing what is "best practice" with regard to how schools should function in the face of the nearly normalized reality of the existence of this evolving virus. But it's teachers who can give us the richest and most honest assessment of the daily and long-term impacts of both this still immediate health threat and how our society has dealt with it, particularly in our school buildings.

Matt, former English teacher: "It's endlessly heartbreaking."

A long-time English teacher, Matt shared his global take on the safety and security concerns that young people are facing now and why young people's sometimes-violent responses are actually quite reasonable:

> Kids do not feel safe right now. And people who don't feel safe react in a variety of ways, one of which is to strike out, to try to protect

yourself. I think because we haven't done the healing work, the community work, the humanity work, kids are feeling wildly unsafe in their schools and they're reacting in ways that are understandable. I'm not denying that these are harmful and self-defeating behaviors, to be sure. But I don't think they're responding in this way for any other reason than we're experiencing an ongoing traumatic event and not being given the space, the tools, the strategies, or the care to feel like anything can change. When a kid feels really unsafe, they act in ways that are not good for themselves. They can't even do basic cognitive tasks.

I think kids do not feel like we're back to "normal" at all in terms of their level of safety. Of course, schools were not particularly safe before COVID if you were queer, if you were Black, if you were Brown, if you were undocumented. And now you throw COVID on top of it…I mean, kids are thinking, "I might die because of these invisible molecules that are in the air? Or I might get my grandmother sick if I bring this home, or my dad or my brother who is immunocompromised?"

Many teachers will tell you that when the COVID-19 pandemic began, they were stunned by the appreciation that so many families, community members, and even politicians expressed for teachers' abilities to "pivot" (Yes, we all *hate* that word now) and do everything professionally – and often personally – possible to keep young people engaged. In that moment, when our most foundational institution – school – simply was not allowed to function in its century-long established manner, teachers modified the very core of their professional practices – their pedagogies – in order to help students continue to learn. And, really, to keep them at least feeling as if some aspects of their lives were still normal. Ultimately, teachers were, again, keeping kids safe.

Matt: "We have completely capitulated to this idea of 'get back to normal'."

But just as quickly as these expressions of support and solidarity began, they dissipated and were replaced by families' pleas for schools to re-open and community leaders' often politically motivated demands that it was teachers' over-reaching appeals and paranoid concerns that were keeping students from their right to a face-to-face education. As Matt shared, both teachers – worried about their students' and their own well-being – and young people knew better:

Kids may be acting out in ways we don't want them to, but they are the only ones acting rationally in schools. Adults, we feel pressure, but we have completely capitulated to this idea of "get back to normal." Kids are screaming out in whatever way they can. Like canaries in the coal mines, screaming that there is toxicity in the air. There is literally toxicity in the air with COVID, but also with other issues – including racism and transphobia and kids just not feeling loved and cared for and supported in schools or in communities. And we, as adults, better start listening, or we're going to continue to see things deteriorate. It's just so disheartening to see that we never do anything differently in education. Which means we really don't understand that you can't learn anything if you don't feel safe and supported and loved in the learning environment.

> **Box 8.1 Your Stories**
>
> What were the "return-to-school" policies and practices in your school after COVID? How would you have felt if you had been required to spend hours a day in an enclosed space with 20 or 30 people? How safe did you feel when you returned to public places during or later in the pandemic? How safe do you feel now? In your experience, who in your community and what students suffered most and gained most from the COVID closure of schools and from the re-opening of schools?

> **Box 8.2 We Can't Keep Kids Safe if They're Not in School**
>
> In the 2017–2018 school year, for every 100 students enrolled across K-12, Black students lost 61 instructional days to suspension while white students lost 14 days. Additionally, students with disabilities lost 100 days per every 100 students while students without disabilities lost 19 days (U.S. Department of Education, 2023).
>
> While restorative justice programs can be difficult to implement and measure, schools with successful restorative justice programs saw statistically significant drops in out-of-school suspensions and violence, particularly for certain Black male students (Darling-Hammond et al., 2020).

Because of the seemingly ever-growing complexity of the safety issues that schools are facing – and which teachers are almost always the first ones to encounter and address – district- and building-level administrators have devised drills to help teachers and kids become accustomed to these threats.

Developed under the guise of preparing teachers to respond effectively, these practices can be traumatizing in themselves and are another example of the "canary in the coal mine" and of normalizing what should not be normal.

Gabby, high school teacher: "If you don't like it, then keep your door shut."

Gabby described a few of the elaborate exercises to which teachers and students have been subjected, all in the name of "school safety":

> Okay, well, you know, we live in an area where a lot of kids hunt. Most of our kids carry guns [outside of school]. So, it's not uncommon for a kid to be like, "Oh, I've got a knife. I need to go tell admin to check it in." I think our district doesn't want to get caught off guard with respect to Code Reds and school safety and gun violence. We'll have one Code Red drill during the first semester, and we know when it's going to happen. The teachers know, and then we tell the kids. And then we know that during the second semester sometime during the first fifteen days another one will happen, but it'll be a surprise. It's really stressful.
>
> In my teaching career, it's always been, you know, leave your classroom open. If a teacher has their classroom door shut, then it's like you're trying to hide something. But now they're always just like, "Shut your doors, lock your doors, keep your doors shut, keep your doors locked."
>
> Probably one of the most emotionally impacting experiences was when they did this drill for the teachers so that we knew what [gunfire] sounded like. They had two different types of guns. We're all sitting there and we're all quiet and you can hear them shooting guns so that we know what it sounds like when it's upstairs, when it's downstairs, when it's approaching. I remember just feeling sick. Maybe it was a good thing, because it could sound like so many different things. But then, also, maybe it was just a little over the top.
>
> There was also one time where I was teaching. I have my door open, and somebody comes stumbling into my classroom, acting all weird, and I've never seen the person. I was standing by the door, and I realized what was happening (it was another drill). But I had to shove them out the door and it wasn't an easy [thing to do]. I found out later they had a body camera on, so they were recording when they entered the building, to see if anybody who encountered them

asked them for an ID. Because if you encounter somebody that's an adult in the building and they don't have an ID, it's your responsibility to initiate the Code Red. Do we really have to practice like that? My administration said, "If you didn't like it, then keep your door shut."

I've gotten caught in the hallways before not knowing [if the Code Red was a drill or not], and that's been really traumatizing a few times. I can just remember being in the hallway, walking towards the copy machine, and all of our administrators are running, and then a Code Red gets called and I don't have my keys. I can't get into a classroom, and we're told not to let anybody in, so I had to beg to get into a classroom, which was really scary.

While explicit bullying and intimidation may not be the most common forms of safety issues that youths and teachers are facing in schools, these incidents do occur. And the primary concern that teachers have in these situations isn't about the threats that kids sometimes pose to them or each other.

Carleigh, elementary school music teacher: "But they're quick to suspend kids who have different skin tones."

As Carleigh describes, teachers' biggest worry is about how they and young people sometimes can't trust administrators to respond effectively or equitably to such threats:

> There's been an issue with teachers not trusting that administrators will appropriately deal with bullying that we've seen in the school. We had a white kid yell to another student in the playground at the top of his voice. He said, "I'm going to beat your f-ing A!" at the top of his lungs, right in the student's face. It took this student two weeks for him to get into any trouble. He did not get suspended. The principal had a conversation with him in the office, and that was it.
>
> But we have an Egyptian student and a Hispanic student – one kicked a student and one hit another student. The principal suspended the Egyptian student and the Hispanic student for three days and not the white student. We also had another white student who bit another student and actually broke skin, and he also wasn't suspended. Ironically, he's on safety patrol and he didn't lose his safety belt – nothing. But they're quick to suspend kids who have different skin tones.

Sometimes, these safety concerns involve multiple issues – outdated and differentially applied policies, overwhelmed administrators who simply don't have the time to serve young people effectively, and what can only be interpreted as racism (intentional or not). At times, the very institution of school can serve to intimidate bright, well-meaning students who are just seeking the sanctuary of a school building. It's moments like these that it can seem as if our school leaders have forgotten that administrative equivalent of the Hippocratic Oath – for doctors, it's "Do no harm," and for teachers and school administrators, it's "Keep kids safe" (Box 8.3).

> **Box 8.3 Your Stories**
> When have you seen implicit bias play a role in how students have been treated at your school? As you think, you might consider if your own implicit biases have ever played a role in a decision you have made, an interaction you have had, or other ways you have treated students. Resist the urge to feel guilty – we *all* have implicit biases. Becoming more aware of the ways we engage them is important for changing our assumptions and behaviors.

Annie, high school teacher: "No one checked to see if these students had a safe place."

Annie, now retired after a 40-year career as a high school English teacher and teacher of multilingual learners at a large, diverse public high school, shared an email (excerpted below) she wrote to school- and district-level administrators near her final day of teaching. In her email, she shared how deeply upsetting it was to watch school administrators target five Black students, several of whom who were leaders in student clubs she advised, and threaten them with handcuffs if they did not leave school grounds during their free period. To protect these youths' privacy, the name of the school has been changed to the fictional Cedar High School.

> A number of students I know, all seniors, were granted early release this year. Guidance counselors and the students' parents allowed these students to drop classes, and counselors changed their schedules. No classes were put in place of the dropped ones. No one checked to see if these students had a safe place, or any place at all to go from the time that they had no class to the end of the day when they caught their buses home, or until the clubs they were participating in started. No one checked to see if the students had cars or transportation other

than school buses. They were not given library or guidance or office aide positions. No study halls or "hang out" places are available.

During the colder months, most of these students did not leave school grounds at their early dismissal time. Many of them do not live near school and many of them did not have cars. They did not wish to leave their "safe" school and go outside elsewhere. They stayed in the library on occasion, but this was not always available. They tried to sit and work at tables in the cafeteria but were not usually able to do so because security shooed them away. No attempt was made by administration or guidance counselors to talk to them or to find the students places to go.

On May 3, five students who just happened to be unlucky enough to be caught, while others scattered, were rounded up from the hallway and brought to the security office. In the security office, the students were each given a paper to sign, and then they were all told that if they were caught "trespassing" on school property, they "would be put in handcuffs in the back of a police car."

NO students, especially students of Color in this day and age, but NO students should be threatened with handcuffs and police cars. This language and this threatened punishment were accepted and deemed appropriate by the school administration. One administrator even said that it was the students' "own failure to adhere to the rules" that put them in a position to be threatened this way.

Box 8.4 Your Stories

In what ways do you see your school treating young people in contradictory ways – simultaneously as children with few rights and few abilities to make responsible decisions and as full-grown and legally culpable adults? Who are the students who seem to experience these contradictions most often? What are their identities? What policies and practices send young people these inconsistent messages? How does positioning young people in this way compromise their safety?

Teacher Strategies

What are teachers doing to keep students safe, in light of this growing range of issues? And what can you do to enhance the security of your own classroom and school in a way that mitigates or stays aware of the ways in which implicit bias can affect students' feelings of safety? A key theme of the insights and practices offered by the teachers who contributed to this book is that they are going further and further above and beyond, out of necessity, out of a sincere personal and professional desire to help their students, and because they recognize that schools are always reflections of our communities' realities. These responses range from the large-scale and conceptual to the minute-by-minute and practical.

Matt: "Healing kids, helping kids feel valued in and through the curriculum."

Matt, who offered that opening reality check to this chapter and introduced us to that "canary in the coal mine" analogy for teachers, students, and schools, argued that schools should be considering wholesale modifications to their curricula and structures, with an emphasis on validation and representation:

> But I do think we'd have less unsafe, violent, bullying schools if we made space for restorative practices – healing kids, helping kids feel valued in and through the curriculum, seeing themselves in the curriculum, and feeling validated and centered.

Such an orientation requires innovative – and real – leadership on the part of school administrators. The list of methods of getting out in the community, of helping kids know and be known by their teachers, and of aiding parents and families to trust teachers are numerous. These strategies can seem like token exercises, but they are ultimately focused on developing those lines of communication and building that sense of collaboration that establish the foundations for authentic forms of security.

Alfonso, high school teacher: "When you haven't even seen their face."

Alfonso shared how his school leadership was committed to these core communication and engagement activities, which were all the more important in a time when some families were questioning the very value of school:

> Our principal also knows that it's important to see students' faces before they come to our school. So, every year he gets a team of teachers for a big bike ride where they go and visit every student's home. That's how you involve the parents and the family because you see that they care. That's kind of the missing piece, when we have all of these debates

about indoctrination and accusation that my child's teacher doesn't really care about them. It's very easy to say that that person's the antagonist when you haven't even seen their (your child's teacher's) face.

Alfonso: "I know the streets."

Alfonso recognized that he was in a unique situation given his knowledge of his community – both its geography and its culture. But he reminded us that it's teachers' knowledge of and investment in students and their communities that can enhance everyone's safety:

> I have the perfect set-up. I am teaching at my old high school. I know the streets; I know the little corners where my students may be hiding in the community. But I know a lot of teachers don't have that.

These commitments also translate to teachers' pedagogies, which are most effective – and result in students' greater senses of security – when they are proactive rather than reactive. Teachers recognize that they have to make the first move to reach families, that often parents' lack of engagement and responsiveness has to be counteracted by teachers' positivity and persistence. And while not all of us have the dual language know-how to translate our messages home to make them accessible to all families, many tools to support teachers in this project exist.

> Something that I like to do when parents are not involved is to give them a phone call, just to say, you know, your son's been great. That way, before the next phone call, if it's a negative one, at least that initial one was a positive one. And finally, as a Spanish speaker, I like to translate every single email I send home, because that is the largest population that I teach. So, in the past parents have reached out back in Spanish. Fortunately, I'm able to do that, but for a non-Spanish speaking teacher, Google Translate exists. It takes a little more time, but the benefits of something like this multiply when you spend five extra minutes.

And when adults in youths' lives – or, worse, adults in the school, including other teachers, administrators, or security guards – are the ones who make our students feel or actually be unsafe, it's imperative that we as teachers attempt to do some of the healing that Matt described.

Annie relayed an experience she had before the COVID pandemic began when some money was stolen from her drawer by a student, in a class for so-called English Language Learners. Most of the students identified as Latino/a/x, and some were undocumented. Annie discussed the shocking, traumatic security team's response, which included them barreling into her classroom, repeatedly yelling at students to remain silent (they were speaking in Spanish to each other, attempting to understand what was happening), and threatening to search each individual student. For young people who have already experienced significant trauma and sometimes violence in their lives, such a reaction is not only unprofessional: it's dangerous.

Annie: "Before we start class, we need to talk about this."

Like any teacher concerned about their students' well-being, Annie did what she could when these students were next in her class:

> And so, the next time we met, which was several days later because of some special events that were going on, we met in a larger room because my room was being used for something else. And I made us all sit at one table, so instead of being spread out in a room where you could sit with your backs to each other, where you could sit and isolate yourself in the corner, I said, "No, we're here at this table." It was a big enough table that we could all fit, but it was also a small enough table that it was pretty intimate in terms of being face to face. And we started to talk, because that was the first time that we had met after security had come into my room.
>
> So, I said, "Before we start class, we need to talk about this." And we did. And I said, "How many of you went home and told your parents?" And two of the kids had, and nobody else had at all. They were just so afraid. And their parents didn't need one more thing on their plates, you know? But no parents were notified. I don't think it would have unfolded that way in an AP [Advanced Placement] classroom or in a class with a bunch of white kids.

Often in schools, we hear one of the mantras of our post–September 11th world: "If you *see* something, *say* something." This is one of the key lessons shared by the teachers with whom we spoke for this volume: If you see a situation that is making – or *might* make – a young person unsafe, do *something*, say *something*. Teachers are not superheroes, but they are often the most consistent adults in young people's lives and have the first opportunity to respond to the challenges they are facing.

Annie: "Better, fairer, kinder policies needed to have been used in this situation."

Annie spoke up often across her career to advocate for her students, to try to keep them safe, whether from themselves and some of their choices, from threatening peers, and from dangers in their families and communities. As she described above, sometimes the most unpredictable or nefarious factors in students' lives are their school leaders, and teachers can speak up when administrators make the wrong, risky call. Below is another excerpt of the email she sent to her school administration after her senior students with reduced school schedules were threatened by security with prosecution for "trespassing" in their own school building:

> Before I finish my 40-year career, since I am retiring, I do have a few final emails to send. In particular I have concerns about how some of our students were treated this year. One specific instance involves students who were threatened with being "put in handcuffs in the back of a police car" if they continued to "trespass" on school grounds.
>
> Better, fairer, kinder policies needed to have been used in this situation. These young adults should have been treated with more respect and consideration. They should not have been threatened with handcuffs and the back of a police car. They should have been included in solutions and problem-solving. They should not have left high school feeling defeated and mistreated and unseen, seeing how power can be unfairly used against them. I can only hope that they will go forth into the world and meet with more kindness, more fairness, and more support than that they were afforded from their school and administration.

Box 8.5 Your Strategies

What connections do you make to what our contributing teachers have described here? If you were in one of their positions, what would you have done? For example, how might you have responded if you were Annie, and your students were being threatened in this way? What were your reactions (emotional, physical, psychological) to any of the situations that teachers described? What are policies or practices in your own context that are similar – or, better yet, that are different and are more effective at keeping kids safe?

Youth Stories

The young people involved in the Through Students' Eyes project echoed many of the insights about school safety shared by these contributing teachers. Then a sophomore in high school, Conner was aware of the fact that he was on a path to adulthood but that he wasn't there yet: "I haven't learned yet how to be an adult. School is pushing you there, but teachers don't explicitly tell us this. School helps you learn to be respectful." Conner and the other project participants longed for teachers to be honest with them about this journey and about the skills they would need to be successful after school.

And Eve – then a high school junior – spoke to the importance of quality, caring teachers motivating students even to show up for school, where they might be kept safe and develop those skills to support that future success:

> If people have bad teachers, it can turn them off from attending school. If you don't feel important or if you feel that no one at school cares about you at school, you might reject school. But doing so is going to hurt you more in the long run, not the teachers. If no one has made it clear that education is important, then you don't understand that it's going to hurt you to not care about it.

In 2023, the high school students who are Youth Research Council Fellows conducted a study that focused on the multiple meanings of school safety, with a focus on what school safety means and feels like for students of Color. One of their major findings was that students do not feel safer because more metal detectors are installed or more security officials are present. In fact, these steps make students of Color feel *less* safe because of the ways that people of Color historically have been (and still are) policed and surveilled.

The Youth Research Council instead found that students of Color feel safest when they have adults in the building they can trust. One Fellow, Finn, shared that the adults they trust the most in their building are the nurses. When they feel anxious, they go to the nurses who talk with them and help calm them down. In fact, last year, Finn shared that they went to the nurse once a week and that practice helped them feel safe and less anxious in school. While relationships with teachers are, of course, important, other school adults should understand that their roles are equally important in helping students feel safe and secure at school.

Taking Action

Across the stories and experiences of our contributing teachers and young people, two themes impressed us. The first is that these teachers are laser-focused on their students' well-being. They feel personally and professionally responsible for not just their students' learning but also their attendance in school, their emotional health, and how they are treating each other and how they are treated by others. This level of responsibility isn't healthy or sustainable for teachers, but they recognize that they are on those proverbial "front lines" and they are sometimes the only witnesses to the threats to their students' safety.

This sense of feeling – or *being* – personally responsible for phenomena that are technically just part of your job is something that we must trouble. Why is it okay that teachers are not only professionally accountable for keeping kids safe but also personally so? It's not. And this is something we should acknowledge and discuss, with each other, in our teacher education programs, in our faculty meetings, and with our school leaders and local and national policymakers. The notion of "intensification" has long been applied to the teaching profession – the idea is that more and more is added to teachers' work, with nothing ever being subtracted. But these safety concerns speak to the idea of "moral intensification": teachers are not just expected to complete these additional tasks to keep kids safe; they are called on to do so because of a moral imperative.

The second theme was one of complexity: the nature of "safety" has evolved so much and so quickly that teachers are often just keeping their heads above water to remain abreast of and be able to respond to this constellation of issues. At the most foundational level, then, what needs to change about society, schools, teachers' roles, and even the teaching profession to *really* keep our children and young people safe? And how can we do this in ways that are equitable for all students and reasonable for teachers?

And, finally, it's important to consider the resources that teachers need to stay on top of and understand this growing range of safety issues. This is both a matter of time and workload capacity and a matter of expertise: we know teachers have barely sufficient time in your professional days to complete your planning, instructional, and assessment tasks, so you will need resources and support to appreciate and address these fluctuating, myriad safety issues. You are already experts in your content areas and with developing relationships with young people, but you will need the input of experts in these safety and security issues to best support children and young people. One way to take action is to connect with these "experts," and we see young people as the experts on their own lived experiences. So, perhaps, the most important action you can take is to listen to your students. Really listen.

Resources

Book: Punished for Dreaming by Bettina L. Love. Dr. Love tracks four decades of education reform to highlight how school discipline unfairly targets Black children. The book highlights what reform in discipline should look like to be fair and restorative for all students and end the school to prison pipeline.

Podcast: *You're Wrong About* by Sarah Marshall, episode: "Juvenile 'Justice' with Josie Duffy Rice". This often-humorous podcast breaks down cultural understandings and historical events to highlight how public perception often differs from the facts. "Juvenile 'Justice'" discusses the American legal system from the 19th century and how it targets and prosecutes minors often to little effect on preventing crime and recidivism. A big picture of the system that school discipline often mirrors.

TED Talk: "Stupid School Security and Discipline Procedures" by Jennie Young (17 minutes). Young makes the case that treating schools like prisons and students like prisoners does not inspire better behavior. Instead, she describes different approaches to discipline that could build community and transform schools. Link: https://www.ted.com/talks/jennie_young_stupid_school_security_and_discipline_policies

Online Resource: Youth Violence Prevention from the Centers for Disease Control and Prevention regularly compiles "Resource for Action" packets that include statistics and research-based interventions about health-related issues. The Youth Violence Prevention packet includes common reasons behind violent behavior in young people and suggested interventions. The appendices have quick reference guides and policy recommendations to prevention strategies. Link: https://www.cdc.gov/violenceprevention/pdf/YV-Prevention-Resource_508.pdf

References

Darling-Hammond, S., Fronius, T. A., Sutherland, H., Guckenburg, H., Petrosino, A., & Hurley, N. (2020). Effectiveness of restorative Justice in US k-12 schools: A review of quantitative research. *Contemporary School Psychology 24*, 295–308. https://doi.org/10.1007/s40688-020-00290-0

Doubek, J. (2021, September 2017). Students are damaging school bathrooms for attention on tiktok. *National Public Radio.* https://www.npr.org/2021/09/17/1038378816/students-are-damaging-school-bathrooms-for-attention-on-tiktok

Mori, Y., Tiiri, E., Khanal, P., Khakurel, J., Mishina, K., & Sourander, A. (2021). Feeling unsafe at school and associated mental health difficulties among children and adolescents: A systematic review. *Children (Basel, Switzerland), 8*(3), 232. https://doi.org/10.3390/children8030232

U.S. Department of Education. (2023). Creating and sustaining discipline policies that support students' social, emotional, behavioral, and academic well-being and success: Strategies for school and district leaders. Title IV-A Technical Assistance Center (T4PA Center). https://t4pacenter.ed.gov/Docs/Fact-Sheets/Supporting_Students_School_and_District_Leaders_508.pdf

U.S. Food & Drug Administration (FDA). (2023). Results from the annual national youth tobacco survey. https://www.fda.gov/tobacco-products/youth-and-tobacco/results-annual-national-youth-tobacco-survey

9

Environmental Justice and Climate Change

It's been nearly five years since a worldwide walkout to protest government inaction on climate change saw 1.1 million students leave the classroom to make their voices heard (Barnard, 2019). Students at the school where Jeff teaches coordinated their efforts, made signs, invited local political leaders, and even communicated with the local press to have the event covered in the newspaper. In all, over 170 students participated. In the online coverage for the event, one anonymous commenter wrote,

> They need to go back to class and stop the BS. When I went to school we were there to learn. Now these kids are there getting brainwashed and indoctrinated as to what the teachers [sic] beliefs are and what the gov't [sic] wants them to know.
>
> (Merod, 2019)

This reaction speaks to several overlapping themes that have appeared in this chapter and throughout this book: a misguided belief that schools are engaged in some form of indoctrination (in this case, related to environmentalism), a flat rejection of the idea that students should participate in any sort of civic activism, and the erroneous view student learning can take place only in a classroom.

Unfortunately, the commenter is not alone in making these unfounded assessments. Environmental education broadly and instruction related to climate change specifically have become increasingly polarizing topics in today's public schools. A New York Times report indicates that many states, including places like Texas and

Florida where the impacts of climate change are most intensely felt, omit or minimize instruction related to environmental justice and/or climate change (Choi, 2022). At the same time, the scientific community continues to ring alarm bells about the threat of climate change and the need for greater environmental justice, and students continue to report feelings of anxiety and stress related to schools' inability or unwillingness to effectively teach about such issues (Will, 2022).

Meanwhile, three of the four final candidates for the 2024 Republican presidential nomination – Vivek Ramaswamy, Ron DeSantis, and Nikki Haley – all acknowledged that climate change is real but asserted that human actions were not responsible. The fourth candidate (and presumptive nominee at the time of the writing of this book), former President Donald Trump, claims he recognizes that climate change is a reality and that humans play at least some part in it. But in the 2016 campaign, he labeled global climate change as a "Chinese hoax" (Wong, 2016) and as recently as April 2023 characterized warnings from the scientific community related to rising sea levels and threats of increasingly severe weather due to the effects of climate change as "nonsense" (Dale, 2023).

It's clear that teachers are navigating myriad issues with regard to if – and how – to teach about climate change and environmental justice. So how can schools provide students with relevant scientific education related to these topics while avoiding accusations of indoctrination or political bias? We think our contributing teachers have some good ideas that might be helpful for you as you grapple with this very question.

Critical Concepts

Political division is not new when it comes to science curricula. For decades, teachers in this country have grappled with different factions warring over what is best in science education, what can and can't be taught in schools, and what kids really need to know about such topics.

Courageous Conversations

Glenn E. Singleton's book (2005) *Courageous Conversations About Race* is a practical guide to navigating pushback about a variety of topics. The first thing to recognize is that when someone challenges one of our beliefs or expertise, strong emotions are likely to rise due to our own philosophy causing us to become defensive. In fact, Singleton says challenging conversations typically occur in one of four quadrants:

- Emotional: I have a strong emotional response around this issue.
- Moral: I have a strong sense of right or wrong regarding this issue.
- Intellectual: I have a need to educate others about this issue.
- Social: I have a desire to take action regarding this issue.

When someone says something that is challenging – perhaps a belief about climate change or what should or should not be taught in the classroom – it is important to take a pause before responding. You may consider which quadrant they are likely operating from. If you are unsure, consider responding with a question:

- This seems to have really bothered you. Can you help me understand why?
- I hear a lot of passion around this, and I appreciate your sharing. Can you tell me more about what specifically bothers you about this topic?
- You saw something I didn't see, please help me understand. I want us to move forward, but I need more information.
- In a perfect world, what would a solution to this look like for you?

Remember the adage "It's not *what* you say but *how* you say it." A curious, nonjudgmental tone is necessary here. Once you have decided where their pushback is coming from, you can tailor your response in a way to best preserve the relationship and move forward.

- Emotional: Acknowledge their feelings with empathy and comfort.
- Moral: Acknowledge their beliefs and offer alternative perspectives.
- Intellectual: Provide more information or data.
- Social: Give them the opportunity to problem-solve

From evolution to climate change, there is no shortage of opinions and debates in science education. Yet often, what science teachers really want to do is help and care for kids in ways that are meaningful to them and their communities. That might look like building a school garden, raising class pets, or studying how the mulch in the playground shifts after a heavy rain. In this chapter, you will learn about how teachers use place-based education both to help students understand – and potentially address problems in – their own communities and neighborhoods and to illustrate larger global trends. Before you read, consider these questions:

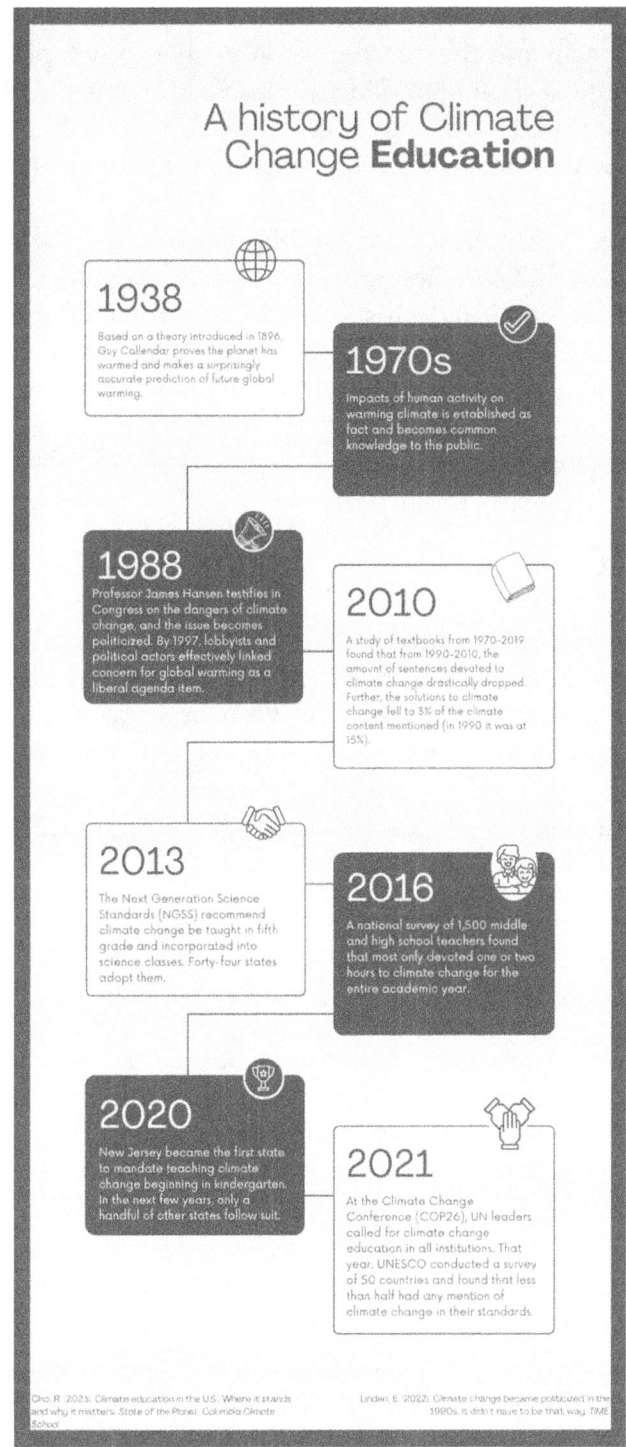

Figure 9.1 A time line detailing the history of climate change education in the United States from 1938 to 2021.

- What was your experience in school related to learning about the environment and climate change? Were there any topics considered "too political" or taboo? Did your teachers ever explicitly address these supposedly taboo topics?
- Who was your favorite science teacher? What made them your favorite?
- How have you seen science learning spark something in students that you hadn't seen before?
- What is the political context related to the teaching of science and particular topics where you live? Have you or any of your colleagues experienced pushback from community members, families, or administrators related to how science is taught or what is included in curriculum?

Teacher Stories

The teachers who spoke with us about environmental justice and climate change have a vast amount of experience – with a combined three decades of teaching in multiple states and contexts. From an upper-class private Christian middle school in metropolitan Washington, D.C., to a large public high school in rural South Carolina, to a Title 1 elementary school in Virginia, these teachers offered insights into the ways they have attempted to rehumanize science and curricula related to the environment.

Aloe, elementary science teacher: "Let's create amazing experiences for students."

Aloe compared her experiences in two very different school settings, suggesting that although needs and resources were very different, it always came back to caring for students in ways that were meaningful to them. She took a humanizing approach to environmental science.

> I've worked in two very different school settings. Most recently I was in a Title 1 school that had about 85% English Language Learners and students who were eligible for free and reduced lunch. And before that, I was at a private Christian school, and there it was upper, upper-class students. And so, my perspectives on environmental justice look very different in those two settings. When I switched from private to

public school, I had all these lofty ideas of what I wanted to do for environmental education at an under resourced public school. And then, after a bit of time, I learned, "Oh, I just need to care for these students and focus on the humanizing and rehumanizing of some of these kiddos."

So that's why I have an interesting perspective, because I feel like, who am I to do acts of environmental justice if I'm not putting the kids first? In a lot of the spaces of research and practice you have those two camps. You have the researchers who are all about that pro-environmental behavior and it becomes almost behaviorism. And then you have folks like me where it's like, "Let's create amazing experiences for students to be outside, to connect with nature, to develop a sense of place, so that as they grow older, they develop more of a care ethic." So, I tend to push against that pro-environmental side. And when I was at that Title 1 school, I did gardening, and I used recyclables to do maker spaces. But a lot of focus was on more justice for the kids.

Aloe: "For me, it's about foregrounding human, holistic well-being and dignity."

Aloe shared that there were a lot of needs among her students, many of whom were newcomers to the United States. Many of the students had experienced trauma before arriving at the school, and so Aloe considered what was most important for those students. Her approach to teaching science was oriented around her students' everyday well-being and human decency.

> So, that's the tension I faced, and I can imagine other educators face when you have students going through trauma. Environmental justice doesn't seem to be the foreground, if that makes sense. So, at the Title 1 school it wasn't so much nervous of pushback from parents. It was more teachers just feeling exhausted and burned out. And so, we tried to partner with people. It was hard to make that a priority when we had such high needs within the student population. So, for me, it's about foregrounding human holistic well-being and dignity, not at the expense of nature and the environment, but almost co-constructed. Together.

Aloe: "I had to be mindful in the language I used."

Aloe shared that when she taught at a well-resourced private school, she experienced pushback from parents about her curriculum. Yet, when she used place-based, experiential learning, the students really enjoyed the learning and there was less opposition. Also, when she was careful with the language she used and emphasized solving problems that students could see in their own community, parents were more accepting of her instruction.

> So, in the private Christian school, if I went too much environmental, there was pushback from a religious perspective – like it was almost seen as too liberal or too hippy dippy or too tree hugger. So, I had to be mindful in the language that I used. But when it was just me and the students they didn't care. But the issues of climate change and anything in evolution, those were topics that sometimes I was like, "Am I going to get an email from a parent?" But for the most part, they were sixth graders. They were just enjoying doing things outside, and a lot of it was place-centered. Place-based pedagogies or land-based where it's more looking at environmental justice from a local perspective rather than global.
>
> In the private school, I did a lot of the more place-based and local stuff. So, for example, I had a guest scientist come and he talked about climate change. My administrator was kind of not too happy about that. But I didn't get any emails from parents. So, in that setting just given the more conservative nature of the school, I just had to edit my language a lot, but I found that rooting it in the local and the place was a good access point.

For the science teachers we spoke with, the political climate was always in the background as they prepared lessons, introduced projects, and responded to parental/family inquiries. Whether at a large public high school or a small private Christian school, teachers felt a constant pressure to say the right words, to not make often entitled people feel uncomfortable, and – at the same time – to prepare students to be engaged and responsible citizens of their communities and the world.

Gabby, high school science teacher: "I just present as much information as possible."

Gabby shared that she navigates the political climate in her school carefully but explicitly. She is upfront with students, clarifying on day 1 of her environmental science class that there is a difference between environmental science and environmentalism so there are no questions about her goals for the class and her students.

> So, I just kind of give a brief snapshot of what students will be learning that year. So, I put up a slide that really does clarify the difference just because I feel that it has a negative connotation. Being environmentally minded is portrayed in our area as something that's a liberal concern or something that's more "hippy." So, I just want them to understand that environmental science is the science of the environment. And then, whenever you get into environmentalism, that's where you look at how governmental agencies are seeking to protect different things when issues arise. So that's pretty much how I handle that.
>
> I don't ever really try to like get the drum out and beat it. I just feel like that's not the best tactic. I always try to go for the backdoor approach. That's one of the things that I really struggle with because with climate and environmental justice, it's like you have to be so concerned, be so depressed, or it's like, oh, we've got this quick little fix. It's not complex. I really just try to figure out how to not do either one of those and just present as much information as possible, and also present things like the Jane Goodall message. She's got the Hopecast podcast. So, discussing that through action, there is hope.

Box 9.1 Your Stories

What do you picture when you think of "hope" in light of teaching kids and young people about science and environmental issues? What do you think about the idea of "rehumanizing" the curriculum? What would that look like to you? How would you go about putting "human holistic well-being and dignity" at the center of your teaching? What would that require you to change? How might you navigate pushback from students, families, or administrators around the teaching of environmental issues?

> **Box 9.2 Take Kids Outdoors**
>
> Since the COVID-19 pandemic, many schools, particularly in Europe and Canada, have experimented with outdoor learning initiatives. These have demonstrated benefits, including improved mental health and increased physical activity (Marsh & Blackwell, 2023). They're an excellent way to connect kids with nature, even for lessons that aren't related to climate.
>
> In 2022, Dr. Claire Warden wrote the book *Green Teaching: Nature Pedagogies for Climate Change & Sustainability*. In it, she makes a case for going beyond just taking kids outdoors and instead embedding a love for the environment into the curriculum. Geared toward elementary and pre-school teachers, *Green Teaching* is full of experiential, hands-on lesson plans and case studies for nature pedagogies. Dr. Warden's goal is for young children to love nature and understand climate change and sustainability early in life, so that they can become future advocates for climate justice.

Teacher Strategies

Even though STEM (science, technology, engineering, and mathematics) teachers may feel some (or a lot of) pressure in today's political climate, our contributing teachers shared many ways in which they – often quietly – push back on divisive rhetoric in their classrooms.

Aloe: "Science identity is a big thing."

Aloe discussed how she used picture books in her elementary classes to introduce the idea that everyone is a scientist.

> You know, science identity is a big thing. I don't know if you've seen the whole "Draw a scientist" thing, how students tend to think of scientists as old white men? Well, I was really intentional with books that we read. There's a really good book called, *Scientist scientist, who do you see?* It's like the brown bear book, but it's all, you know, different scientists. The first time I read it the last page shows all of the different scientists, and the first class I read it to, they're sitting on the carpet, a bunch of first graders, and they start to say, "Oh, that one looks like me, that one, look!" And then they all wanted to share which one they thought looked the most like them, and every single class afterwards, when I showed them that last page, they did the same thing, and these little kids just wanted to do that. And so that meant that even if they don't remember any of the content, if they see themselves as scientists or engineers, that's it!

Box 9.3 Draw a Scientist

From 1966 to 1977, social scientist David Chambers asked almost 5,000 children, mostly from the U.S. and Canada, to draw a scientist. Most of the drawings had similarities – they depicted chemists with lab coats and eyeglasses – and almost all of the scientists were male. Of the 4,087 drawings, only 28 featured female scientists, and all of those were drawn by girls (Yong, 2018).

This experiment was repeated in 1985, and 33% of the girls drew female scientists. When it was repeated again in 2016, 58% of the girls drew female scientists. While girls today are more likely to recognize that scientists can be female, that number lowers with age. Kindergarteners were more likely to draw female scientists than high school girls were. When asked to draw a scientist, 70% of kindergarten girls drew a female. In high school, only 25% of 16-year-old girls do (Terada, 2019).

This study is evidence that implicit bias still exists in STEM. Some proven ways that teachers can help level the playing field would be to incorporate diverse role models in books, curricula, and classroom decorations. Additionally, be mindful of gender bias in language and impart a growth mindset on students. Being "good" at math and science are skills, not innate talents, and it's important to reinforce that on students through language and feedback (Terada, 2019).

Box 9.4 Your Strategies

How might you replicate this "Draw a scientist" activity in your own classroom? How might you use a similar strategy to call on students to "picture" what they see as a healthy environment or climate? You might have students choose images rather than have them draw them. Why is identity more or differently important for children and young people when we are considering science topics?

Just as what we *see* who scientists are and might be, teachers consistently reminded us that the words we use when discussing science and environmental topics need to be carefully chosen. Choosing the "right" word is both about avoiding potential negative responses from students and parents or family and avoiding explicitly political issues and about being accurate with how we are representing these issues. One ready example is helping students to understand the difference between "global warming" – the indisputable rise in global temperatures – and "climate change" – the also irrefutable evidence of the long-term changes in measures of the climate (e.g., precipitation and severity of storms).

Aloe: "There are certain words that actually trigger visceral reactions."

For Aloe, this concern extended to recognizing the fraught nature of teaching science given the current political landscape: Teachers simply need to be aware of these contexts. For her, sometimes it was just about being aware that certain words would be problematic for her students. She didn't necessarily avoid those words altogether, but by being aware of what might trigger certain negative reactions, she was prepared to contextualize comments or answer questions she knew would come up.

> I think like within my experience teaching, there are certain like hot buttons that you either just avoid, or there are certain words that actually trigger a visceral reaction in some students and families like "Trump." You say that word, people have a response, right? So, it doesn't necessarily mean I avoid it. It's just being aware of that in today's climate. Words carry, I think, a lot more weight than maybe years ago, or when I was growing up. I don't remember ever hearing a word and having this visceral response to it.

In terms of pedagogical strategies, our contributing teachers shared how they were more intentional about what they would *say* about environmental and science topics, how they employed methods to help children and young people *see* these topics, and how they helped students to actually *experience* these issues, in their own contexts. These were safer and more relevant approaches to helping kids and youths recognize environmental realities.

Aloe: "These are ways to engage that are safe for teachers."

Beyond using different books or being aware of how language can trigger negative reactions, Aloe shared how she used place-based pedagogies to show parents and community members that environmental education doesn't have to be so abstract with discussions of places far away – places most students will never experience. Place-based environmental education is about solving real problems right outside students' doors.

> So, when I'm saying place-based, here's an example. There's so much concrete everywhere, right? All these buildings and roads. The ground itself is not permeable. So, when you have heavy rains, instead of just

soaking into the ground like it would have hundreds of years ago, it moves different places. Or if you have earth that's hard packed because of overuse. So, a big issue all across the globe is flooding, which is mostly caused because of how humans have altered surfaces. So, in a place-based perspective, we went out when it was raining, and watched where water was collecting on our own property, and it was always where it was hard-packed. We talked about why this is happening, how humans have impacted this. And then I made a partnership with our county's stormwater management, and we did a water retention pond project. So, they came, and they brought plants that are good for water retention, and we planted them as a class in the area that kept getting flooded on our property, and then every year they come back and refreshed that. So that was super local – literally on our own property. We tied it into how we humans have a negative impact, even if it wasn't us specifically. But also that we specifically could have a positive impact.

And then students were making connections like, "Hey, I was coming to school, Miss Aloe, and I just saw all this water running because the ground wasn't permeable." So, yeah, I could have taught that more from a global perspective. I could have drawn examples from other countries that might not have programs like our county to plan a water retention pond. But this made it real to them.

So, these are ways to engage that are safe for teachers to solve real world problems that are local. Because it's not some theoretical, abstract idea that sounds dangerous or political. We're actually doing it to solve real problems.

Gabby, high school science teacher: Keeping it local

Gabby approached her lessons in a similar way – always tying it back to local problems and real-world solutions.

> Our students are extremely interested in our water quality initiatives that we do that are part of our environmental science curriculum. In fact, I wrote a scholarship with a nonprofit organization that works with a lake where all of our water drains to. There have been a lot of students that have gone on to apply for that scholarship and then maintain their adopt-a-stream certification.

Aloe: "Starting kind of local and then expanding."

Our contributing teachers agreed that when they tie what they're doing in the classroom to state-mandated standards of learning, it becomes difficult for parents and community members to take issue with them.

> With weathering and erosion, I always tied into the playground. Because at any school you're going to see mulch, right? So, it's making that place-centered. And then they're designing possible solutions, understanding that every solution costs money, or it will have another negative impact. And then, looking at other examples of weathering and erosion in other parts of the world, see us starting kind of local and then expanding so that it's also more accessible, I think, for kids. And they're understanding the environmental problems we're facing. Tying it into science standards, for the state is also a good way to be like, "hey, here's why I'm teaching it."

Box 9.5 Your Strategies

Have you ever felt like what you were teaching was unsafe in any way? Like, you might get in trouble for teaching about the environment? Does Aloe's example spur any ideas for you? What is one example of how to make a lesson or concept one that your students can see or experience – one way that you might make a lesson "place-based"? What other strategies might you employ that focus on students seeing, discovering, and caring about the current and future state of our environment – rather than your explicitly *telling* them about these conditions?

With what seemed like a reasonable amount of research, these teachers were able to identify numerous community resources – bringing in their friends and neighbors – to connect science and environmental issues back to real people. One of their objectives was to make these lessons as authentic as possible – that is, to make science instruction matter to something other than a classroom quiz or a high-stakes test. One of the ways to integrate that authenticity was to turn the tables on students: to call on them to switch from being the learner to being the teacher, choosing with whom they would want to share the new science concepts or facts they had just encountered.

Gabby: Green Steps and Monarchs

Gabby gave her students incredible opportunities to complete various projects related to the local environment. By giving them these opportunities, she was making environmental education attractive in a new way.

I created a class called Green Steps. It's actually an environmental designation that any school in South Carolina can earn by completing projects. You have to complete six projects in three different categories. There's a conserve category, a protect category, and a restore category. Within each one of those categories, you have to do two projects, and those projects have to be formatted such that you have evidence of your learning, evidence of your doing, and evidence of your teaching. So, it always has a teaching component at the end, where students have to take responsibility for what they've learned and what they've done, and then teach somebody else which I really like that as far as the framing goes. The program's been around for, I think, like 25 years.

As a part of this program we interface with mentors, like our local university has a Center for Watershed Excellence and a 4-H Extension program. We also work with our County Beekeepers Association. We also have master gardeners that we build gardens with. We also work with our solid waste and recycling department. So, we interface with those organizations and students get to kind of commingle and get exposed to people in different occupations that are doing various aspects of some sort of environmental work that might be more science related, but definitely has an environmental slant to it.

I've been working on doing a lot of vertical alignment to build butterfly gardens at each one of the district's elementary schools and to train the elementary students and some of the teachers that are going to be passionate about the program about how to do the citizen science projects that we're doing with the butterflies.

We also got a grant to sponsor all of our cross-country runners to track their mileage during the season and then superimpose that on a map of North America, to show how the runners' miles map onto the migratory pathway of monarchs, and then we engaged our entire school body with like, "This is how many miles that our track team has run in conjunction with the migration of the monarchs." We did that for five weeks. It's like a 3,000-mile migration, and I think they ended up running a migration and a half, or a migration and a quarter or something like that. So, we did that. And then we're also partnering with our Spanish classes to grow milkweed, and then to have seed packets that are in both English and Spanish. So, it's like a multi-tier, multi-phase project.

Some of the most compelling strategies that our contributing teachers identified were ones that were relevant across subjects and that focused not on particular curricula or subject areas but on skills that mattered in school but that were even more important beyond school.

John Brown, social studies teacher: "Take two steps back from whatever the end goal is."

While not a science teacher – he was actually a social studies teacher, which is reasonable given that environmental and climate students are as much social issues as they are science topics – John shared pedagogical processes that focused on dispositions, including being open to people who had different perspectives, even on very important issues.

> If the disposition I want students to have is to be open to people who are different from them and their ideas, I can't tell students that. As a teacher, you have to take two steps back from whatever the end goal is. If you want your kids to be able to advocate around an issue they believe in, you can't tell them that. How do you go two steps back from that and get them the skills and the groundwork and the ideas that would then lead them to that conclusion – to be an advocate – in the future? Issue content doesn't matter because they're going to be dealing with different stuff in the future, anyway.
>
> But if I want my students to consider other people as real people who are different from them, then I have to kind of work them up to that through levels of difference and think about difference in lots of ways. The way I did in that class was by just starting by having them describe something that happened between them and a friend. I had them write about it, and then go and interview their friend – or a parent or sibling – about whatever the topic is and write the story from both perspectives. And they would say, "Oh, wait! They saw it totally different than me!" That was a revelation for a lot of my students, and then we could work through other topics by considering different viewpoints, and most of them got there.

Box 9.6 Your Strategies

Are there opportunities in your area for offering exciting extracurricular projects like the ones discussed here? Who are the potential partners in your area who could support you and provide you with resources? Who could you work with to bring something like Green Steps – or even something on a smaller scale – to your school community? How might you give students an authentic task of teaching something they've learned in your classroom to someone else in their lives? And how, in all this, can you work to develop those dispositions that allow the kinds of courageous conversations and navigating pushback we discussed earlier in this chapter to emerge?

Youth Stories

Overall, the young people we have worked and interacted with through various knowledge creation projects and in everyday classrooms agree that the best environmental education is done in ways that are relevant to their lives.

Hazel, Through Students' Eyes participant: "I was so engaged."

Hazel, a participant in the Through Students' Eyes project, shared about her experience during an Advanced Placement (AP) Environmental Science project.

> For the project our teacher, Mr. Earle, took the entire class outside to take a nature walk and remove invasive species. This was because he said, 'it was such a beautiful day that we shouldn't be stuck inside.' This was a very engaging and fun project because it allowed us all a break from being stuck inside for the 8-hour school day. Since I was so engaged it allowed me to learn a lot about invasive species and how to remove them, which was very helpful on the AP exam at the end of the year. This project was a great example of things that make students want to come to school and learn."
>
> I identified two main reasons for why students refuse to engage with school. This photograph symbolizes the first: rejection of school for other pursuits. To many students, the sterile school building and seemingly uncaring administrators and teachers pale in comparison to what's out there right now. Fun, a social life, relaxation and ease can be extraordinarily compelling to schoolchildren without an understanding of the deeper importance of school, without which many school rituals like pop quizzes seem pointless. I chose to communicate this refusal to engage with school by focusing on how compelling things seem outside it; using the symbol of a bright blue sky that evokes a beautiful day outside. That clear blue makes sitting in uncomfortable chairs for 6 hours to achieve some vague educational goal seem extremely unappealing.

At the same time, young people we know are fed up with being told that they should be the ones to solve the world's problems – including climate change.

Figure 9.2 Blue sky shining through green leafy branches. Photograph by Hazel, a student.

Cypress, Youth Research Council Fellow: "They are still alive! They can still do things to make change!"

For example, after listening to a discussion about how young people have the opportunity to make change through justice-oriented research, Cypress, a Fellow in the Youth Research Council, raised her hand:

> We see and hear a lot of older people say, "It's your generation. It's your duty to fix everything. It's your generation's duty to fix racism, environmental issues, climate change, the prison system. Your generation. You guys have to do all of this."… These people – people who are in positions of power – they are still alive! They can still do things to make change! We see these big people with big power in Congress and elsewhere. They could be making big changes, but when it comes to the work that needs to be done, they are not showing up.
>
> (Call-Cummings et al., 2024)

Box 9.7 Your Strategies

How will you balance offering opportunities for your students to feel empowered to make change with fostering in your students the willingness and ability to advocate for adults who are in power to do the jobs they were elected to do? Could these be done simultaneously? Looking back on Chapter 3 (focusing on civic and community engagement), what would (or could) happen if science teachers got together with social studies teachers – and then members of their communities – on these very questions?

Box 9.8 Young Climate Activists

Fifty-eight percent of young Americans, ages 13 to 29, believe it is possible to prevent the long-term negative effects of climate change through appropriate action. About 15% said they don't expect climate change to impact their future at all (Isaacs-Thomas, 2021). Giving students opportunities to engage in this issue could be critically impactful.

Action for the Climate Emergency (ACE) is a nonprofit networking organization that connects students across the U.S. around national and local campaigns to fight for legislation and climate justice. Their Youth Action Network boasts over 500,000 high school participants. Their most recent campaign pushed to register young people beyond high school to vote, so they can continue to advocate for climate justice at the polls.

In addition to encouraging students to join their network, their website (www.acespace.org) has a digital library of well-produced videos explaining different facets of climate change and climate advocacy, including explainers on fossil fuels and tips for talking about climate change with others. These videos could be useful in a variety of classroom lessons about science or advocacy or both.

 ## Taking Action

As we spoke with teachers across the country in preparation to write this book, one of the things we realized is that in some ways political rhetoric and tactics have changed drastically in the past decade. We also recognized – and were troubled – that in other ways, this rhetoric has remained eerily similar to that employed decades ago, when we were kids, making our way through public school. In the context of environmental justice and science, this seems like a case of different singers, same old song. There might be a different cast of characters calling for teachers to not say "climate change" in the classroom or to not "indoctrinate" their children, but it feels like the same fearmongering, power-laden tactics we grew up with. Back then, it was evolution and the Big Bang, now it's climate change and social justice. Underlying all of this is a desire of a few to control the many and to embed fear into the content of schools' instruction – to silence courageous conversations.

That said, we can't minimize the political, professional, and increasingly personal pressures that teachers are experiencing today. While it might feel to some like the same old thing, there are real fears and tangible outcomes associated with the current rhetoric around what you can and can't say or teach in science – and all – classrooms today. We have to acknowledge – and talk about – this courageously. Max hit the nail on the head when he said that all teaching is political – whether we are teaching about climate change or not.

Max: "We have to ask the big questions and then…trust them to do something about it."

We agree that the best education we can offer young people will allow them to wrestle with big ideas – in the science classroom or the lunchroom, as they play at recess or compose a poem for the first time. It's all political. We are trying to change the world – and to help young people know they can change it, too.

> I still believe that the best learning is done with people and groups grappling with big ideas. And I still think about, why did I become an educator? There's something still so very mundane but also magical about this idea that you have 25 to 30 totally different people made to be in this space together and we can consider, "What are the possibilities that otherwise would not happen?"
>
> I think education is where we have to ask the big questions and then have students grapple and talk about those big issues and then trust them to do something about it and to and to create something together. I was trained in a co-taught classroom, with two teacher mentors and 40 plus students in the same classroom. My sense of sharing space and creating and bigness comes from there. Sharing happened with a co-teacher and then sharing the space with the students. I fundamentally believe that we have a whole lot of things that we're not figuring out as adults. We might as well be very open with our students and bring those actual issues to them.

I believe that all teaching is political, and yet I believe in critical thinking first. One of my biggest criticisms with the way that some teachers have approached some of these issues – like the Israeli/Gaza conflict – is that if it's truly something that students want to learn about and are bringing to school, then my responsibility is to actually have them learn stuff. The two biggest pitfalls are that, one, the teacher tries to make the students feel better about these issues, and, two, the teacher feels that they have to have an out when they are asked about their direct stance on the issue. I still believe that it's my responsibility to actually complexify the issue more rather than to try to resolve the issue. And so, my approach is, "Well, let's not just talk about how we feel about these things. Our lived experiences are important, but that's just one piece of the inquiry."

We join Max as we urge all of us to engage with complexity – in developmentally appropriate ways – in these difficult conversations. Hopefully, the resources and ideas our contributing teachers have provided in this chapter give you a place to start or spark a new idea for you.

As always, we believe what is most important is that you build relationships with people around you who can (1) help you cope and manage the stress that comes with navigating pushback from sometimes hostile parents, family members, or others; (2) partner with you to offer new opportunities to your students; and (3) build a coalition to advocate for changes that center the needs of your students and their families.

Resources

    Book: *The Intersectional Environmentalist* by Leah Thomas. While not directly related to teaching, this book examines the intersections of privilege and climate justice, using research to demonstrate how climate injustice harms people of color most often. Interwoven are practical ways to get involved and empower everyone to fight for a better world.

    Podcast: *Stories from Home: Living the Just Transition* by Climate Justice Alliance. Host Keenan Rhodes interviews diverse groups across the world to highlight the intersections between climate change, art, culture, and social justice. The story-like structures of the conversational interviews allow these primary accounts to shine, elevating frontline communities that strive for climate justice.

TED Talk: "Climate Change: From One Kid to Another" (9 minutes). Eight-year-old Bandi Guan explains the basics of climate change and the impacts for children all over the world. He then discusses how kids can fight for climate justice. Link: https://www.ted.com/talks/bandi_guan_climate_change_from_one_kid_to_another

Online Resource: Students for Climate Action (S4CA). A nonpartisan, nonprofit dedicated to fighting for legislation that protects the environment and fights climate change. The organization is a database of information on pending legislation and activism opportunities. Schools can start or join local chapters. Link: https://s4ca.org/

References

Barnard, A. (2019, September 20). 1.1 million can skip school for climate protest. *The New York Times*. https://www.nytimes.com/2019/09/16/nyregion/youth-climate-strike-nyc.html

Call-Cummings, M., Best, A., Keller, J., Gray, N., Khalid, W., Kalinichenko, O., Berhe-Abraha, S., Kodwo, M., Martah, S., Rotherham, L., Davis, K., & Dazzo, G. P. (2024). Community-based research as civic engagement: An example from the Youth Research Council. Unpublished article.

Choi, W. (2022, November 10). What do middle schools teach about climate change? Not much. *The New York Times*. https://www.nytimes.com/2022/11/01/climate/middle-school-education-climate-change.html

Dale, D. (2023, April 24). Fact check: Trump's latest false climate figure is off by more than 1,000 times. *CNN Politics*. https://www.cnn.com/2023/04/24/politics/fact-check-trump-sea-levels-ocean-climate-change/index.html

Isaacs-Thomas, B. (2021, November 5). How young people feel about climate change and their future. *PBS NewsHour*, https://www.pbs.org/newshour/science/young-people-are-optimistic-that-theres-time-to-prevent-he-worst-effects-of-climate-change

Marsh, K., & Blackwell, I. (2023). 'COVID couldn't catch him there': Can outdoor learning benefit primary school-aged children after a global health crisis? Education 3-13, https://doi-org.mutex.gmu.edu/10.1080/03004279.2023.2182162

Merod, A. (2019, September 21). Handley students join global climate strike in walkout. *The Winchester Star*. https://www.winchesterstar.com/winchester_star/handley-students-join-global-climate-strike-in-walkout/article_1edd75f8-cf68-5780-ad92-8c98286d94c8.html

Terada, Y. (2019). 50 years of children drawing scientists. *Edutopia.* https://www.edutopia.org/article/50-years-children-drawing-scientists/

Will, M. (2022, December 7). Teens are struggling with climate anxiety. Schools haven't caught up yet. *Education Week.* https://www.edweek.org/leadership/teens-are-struggling-with-climate-anxiety-schools-havent-caught-up-yet/2022/12

Wong, E. (2016, November 18). Trump has called climate change a Chinese hoax. Beijing says it is anything but. *The New York Times.* https://www.nytimes.com/2016/11/19/world/asia/china-trump-climate-change.html

Yong, E. (2018). What we learn from 50 years of kids drawing scientists. *The Atlantic.* https://www.theatlantic.com/science/archive/2018/03/what-we-learn-from-50-years-of-asking-children-to-draw-scientists/556025/

10

Caring for Kids

Closing: How and Why Teachers Care for Kids

As we have noted throughout this book, schools are always just representations or microcosms of society, of its best and its worst. We would be disingenuous if we did not acknowledge that in the past several years our society has encountered something of a crisis of confidence in its institutions – government, churches, and schools among them. *Why* this is the case is something we could debate for days.

Max, high school assistant principal: "What is the center?"

But, as Max articulates, this crisis of confidence has bled into the ways teachers operate and how they consider their work.

> I think most of us who are good educators are trying to be reflective, and we're trying to inquire into how to best serve our students. We know that we're not doing a very good job in many ways across the entire country. In some ways this sort of lowered professional confidence is one way to explain it. Yet once educators come down from an idea of confidence, then what is the center? Where is it going to hold?

> I remember looking up to my department chair and to my principal when I first started teaching about 25 years ago, and I knew that they were like real people. But I always felt like they had the answer.

We opened this volume with an acknowledgement that because of who schools serve – our children and young people – they are often subject to intense, daily scrutiny. Because we send the most vulnerable of our society to be served by this most unifying of institutions, we – parents, families, community members, and policymakers – are also hyper-protective and sometimes irrationally sensitive to the moves teachers make. But the premise of this volume is that if and because this institution is *so* common, we have a shared obligation to defend it, to be gentle (and still firm) in our criticisms of its structures and players, and to engage in the most civil of conversations around it.

One of the flaws of this commonality, though, is the way in which it seduces us into assuming expertise as a result: we all *went* to school, so we all know what's best *for* schools. But in this text, we have attempted to remind readers not only that schools are *places* where we go ourselves and where we send our children to learn new, important things but that these schools are served by *people* who have and share that knowledge. Perhaps even more importantly, these people – teachers – have cultivated expertise not only in their chosen content but also in the skills associated with caring for the younger, smaller, and more vulnerable members of our families and communities, our children. These individuals know what comes first: they teach *kids* content, not the other way around.

We have illustrated over and over again, chapter by chapter, teacher by teacher, and issue by issue just what these teachers' expertise is and how they are helping young people to navigate some of the most complex topics our society might present them. We have depicted the myriad moments when teachers are called on to go above and beyond the subject matter in which they are experts and help children and adolescents make sense of the controversies that must be considered – and must be considered together. Sometimes over the protestations of the very people who dropped off their kids that morning. But, again, it's because students *arrive* in school already living and attempting to understand the issues we've explored here that teachers take these on. Our ultimate aim has been not to debate the political issues that simply can't be avoided in our classrooms but to highlight how teachers help children and young people examine and address these with the grace they need and deserve.

With these goals and realities in mind, in this closing chapter we again highlight and honor the voices of our contributing teachers as they offer their thoughts on how – and why – they care for kids.

Annie, recently retired high school teacher: "Kids needed something to eat."

We asked several of our contributing teachers how they signal to young people that they care. For Annie, she recognized the basic needs that were often not filled by school.

> I had peanut butter and jelly sandwiches because kids were hungry, and so you could come in and make a sandwich when you needed one for like 25 cents. I mean, we were up to 20 loaves of bread a week at one point because kids would come in constantly. And none of that went into my pocket. All of that went straight back into the rebuying of the supplies. There was never a profit.
>
> So there were always other people besides my students in and around my room. Kids would come in and sit down in my room somewhere. They would sit beside my desk, they would sit at the table and even eat their lunch in my room. I would let a couple of them that were in real need eat their lunch in my room, even when class was going on because we had different lunch times.
>
> One of the boys that I had in tenth grade came back in eleventh or twelfth grade, and said, "I never understood why all those people kept coming in and out of our room all the time until I was one of those people."

Annie: "I'm not going to pretend like I don't see them."

Annie emphasized how, in addition to filling some of their most basic needs, she worked hard to make sure students knew she saw them, she recognized their humanity, and she valued their mental and physical health above everything else.

> During COVID there was a place in my Canvas module where I would say, "This is kind of our mental health module. And if there's something you need, or something you want, or something you want to say, you can have it there, and they never really used it, but every assignment that we did I would say, "Well, so how are you feeling now? Or how did the first quarter go?" And those were things that I have done for a large part of my career. But during COVID I needed a point to stop every week, or to stop every time and say, "Here's a mental health module. If you need to tell me something, nobody else knows." And that happened with one of the girls. We

had a class, and she didn't sound right, and I said, "Can you stay after class in a Zoom? And it turns out she was suicidal. She was in charge of her 2-year-old niece who was in the room with her 24/7. She was the caregiver. She was always muted because Emily, her niece, was always in the room watching television and stuff. But I got our school psychologist on the Zoom, and the three of us sat in the Zoom together and he asked her a series of questions and then called her parents to come home.

So, I just listened for those things. I'm not going to pretend like I don't see them. If a kid's crying in my room, or even in the hall, and I don't know them, I'll turn around and go back and say, "Hey, what do you need? Are you okay?" Or, you know, "Did you just get hit in the head, and you're crying, or is there a crisis?" And so, I was always available. If a kid came to my door and said, "Can I speak with you for a minute?" I would always be available, and my classes saw that, and some of them might have thought, "Well, why are they getting more attention than we are?" But when they became the one that needed that attention, then they understood. So, the constant flow of traffic was a good indicator of what was happening in my room.

That constant flow of traffic Annie described was an indication to students – many of whom didn't even have her as a teacher – that she cared. As she said, she would stop anything and everything to make sure the young people around her knew she cared.

Aloe, STEM teacher: "It always come back to loving and caring for the individual student."

For Aloe, just like for Annie, teaching was love. There was no difference. She wants to make sure teachers never lose sight of that, even "amidst all the craziness."

> For me it always comes back to loving and caring for the individual student – the kid. If we let all these things overshadow that little one's heart, then we're losing sight of why we're doing this. In environmental justice we do it so that future generations have an Earth to call home. It can get really polarizing in that space but it's like we're all interconnected. And I want my students, whether they're pre-service teachers or little ones, to also care for the Earth. So, it's all part of it to

me. But yeah, honoring the whole child and not losing sight of that amidst all the craziness.

Carleigh, elementary music teacher: "I just love the kids."

As a Black woman whose principal has repeatedly shown discriminatory, anti-Black behavior, Carleigh expressed her frustration and the difficulty she feels almost constantly as she battles toxic professional relationships. So, why does she come back?

> It's been very difficult to go to work where the principal doesn't like me, the assistant principal doesn't have my back, and I can't rely on them if there's an issue. The only thing that keeps me coming back is that I just love the kids. I've been teaching there for six years. My fourth graders, I've had them since they were in preschool, so I've been able to watch them mature and grow individually and musically. Seeing the kids who were very quiet in first or second grade and now they have these full personalities, that's what keeps me coming back. I just love the kids. I love seeing them grow. I have kids with speaking parts in our concert or with piano solos, kids who a couple years ago would have run away from being on stage and now they're proudly taking their place on stage. That's what keeps me coming back – seeing these kids mature and develop confidence they didn't have before. Just being able to nurture that love of music in them. But it's been very tough. I won't be back next year. I can't do it another year. It's causing havoc on my mental and physical health.

For Carleigh, perhaps like some of you reading this book, it's just been too much. You need to take care of your own mental and physical health, even though you also care deeply about the health and well-being of your students.

Frankie, former teacher of students with intellectual disabilities: "I want their expectations to lead."

Initially, Frankie left the classroom because she wanted to pursue a doctorate in education. As she took classes and began her dissertation, she had every intention of going back to the classroom to be with her students. And yet, upon completion of her degree, she realized it would be so hard to go back. She described to us how much needed to change in order for her to even consider going back.

> I can't picture going back without a lot of changes or a lot of power that I'm never going to wield. It feels very problematic. A lot of the classroom is just, "Sit down, obey, and don't be your true selves, don't have those behaviors, don't communicate like that. Don't have those interests and just conform to what's happening upstairs or down the hall with students that don't have disabilities." It's a part of a bigger piece of schooling and education. So, I would be fighting more battles to be creative and let students lead their own learning. I want anything I do now to be fueled by what students or the community, or whoever I'm working with, I want their expectations to lead.

Administrators, as you read this book, we urge you to consider making changes – both simple and potentially complex or hard – to make it easier for amazing teachers like Frankie and Carleigh to stay in the classroom, caring for kids.

Max, high school assistant principal: "Teachers are staying at our school."

Max gave an out-of-the-box example of how his school is keeping teachers in the classroom: they've changed the schedule so that teachers have smaller classes and appropriate time for planning, assessment, and collaboration.

> At my current school, teachers teach two classes and an advisory, but two classes a day that are longer, and they have a two-hour prep, which in California is unheard of. There's also the design of collaboration time, an hour a day, which is cross disciplinary as well. It's the simplicity of a schedule along with a lot of time for teachers to collaborate, to observe each other, and to do the planning and the assessment that's truly necessary. I mean, it's seemingly very small, but because of these two classes along with advisory, teachers are responsible for about 50 students in a public school in California. My first year I had four classrooms, 165 students, and a 50-minute prep. Teachers are staying at our school because they think it's somewhat possible to be really successful.

Max: "That just doesn't work."

Max went on. He advocated for real, deep investment in teachers as opposed to quick "fixes" that policymakers and education leaders purport to be the answer.

> Too many education leaders think about teachers and decide, "You're a professional, and we'd better be hard on you because we want you to be better teachers." But that just doesn't work. Fundamentally, the only way that teachers are going to be better is if somebody truly invests in them in a real way with some deep coaching, and actually believes in them rather than tries to "fix" them.

We all know these things need to happen. It's not rocket science – giving teachers time to collaborate or actually believing in them. So, why do we all feel so caught, like we have no autonomy in our current system? Yes, these changes will be hard, but they are not impossible. As we grapple with how we can change our system, we would do well to remind ourselves why we are doing this work.

Bjorn, an administrator in a private school: "They had to see me wanting to work for them."

Bjorn said what all of our contributing teachers said: relationships are crucial. Seeing students and centering their humanity are paramount. Caring for kids is what it's about.

> As a Christian who is fairly conservative, walking around the halls of my school, I felt like there was a target on my back constantly. But I realized that I had to work hard on establishing a relationship where students knew that I valued them, regardless of anything that they believed or thought, because there was work to be done, and they had to see me wanting to work for them. It had nothing to do with any agendas: I had to model not buying into this division thing for me to value and work hard for students, and hopefully get them to a place where they were emotionally available enough to learn.
>
> That's kind of a big thing that I've always felt is important for newer teachers to focus on: Unless a student is present enough, emotionally, or socially, whatever you have to teach them ain't getting anywhere. Maybe when you and I were growing up if we had a bad day teachers would say, "We don't care what mood you're in. Do your work." And we did it. But these days young people are built very differently. If they're not feeling like you care about them, or that they're somewhat in a safe environment, then they're not available to learn and to make these higher-level thinking connections, and to think critically.

Do I care about these political topics and conflicts? Sure. But they can't be the reason why I don't do what really matters the most, and that's allowing students and adults the opportunity to know that no matter who they are, where they are in their ideological thinking, or where they are in life, that they matter, they mean something. Because students don't need to necessarily know where I stand ideologically for me to love them, care for them, and work for them.

I'd like to help future teachers become not better at the content – I've never met a chemistry teacher who didn't know chemistry. But I *have* met chemistry teachers who just didn't understand how to connect with students so that they can learn chemistry.

> **Box 10.1 Your Turn**
> You're almost through the book. Perhaps it's been a while since you jotted down some thoughts in the notebook we suggested you have with you. Pick it up – right now. Record your thoughts, your ideas, your impressions, your goals in this very moment. What do you want to do? What are you committed to? *Whom* are you committed to? Then never lose that notebook.

Youth Stories

As we grapple with the many, many changes we want to see in our education system in the United States, we should listen to our youth. Really listen.

Rachel, Through Students' Eyes: "Education just tends to provide the taller blocks."

Rachel, a participant in the Through Students' Eyes project, compared education to Legos as she talked about how young people build their futures).

> I took a picture of my sister and me building Legos. Education is like this. Attending school provides kids with the block of Lego they need to develop their own future. Many times, though, one may lose this Lego block for various reasons that may arise in the way of their education. This only leads to the need to find a new block and why many tend to give up. Some people believe that they need specific blocks to create the future they desire to live in. In reality, there are many different ways one can get to the same place; education just tends to provide the taller blocks.

206 ◆ Talking Equity in Polarized Times

Figure 10.1 A pair of hands building Legos. Photograph by Rachel, a student.

Mahmoud, Through Students' Eyes: "You should hang around people who are better than you."

For Mahmoud, it's important to surround himself with positive influences. While he talks about his friends, we also think those influences are teachers he trusts and respects.

> I'm trying not to hang out with negative influences. My friends help me make good choices. I surround myself with people who are "better than me" – academically – and it works. They influence me just by being around me...you should hang around people who are better than you, at least in some ways – better without being egotistical. They teach me a lot, sometimes with some nice competition, like with my friend in math class. This also makes you become a good influence yourself.

Taking Action: Ten Ways to Start Now

We end with a "top ten" list of sorts:

1. Administrators and policymakers: *Talk* to our teachers. Talk to them about what they need in order to best serve our kids. Talk to them about what they are teaching and how. Talk to them about the issues they are seeing our kids encounter and about the help they need to support *our* kids.
2. Administrators and policymakers: *Listen* to our teachers. Listen *more* than you talk to them. Listen to their expertise and their ideas. Listen to their dedication and their optimism. Recognize that effectively serving 30 students in every class, every day is an almost impossible task. Give teachers the tools to do this better.
3. Administrators and policymakers: Make space to listen to and talk to students in genuine ways. Students get it. When decisions are explained in kid-friendly (and honest!) ways, students can understand just about anything. When problems are presented to students and their help is solicited – again, in genuine ways – often the solutions they provide are better than anything adults could have generated.
4. Parents, administrators, and policymakers: *Trust* our teachers and our schools. Assume the best about their knowledge and their intentions. Trust that this foundational institution should be not a political football but a community center where our most precious and most vulnerable members of society go to become better, for themselves and all of us. Let's trust our teachers and our schools *by* talking and listening to them.
5. Teachers: Talk to your students. *All* of your students. Check in with them. Listen to them. Hear them. See them. Try – *hard* – to build appropriate relationships of trust and care with your students. Help them see themselves in your classroom and in your content.
6. Teachers and administrators: Take the risks you can. Yes, we are caught in a system that is inequitable and unjust, but if we throw up our hands, when will it ever change? If you feel concerned about taking risks, work to develop relationships with others to form a squad of sorts. Be strategic.
7. Teachers: No, seriously, find your squad! Trust each other. Lean on each other. Help each other. And perhaps most importantly, hold each other accountable for this hard work of being equitable. You create the climate of the school. You shape what is or isn't acceptable

in your classroom and in your sphere of influence. Build your network and work together.
8. Administrators: Remind yourselves of why you are where you are. Is it to ensure that your students get in the top 10% in the standardized test rat race, or is it something else? Remind yourselves that you are there to care for kids, *all* kids. Then act on that – every day. Interrupt. Take risks. You have power. Use it for good!
9. Students, young people: Talk to your teachers. Be honest with them if you feel like you can. Find the people you can trust and ask them to help you make the changes you seek in the world, but begin in your own classroom, your own school. There are so many people who will join you.
10. All: If you're reading this book, you likely care deeply about public education. As Annie emphasized earlier in this chapter, we must recognize the humanity in each other and that we are all intimately connected. Anonymous comments online and easily shareable clickbait articles have made it too easy to demonize one another. We need to do better. The stakes are too high. Our kids and our communities deserve our best.

Bobbi: "Then you can start advocating for the kids a lot more effectively."

And because this book is, first and foremost, for teachers, we will trust their expertise once more and trust that their – in this case, Bobbi's – sage advice will help us find that way forward.

> I know it's a cliche, but it is a marathon, not a sprint. You have to pick your battles. And you're not going to fix the systemic issues with public education in your first couple of years teaching. I think that new teachers sometimes don't recognize how important it is to build your reputation first, and then become a squeaky wheel. Like I can get away with making my principal cry at a meeting. But a brand-new teacher who's been here for two months cannot get away with making their principal cry in a meeting. Your reputation means a lot, and good principals take care of their good teachers. So, if you can prove that you're a good teacher, then you can start advocating for the kids a lot more effectively. And it doesn't mean like, put up with a bad principal by any means, or put up with a bad administration, but try to earn some street cred before you start throwing your weight around, because then you'll get a lot done, and people will really listen to you.

Appendix A: Self-Reflection Worksheet

Topic, question, interest:

What are my current practices? Are there any assumptions I'm making?

What is my ideal situation?

What are constraints in achieving my ideal? (Time, financial, legal, social, administrator buy-in, personal knowledge, connections or relationships, comfort level, etc.)

What or who are my resources in making change? (Knowledgeable colleagues, available professional development resources, laws or regulations, practices in other schools or districts, relationships with experts, etc.)

Now, make one concrete goal or plan:

Finally, how will I hold myself accountable?

For Product Safety Concerns and Information please contact our EU representative GPSR@taylorandfrancis.com
Taylor & Francis Verlag GmbH, Kaufingerstraße 24, 80331 München, Germany

www.ingramcontent.com/pod-product-compliance
Lightning Source LLC
Chambersburg PA
CBHW081202240426
43669CB00039B/2780